LAST CALL

JULIE PEPPER

ISBN-10: 1481939467
ISBN-13: 9781481939461

DEDICATION

In loving memory of Kim Klusman, one of the best friends
I've ever been lucky enough to have—in honor
of all those people who loved her and miss her daily.

ACKNOWLEDGEMENTS

'D LIKE TO thank my loving family and friends for all their support in writing this, my first novel, and for their encouraging belief in my ability to transcend, if not all tough situations, many, through the written word. I'd like to thank Dennis Lim, for providing me with the wondrous gift of financial freedom to write, and my children for sleeping some of the time so I could. I'd like to thank Jonell Serra for being a great friend when I was in great need of a friend. I'd like to thank Beth Sullivan for being my roomie in that first railroad apartment on Sixteenth Street between Eighth and Ninth Ave. I'd like to thank Holly Beverly for braving the cold while maintaining writer's focus in those adjacent cabins in Yosemite and, of course, for helping us both see another day, in our brilliant escape from that pool hall in Taos. I'd like to thank Laura Clemente for the late night talks and in depth analysis of what it means to be the recipient of "the look"—you know which look I'm talking about. I'd like to thank my professors in college and graduate school, especially my committee, Dr. Mercilee Jenkins and Dr. Amy Kilgard, for all of their critical analysis in making me a better writer, and all of my teachers for letting me know that I was one in the first place, most especially Dr. Weir, Ms. Capo and Mr. Orefice for recognizing something in me to be valued at an early age. I'd like to thank ADL, my writer's group, for hearing me and helping me with anything I needed help with. I'd like to thank David L. Ulin and Kaylie Jones, respectively, for taking time out of their busy writer lives and fielding my excess of questions while painstakingly working with me on two separate drafts of the many drafts I wrote. I'd like to thank Annie Gottlieb for her fantastic editing work and kindness, and Michael Reynolds for introducing me to Annie and for encouraging me to publish this book in the first place. I'd like to thank Peter Zibelli for answering my call for help in creating a book cover design through brainstorming sessions and trial and error, over Facebook, as if we had just talked yesterday, when it had been a lot longer, and for ultimately rising to the challenge of creating a really cool book cover for me. I'd like to thank Ryan Muir for his beautiful, gritty photo gracing the front cover and making it so cool and David Sorich for his lovely back cover photo creating that film noir finish. I'd like to thank Denise Lescohier Tung for reading two different versions of this piece I wrote previously and for hopefully reading this final, *Last Call*, version, too, and for being that big of a fan and not just because she is a dear friend. I'd like to thank Nicole Mott for being a great neighbor and also reading every word of my book, just because she was genuinely interested. I'd like to thank Cheryl Pole for being a huge part of the village it takes and giving me the precious time away to do what I needed to do to get this book done. I'd like to thank Lupe and Viridiana Razo, Maria Rodriguez, Flor Rabago and Gloria for taking care of my children and my house so I could work. I'd like to thank my mom, Llewellyn Berk, and my dad, Lee Fliegel, for always insisting I speak my truest most authentic truths no matter what other people might think and no matter who it might hurt, and again, all of my family members and those people close to me for putting up with what I think is true. I'd like to thank Len Berk for sharing his writing with me and reminding me how the simplest thing in a story can make it the most moving. I'd like to thank my stepsister Gail Harris for paving the way as a published author and making me think I could follow her lead. I'd like to thank my sister Laurie for loving my work and thinking I'm smart even though she is *the smart one*, as anyone who knows her will tell you. I'd like to thank my brothers and sister-in-laws on both sides, as well as my brother-in-laws on both sides, for loving bars and sometimes hanging out with me in them. I'd like to thank my aunts, uncles, cousins and extended family for their love, support and expertise in the fields of psychology, literature, education, human resources, law and medicine. I'd like to thank Ed Queair, for supporting my interest in writing and never diminishing it, even though he had years on me as a great poet and playwright. I'd like to thank Dave Minoli for always making me feel like *I'm* the smart one and pushing me to do the smart things, like getting this book out so at the very least people can read it. I'd like to thank Kristi Larson for being the very best friend through sickness and in health, in good times and in oh so bad. I'd like to thank *Tikkun* Magazine for getting me excited about words all over again, reminding me that stories exploring and fighting for social justice can be incredibly healing and energizing and allowing me to be a part of all of it. I'd like to thank Joie and Sean for making me so extraordinarily proud of them that I am always looking for ways to make them feel even a fraction as proud of me. I'd like to thank the Ressler brothers, Tom Swanson, Andrew Nathan—chef extraordinaire, Chelsea Place, the Noho Star, and Suzie and Matt in Queens for helping me support myself in the 1980s; the Broadway Deli and Tribeca's in the 1990s; the Yountville Hotel and the Fog Harbor Fish House in the 2000s; and Larkspur Hotels, MetWest Terra and the fantastic staff at the Tiburon Tavern/Lodge, (past and present), notwithstanding the extraordinary and talented chef Jamie Prouten and his entire crew, for providing me with a home away from home that afforded me the opportunity to be surrounded with the warm community of people living in and around Tiburon. I'd like to thank the Tiburon Fire Department and all of the firefighters and volunteer firefighters for being right next door—because who wouldn't be grateful for that? I'd like to thank anyone who has ever loved bar life, or hated it, had an addiction or battled one away, been caught in a place they didn't want to be but somehow found something about it they did want, anyone who has lost someone they loved, and certainly the many amazing people whose paths have crossed mine in my eleven years behind the stick and whose stories I've never had the privilege to fully know...

CHAPTER 1

C ASEY COMES IN and plops her leg up on the lip of the pocked bar.

"Look at it," she says. "It looks like I'm going to have a fucking Frankenstein scar."

A few of my regulars stare at her, checking her leg out, checking her out. As usual, she looks cool. She's got brown platforms on and an old vintage jacket with weird patches on it, a cabbie kind of hat. Her lipstick is a deep, burnished red.

"Did he say you would have a scar?" I ask.

"He didn't say anything except that I should call my mother. And I told him no. But the next thing you know, my mother is calling me in a panic, telling me to come home. What I don't get is, I'm not a minor, he can't call her without my permission." She's practically crying and she never cries.

"Well, of course not. But why did he?"

She lowers her voice. "Probably because I'm going to die and he thinks my mother should know."

"Shut the fuck up," I say, because she's scaring me and I don't even want to consider that she's not kidding. She has this way about her where she kids about the gravest things, which is one of the things I love about her but not particularly at the moment.

"You know my mom has a heart condition, which this phone call didn't particularly help. Anyway, I have to get to work, but I'm so pissed I just had to show you. Also, this guy's a dick and I have to get a second opinion, so if you wouldn't mind going with me, I got a reco but it's up north, so it would mean a road trip."

"Of course," I say. "And if it turns out this guy fucked up we can sue his ass later, you know? But try not to worry about it now."

"Yeah," she says. "I couldn't work yesterday the damn thing was bleeding so much. Now I have to pick up as many shifts as I can, but I'll call you about when."

"Okay, but don't overdo it. You don't want the thing to swell anymore than it is."

A jagged scab spanned a good chunk of her inner thigh, and the thing was, the ugly brown mole was still there; only a piece of it was missing. It didn't look good. "He fucking shaved it. They're not supposed to shave it," she says, shaking her head and grabbing a smoke out of her purse as she makes her way toward the door.

"I'll call you tomorrow," I say.

"Your eyes look better," she says, getting closer to examine.

"I'm careful not to touch them. It seems to help," I say.

My eyes have been doing this weird thing lately. They swell a little; then they get a little red and scaly, flaky and spotty, and if I rub them or even just touch them, they grow into large golf balls where the eyes used to be. (This looks scary if I'm wearing mascara, or any eye makeup at all. Of course, without it I just look sick. But today they seem better.) In a strange way it seems like my eyes' way of telling me they've seen enough.

Casey lights up in the doorway and waves her smoke goodbye at me.

Steve, one of my regulars, has been inhaling our every utterance, but when I catch him, he drops his eyes and pretends to be deeply absorbed in his Absolut and Cranberry, dipping his pronounced nose into the ice, making his salt-and-pepper hair fall over one eye. But then he looks up and casually says, "Hey, Nicky, what's with your friend? She's cute, but a little angry for my taste."

"Who are you kidding?" I say.

"No one, I guess. Talk about angry, you should have seen this babe last night. She says to me, who do you think you are, anyway? And she says it real snotty, like she's trying to pick a fight."

"And you loved it."

"Well, I could tell she liked me, so yeah."

"How could you tell?"

"Well, she keeps looking over at me, and every time I say something, anything, she nudges her friends, going out of her way to show that she thinks I'm a jerk. You know, rolling her eyes and making some smart-ass comment."

"And this behavior was a dead giveaway that she liked you?"

"I'm not even talking to her. If she's as offended as she's trying to come off, why does she bother with me?"

"Yeah, okay," I say.

"Anyway, the next thing you know, her friends are leaving but she's not. She asks me to come over to her table."

"So of course you do."

"Of course. She's hot. She's wearing this little yellow skirt and she's got those come-fuck-me heels on. But she starts in on me, 'I've seen you around here before. You really think you're pretty slick, don't you?' She pokes me. 'Don't you?' So I tell her, no, I don't know what she's talking about, but she won't let up. 'You're always talking so loud all the time. Can't get enough attention, can you?' But even as she's saying it, I feel like it's some weird kind of foreplay. And sure enough, before I know it she's buying me a drink."

"That's kind of funny, Steve. Like she's been watching you for a while, when you didn't even know she existed. It sounds like she's jealous of you. Maybe you've been stealing her limelight and she's out for revenge."

"Yeah, maybe," he chuckles with pride. "I asked her out anyway."

"So I figured. When you going?"

"Tonight. Maybe I'll bring her by."

He throws down a ten and heads out. He walks and talks with a rock-and-roll type of rhythm, quick and boppy. I watch him. He's putting on what looks like an exaggerated Don Juan act, stopping at select bar stools, attempting to tickle the urges of the ladies he would most like to love, or fuck. I think he keeps the volume turned up high in his head so that he won't ever have to stop dancing and slow down.

The soles of my black combat boots pull stickily up and down on the rubber mats as I make my way back and forth. The mirrors surround my back, and warm lights shine down from overhead, dimming now for that special evening effect. I take my glass mixing cup and design the napkins into fluffy uniform spirals, dropping a stack every few feet along the bar. It's a long bar, trimmed in brass, with an old–fashioned, old-movie look. I stir a Martini till it's icy cold, light a smoke, then stand still and listen. Early in the evening like this, you can actually hear the conversations over the music, and it's oddly soothing.

Ludwig saunters up to the bar, his trademark cigar dangling between his lips.

"Nicky, I'll have a Beck's," he says, gesturing with his head toward the cooler.

I put it up on the bar and his little sun-spotted arm reaches over for it. His sleeves are short, and I'm struck by how he doesn't even try to cover the numbers on his left forearm, from Auschwitz. The first time I saw them I wanted to stare, count the numbers, touch them to see if they would smear like ink, but instead I quickly averted my eyes, careful not to get caught gawking.

"You far away today," he says smiling as he grabs his Beck's.

"Not far enough," I tease him, as I walk away.

At around ten Steve struts in with his usual cocky bop, only now he has this woman flung over his arm. She has no trouble keeping time with his strut even though her eyes are darting to every corner of the room.

They sit down in front of me.

"Hey, how about some service?!" he yells.

I stick my finger in my ear as if to check if my eardrum's ruptured, then ask him what he wants. He smiles, kisses my hand and introduces me to Janine.

"Hi, Janine," I say. "Nice to meet you."

"Hi," she says all smiley, fluttering her eyelids. But then she gets right to the point: "Can I have a glass of Chardonnay, please, Nicky?"

"Sure," I say. "And what about you, mister? You want your *usual*," I say, emphasizing Steve's status as a regular, "or would you like to join the lady in a glass of Chardonnay?"

"You know, I think I'd like to join the lovely lady," he says, and I think, yeah, I know you would.

"Two Chardonnays, Nikolai, and please put it on my tab."

"Certainly, M'sieur," I say, going about my business, but suddenly acting as though I'm his butler.

When I return with their drinks, I let them fill me in on their evening so far. They giggle like schoolkids as they relay it to me; the more obnoxious the one's behavior, the more appreciative the other.

"And then we went over to Tatou and you got us that table, just like that," she says, snapping her red-manicured fingers. "Just like that," she says again, this time to me. "He went right up to the maître d', and I don't know what he said, but the next thing you know we had a table for two and a platter of canapés in front of us."

I figure what he said might've been something like, "I really need to get laid tonight, can you help me out?" As I'm figuring this, I'm watching Janine twitch.

She twitches a lot. Just above her lip and under her eye. A twitch for each side of her face, and sometimes just her eye will start to flitter around by itself, creasing her cheek unendingly until it finally stops.

Once this old guy in a bar, I think he was the manager of the bar, was talking to me and a girlfriend of mine about the effects of cocaine on the nervous system. He claimed to know quite a few young women who developed permanent twitches in their faces from using cocaine. It so happened that I had just snorted some, and my face wouldn't calm down, especially that teeth-grinding thing, and he just kept on about it.

It made me paranoid that the twitching might never stop, even though I suspected he knew I was high and was just trying to scare me. I thought he was full of shit, because why would only young women be afflicted with this unending twitch? I actually asked him that, just to see what he would say, and he came up with some bullshit story about how a woman's nervous system is different from a man's.

But now I wonder if I wasn't just too fucked up to get his point, because Janine looks like she has a permanent twitch. I wouldn't be surprised if it was caused by cocaine use when she was a young woman (which she's not particularly now), or if she's just really coked up tonight. She wears a lot of makeup and she talks pretty loud. Somehow her loud is more glaring than Steve's. I guess between her nails and her bright white hair, her come-fuck-me heels and her miniskirt, she wouldn't exactly vanish into the woodwork anyway.

It doesn't bother me, though, because the more flamboyant her behavior and attire, the more she draws attention to herself, the more comfortable I feel fading away, vanishing into the woodwork while I scrutinize the details of her gestures and attitude. I allow myself to indulge in this character study even though I don't know if I'll ever get to use it, because, frankly, I may never get another part, much less one like this. Still, it's good to have it in my repertoire.

Right now, for instance, she's stopped on her way to the ladies' room to try to buddy up with one of the waitresses. She's bent over Sandy's neck, admiring her ("Oh, that's gorgeous!") necklace. She doesn't know Sandy. They've never met before, but Janine continues to converse with her, saying something else excitedly, which I can't hear, and then grabbing poor Sandy's hand like she's going to take it home with her.

Of course she smokes. I light her cigarette for her. She seems to expect this. Or pretend to expect it. I don't mind that either, because that's one thing I love to do, light people's cigarettes. I like it when people light mine for me, too. There's something romantic and sexy about it. I guess part of it is that they don't know it's coming. They're in their own little world, ritually preparing to cut a few minutes off their life, and then suddenly another person is there doing it with them, giving them something they need. It's like everyone's admitting it's a bad thing, but in the same breath everyone's admitting we all do some bad things, and since I can't talk you out of it, I can make you feel more comfortable doing it. Or maybe none of those thoughts cross their minds and it's just a moment we share.

Between drags on their cigarettes, Steve and (back from the ladies room) Janine kiss. They really go at it. I can see the tongue exchange. When it gets too disgusting, I lean on my elbows right in their faces and say, "I hear they're having a special on rooms over at the Peninsula."

They both come up for air, and Janine laughs like she's sooo naughty.

"Nick, what's the matter, baby?" Steve says.

"No kissing at the bar," I say.

"Is Phil working a lot of overtime lately, or what?" I guess he's implying that maybe I'm lonely. I'm not lonely, though Phil actually has been working a lot of overtime, in preparation for a trip he's going to take in the next couple of months or whenever he gets the money. He needs to go visit his family and pick up a used car some cousin of his is selling. But ever since he's been working all those extra hours, I've noticed how peaceful the place is without him. It's a shame I'll have to tell him about the road trip to San Francisco with Casey. He'll take it personally, like I'm abandoning him, and that will certainly disturb the peace. I would think he'd like the space; time to write, smoke pot, whatever. But I guess without me around, there's no one for him to torture but himself.

Ricky, my bar back, walks by and cleans Steve and Janine's ashtray, murmuring under a covering hand, "Get a room."

Then we're all laughing, except Janine. She's off and running to return a call from her beeper.

"What do ya think?" Steve asks me.

"I think . . . trouble," I say, watching Janine bump into another waitress and hug her with an excess of "I'm sorry" excuses while simultaneously offering gum all around.

"Yeah—*grande* trouble," Ricky agrees.

But Steve just says, "Yeah, I know. We're made for each other."

And in a way I understand. It's that thing you see at some point in your life that looks so good to you. You're not sure why, but you're totally drawn to the thing. And once you touch it, or it touches you, you want to stay around it. You like the way it smells, looks, feels, makes you feel. The more you like it, the more it scares you. And the more it scares you, the more you start to think, *This is a bad thing. I've got to give it up.* But the more you know you should give it up, the harder you cling to it. And in your most hidden thoughts you say, *nothing will make me let go of this.* And then you're secretly proud of yourself for having the strength to hang onto what you believe you deserve.

CHAPTER 2

THE FIRST TIME I SAW the big, ugly, brownish-black bump of a mole in the middle of Casey's thigh, I never imagined it would end up being such a big deal.

I was walking down the street with her on one of those bright, sunshiny California days. She had on a cute little pale-green-and-beige sundress. It was short.

"What the fuck is that?" I asked.

"What the fuck is what? This thing, you mean?" She pointed to it.

"Yeah," I said. "That thing."

"I know. I gotta get it checked out," she said, laughing. "I have an appointment. Actually on Wednesday."

"But did you always have it?" I asked. "Or is it new?"

"I think I always had it. But I don't remember it looking quite like this."

"God. I think you'd remember it looking like that if it did."

"I know," she said. "It's kind of scary."

And suddenly now it was, very scary. That dickhead she went to that shaved it shouldn't have. The San Francisco clinic explained that to us over the phone before we even got there.

So we drive the six or seven hours up to San Francisco, to this clinic known for its specialization in skin cancers, and especially in malignant melanoma, which is what Casey has. (Which is why that doctor had told her to call her mom.) We drive, fighting over the wheel, because we're not taking the scenic route and it's much less boring when you're driving.

"What did Phil say about you taking this trip?" Casey asks me.

"Not much," I say.

"Is that a good thing?" she asks.

"It's good for me," I admit. I was surprised he didn't have much to say about it. Maybe it was the reason for the trip, maybe the way I presented it. I don't know.

When we arrive at the clinic, they ask us why we didn't just go to St. John's in Santa Monica, and, grumpy from the ride, I want to say because we're assholes. But the real reason is that someone Casey's mom knows at a famous hospital in Philly, where they're from, had recommended a famous doctor at the San Francisco place.

The clinic doesn't seem particularly impressed with our efforts, which kind of bugs me. But they're not going to turn us away, which I suspect St. John's would. They do, however, advise us that if any major procedures need to be done, they'll probably recommend we do them in LA. This is not great news, but it's okay, since the only place Casey seems determined to avoid is her hometown, Philly.

We spend the whole day in that clinic, sometimes waiting, sometimes talking to the doctors, and sometimes I just sit there while Casey gets looked at under a microscope.

The doctor that examines Casey and leads us through it all tells us exactly what he is doing as he does it. He tells us what the other doctors will be doing. He never speaks in that medical language that escapes laymen's comprehension and makes them worry that it's all bad. He even makes Casey laugh a few times.

But as he wraps up his exam, he says, "I think it's important that you get the procedure done close to home." "The procedure" is surgery.

"Oh, why can't you do it?" "Yeah, why can't it be you, please?" we blurt out on top of each other.

"You'll need some recuperation time (which we all know she can't afford to spend in a hotel or in the hospital), and then there will be the monthly visits and the constant watch on your health. I just think it will be more manageable close to home," he says.

Then he, too, suggests Casey go back to Philly. But I'm beginning to think going back to Philly represents a kind of death to Casey—death to her costume design, her Hollywood apartment, her independence, her lucrative waitressing gig, and somehow to her quest for life. I guess Philly feels to Casey like my hometown, Armonk, New York, feels to me—like if you don't get out, you'll get sucked in and die there.

Then Casey's doctor sends us to meet with the clinic therapist, who by now assumes that I'm Casey's lover, as do most of the doctors before him. He explains to us that after Casey gets the surgery to remove the tumor (which is what they are now calling it), she will have five years of watchful waiting before she will know if she is in the clear. He explains that if she makes it through those five years, she can consider herself cured. He tells us that there are support groups for exactly this illness and the stresses and strains that not knowing can bring.

We think he is very nice, but neither of us understands why we would need a support group. I mean, Casey feels absolutely fine, except that she's anxious to get the big, ugly, dark brownish-black bump of a gnarly mole, which now turns out to be a possibly fatal cancer, off her leg.

Finally we leave the clinic with our little booklet of contacts and the clinic's assurance that Casey's file will be sent as soon as we find a doctor to do the procedure. We have a lot of information about the best doctors to perform the surgery down in L.A., but we both cling to the fact that we want the doctor that examined her today to be the one.

We leave, stunned and disappointed that we can't leave it all behind us right then and there. Then we head for Haight Street, because Casey feels shopping for vintage clothing is the only thing to do at a time like this. After picking up a few essential items like hats and scarves and old boots, we go back to the Pacifica Motel on Union Street.

We take turns taking long showers and sit around in our pajamas talking, tired from the driving and the doctors and the diagnosis and probably the shopping. We hit the little motel beds hard, knowing that first thing in the morning we'll hit the road back to L.A. in search of surgery.

Just a couple of months before Casey noticed Mr. Cancer Mole, she and I had tried to get Halle's, the restaurant where she worked (and where I had worked, too, until I got sacked), to assist us in getting some kind of health insurance for the whole staff at a group rate. They provided no insurance just for being employed there—claimed it would cost them too much for part-time employees, which just about everyone was. So we hoped they would just allow us to hold a meeting with an insurance group and let any interested employees attend. About two hundred employees worked there at the time, and most had expressed an interest in insurance, especially if they could get it cheap.

It took Halle's so long to let us know that the meeting never took place, and unfortunately, some of us never got health insurance at all— some of us like Casey, who now had a preexisting condition: cancer.

So after calling places like John Wayne at St. John's, who refuse to do any procedures unless you have cash upfront or a super medical plan, we end up on a County Hospital waiting list, thanks to a connection of one of my bar clients, who's a doctor.

Paul is his name, and he's a neurologist. He only comes in once in a while, but he's the nicest guy, and when I tell him about Casey's problem he acts immediately. It's tough to get in, he says, but once you do you will get excellent care. He must have some kind of clout, because even though the list goes on forever, we only have to wait two days and we're in. Unfortunately, once you're in you have to wait forever to be seen. Hours and hours of sitting around the waiting room, agonizing over what will happen when the doctor actually gets to you and your black mole and what happens is, biopsies and more biopsies and probing.

Except, this one time, Casey gets in right away. This time, this last time, I go off to park while she goes in to claim her place in line. After I finally find a parking space, I run up to the waiting room to find her. But she isn't there. I wait in the check-in line for a chance to ask if Casey has gotten in to see the doctor. The nurse thinks she has and allows me to go back and look.

I run up and down the halls, peering into the examining rooms, and just when I'm starting to panic, I see her. She is in one of the rooms with a doctor and she is crying. Not a little bit, but big crying with difficulty breathing. She beckons me into the room.

"Hey, what's going on?" I ask not just her, but the doctor, too.

"This is my friend, Nicky," Casey says, struggling to calm down. "Tell her what you just told me."

That's when the doctor, this Filipino guy, says, "It's too late for surgery. There's no point."

Casey starts crying again, but this time I can see her tears are from frustration with this doctor, whose English is somewhat incomprehensible and whose bedside manner is nonexistent.

"It's a projection," she says. "You can't tell from a projection!" She is practically screaming.

"Yes. A projection. The projection says six centimeters. It too deep—" He is practically yelling back at her.

"Wait a minute, please," I say. "Let me understand this. You have a projection here that indicates what?"

"The projection indicate the cancer is very big."

"Excuse my ignorance, but what is a projection exactly?"

"It's part of the tumor, biopsied."

"The top part? The bottom part?"

"It's a piece that could mean the cancer is as deep under the surface as it is on top."

"But I thought you can't tell how deep or big it is until you operate."

"Well, not for sure, but—"

"But what? If the only way we can know for sure is to operate, what are we waiting for? Let's get her on the table."

"Well, we have to see if there is a surgeon that would do it, and—"

"You're not a surgeon?"

"No."

"Can we please speak to someone who is?"

"Well, I can try to set up an appointment."

"We would like to speak to a surgeon now, today," I say. "Well, I'll call right now for you, but I don't think—"

He would have gone on, revealing openly and without emotion his verdict that Casey was on the brink of death—no matter how wrong he might be—but I notice a white phone on the wall that I've seen the doctors use before to communicate with each other. I go over and pick it up.

"What are you doing?" the Filipino doctor asks me. "Who do you think you are going to call?"

"I'm not going to call anyone. I'm just trying to help you out. You said you would call someone for us, and I think that's an excellent idea. No time like the present," I say, holding the phone out to him.

Next thing you know we're meeting with a surgeon, whose name is Dr. Levine. No sooner does he come in than he starts cracking jokes—silly jokes, but he gets Casey laughing, which is a feat under the circumstances. He's very nice as he gets the preliminary information out of the way. "Where did you go?" "Who did you see?" "How do you feel?" "How old can you be, anyway?" He listens carefully, speaks highly of the doctors we've met in San Francisco, and makes fun of Dr. Tong, our Filipino friend, which really helps to break the ice. Then he examines Casey and sets a date for surgery.

The only problem is that the surgery is scheduled for Easter Sunday, and Casey will have to be admitted on Good Friday and miss out on all the traditional Easter festivities. This really bums her out because, though Casey isn't the churchgoing, Bible-quoting kind of religious, she truly loves God. She talks to him, prays to him, and believes 100 percent in his existence. So missing, I guess, the celebration of his resurrection is really disappointing for her.

I, on the other hand—maybe due to the fact that I'm Jewish, but I don't think so—am glad. It's Thursday now, and Sunday is the first day that the hospital can squeeze her in for surgery. I wouldn't have cared if it was my birthday, wedding, or belated Bas Mitzvah. I don't want one more day to pass when that thing will have a chance to grow and spread. The one thing all the doctors agree on is that at Casey's young age of twenty-two, cancer spreads at breakneck speed. And even though I know, just by the fact that Dr. Levine has agreed to do the surgery, that Dr. Tong was wrong to say what he said, it still scares the shit out of me, and I wonder what he saw that made him say it.

CHAPTER 3

I WEAR A LONG silky sleeveless dress with little peach flowers splashed all over a black background. On my head I wear a hat, floppy, felt, and plum-colored. It's Casey's. I borrowed it first thing this morning, just before I drove her to the hospital.

I run in, panting, my cowboy boots clunking.

"Hi. Are you guys ready for me?" I ask. "I'm Nicky Ferrer."

"Well, the sides haven't arrived yet," the woman sitting behind the table says.

The sides haven't arrived? How am I going to get out of here on time if the script isn't even here yet?

"Well, I have a time conflict. I need to be out of here by 12:20. My agent said you guys knew that," I say.

"Uhm . . ." The lady with dark hair fiddles with something on the table. "Can you wait a few minutes?"

"No, I really can't. Do you have any sides at all?" I ask, refusing to drop out of sight.

"Just this one copy," she says, waving the white pages with black print.

"May I look at those for five minutes? That way when the sides get here I'll be ready for you, and we can get me in and out in no time."

I was being pushy. But it felt good, because normally I'd wait hours for those sides and when they finally came, I'd just walk in pissed, my attitude killing any chance I had. Today I really was in a hurry. I wanted to get back to the hospital, but first I had to teach an aerobics class. I was doing a favor for somebody who'd covered for me when I went on the road trip to San Francisco, and I couldn't get out of it, and now I was glad. The thought of all those students standing there in their leotards and tights waiting for me made me feel less desperate.

"Okay," the woman says. "Sorry about this." She was apologizing to me.

"Oh, that's okay, I'm sorry. It's just that I have a class to teach." I don't mention it's an aerobics class. Let her think I'm a scholar.

She hands over the sides and I go out in the hall, where all the other hopefuls are now waiting, too.

"Oh, do they have scripts in there?" a tall, chiseled man asks me.

"Not yet," I say. "You can have this one when I'm done with it."

"Thanks," he says as I move down the hall, attempting to focus.

The character is a tomboy from Ohio. It's only for a stupid music video, but the dialogue is pretty good. I like her. I read it over three times and when I look at my watch for the millionth time, it's 12:12. I walk over to the now closed door and knock.

"They're not here yet," the man at the door says. I guess he's her assistant.

"Well, you know what? I don't need them. Was one of you planning on reading with us?"

"I was," the woman says.

"I'm ready. You can have these," I say, handing the script over.

"Oh, all right. That's a good idea. If you need a line I'll give it to you."

"Great," I say.

"This is for camera," she says.

"Okay," I say.

We start the scene. I say something. She says something. Then there is a break in one of my lines and I pause. Not long, just long enough to find the next beat of the action. The stage direction says she takes a moment, so I do. But she interrupts me.

"Your line is," blah, blah, blah.

"I know, I was just—"

"Oh, I'm sorry. You—you were acting. That was great. Take it back before the pause."

Just as I do, a guy comes bursting through the door with a large package.

"Here they are," she says. "Hang on a sec," she says to me. She rips the package open and stacks the scripts on the table, beginning to sort them for different characters, but then remembers that I'm standing there and I'm in a hurry.

"Okay, we were right at the part where—oh, here. Take your own, now that they're finally here," she smiles.

"Thanks," I say taking one of the freshly printed scripts. "Do you mind if we take it from the top?"

"No. That's fine."

So we read through it, and when I get to the part with the little pause, she lets me have it and it makes the rest of the scene make sense.

When I'm done she says, "Nicky, that was really, really nice." (Which I've heard many times before, from many different casting people, for many different parts I didn't get.)

"Oh, good," I say.

"I really mean it," she says. "I was wondering if you could take your hat off. It's great, but the producers are going to want to see your hair."

It's a simple request, but the reason I'm wearing a hat in the first place is because I'm growing my hair out and it's not looking its best. The first thing Casey did this morning when she saw me was throw the hat at me. In my headshot I still have short hair, that's probably why they called me in, but I want long hair. I want it to flow down my back and over my breasts in front. Short hair looks better on me, but it doesn't feel better. In spite of my breasts, short hair does kind of make me feel like a boy.

"I don't mind, but you might," I say. "It's kind of a mess, because I'm growing it out."

"That's okay," she says. But when I let it tumble out, she doesn't look happy.

"Are you sure you want to grow it out?" she asks.

"I've been working pretty hard at it," I say.

I have been working hard at it, and it's only a music video. What about the next project when they want someone with long hair?

"Well, thanks, Nicky, really good work. And I'm sorry about the time thing."

"Thank you," I say.

And I take off. I'd be late, but not very.

I haven't had an audition in a while. Because of the recession, people like Laura San Giacomo and Holly Hunter seem to be reading for roles I used to get a crack at, and now I'm reading for music videos and only if I'm lucky. But I like zipping in and out like that. Like it isn't the most important part of my day and everything doesn't just roll over and die for it. I'm tired of dying for it. Everyone loves my work, but no one will give me a job. We all kid about it at the bar.

"How's the acting going?" one of my fellow actor/bartender buddies will say.

"I'm out," I'll say.

"You're out?"

"Yeah, I'm out," I'll repeat.

"Yeah, me too," they'll say.

But I really am on my way out. This audition was like a test for me to see how much more I can stand. They always say when you don't care anymore, that's when you'll hit it. I never thought that day would really come for me, but I'm beginning not to give a shit at all.

So it's a Friday morning audition, and I get the call on Friday night. Usually I count off every day I don't hear back starting the day after. But this time I don't have time. I'm just back from the hospital and I think it might be Casey calling me because she's bored.

"Hi Nicky, it's Sharon. From the Richard Marx video?!"

"Oh, hi," I say.

"Listen, the producers loved your tape. They want you to come in and meet them. They really liked you."

(These are the kind of statements that it's dangerous to believe. Because if they call you back because they really liked you, doesn't it stand to reason that if they then don't give you the part it's because they really didn't like you after all?)

"Wow, that's great," I say.

"Yeah, but listen, about your hair . . . they really picture Mary with short hair. She's, like, a tomboy, and they love your short hair in your picture. I know you're growing it in, but would you reconsider for this?"

"They want me to cut my hair?"

"Well, it would work better for this role, they think."

"I'm not sure I understand, Sharon. Do I have this part if I cut my hair?"

"We're having callbacks on Sunday and they want you to come."

"Okay."

"But I just wanted to tell you that if you'd be willing to cut your hair for this, you really have a shot. If you're dead set against it, we understand, but you know, I think you look really cute in short hair. I know how you feel because I was growing mine in and then I cut it, but after all, it grows back, right?"

"Yeah. Takes a long time, though."

"I know what you mean. But could you just think about it?"

"Sure, Sharon. But they don't want me to cut it off for the callback, do they?"

"No, no, no. Don't worry about it for the callback. But don't wear a hat and try to neaten it up a little, you know?"

"Oh, yeah," I say. It really was a mess that morning at the audition.

"Okay, so three o'clock on Sunday. Everybody's dying to meet you. Richard'll be there, too."

"Isn't that Easter Sunday?" I ask.

"Yep. Sorry about that. See you then," she says and quickly hangs up.

"Great, Sharon. See you Sunday," I say to myself.

Surgery and a callback on Easter Sunday? I know Casey wouldn't approve of my saying it, but . . . Jesus Christ.

When I get to the place, there are already at least five other girls there and we're early. About five more arrive after I me. I look around and not one person has the same hair. Reds and blondes, big hair, curly, straight, short, long—basically they have no idea what they're looking for, and yet they were pretty sure they wanted me in a pixie.

I sit down with the script. I read it over in my head a few times, thinking about what I'll do with it if I actually get it.

I can feel my face curling into a grin one moment and sulking down into a frown the next. I will look right at him when I speak, and sometimes I'll refuse to look at him at all. I can really hear someone talking to me as I sit there, and I can feel myself sitting and listening as she would. I think about when she'd sit and the way she might plop herself down, letting her legs fall open and stretch out, her whole body relaxing into the comfort of boyishness as she plays with a rock by the river.

I have the script well memorized by now, but I find when I'm at one of these things it's best to keep busy, so I continue to toy with it as I wait.

The call is for three and it's pushing four. But the doctors told me not to bother coming to see Casey today anyway. Pre-op, surgery, post-op, I won't get to see her till tomorrow, which is kind of good, since I'm thinking I might actually have a shot at this—so I do what I can to push Casey completely out of my obsessing thoughts about her until tomorrow.

After a while, I just sit around checking out the competition. Some of them are not remotely tomboyish—hair done, nails painted, frilly dresses. Some look really cute—big sweaters, ripped jeans, worn leather shoes, and great hats. I'm wearing the same thing I wore to the first one, minus the hat. They say you're supposed to do that. Wear the same thing to the callback that you wore to the audition.

I'm getting pissed just sitting here. Some lady keeps coming out and apologizing to us. But the last time she came out, she said, "We're really sorry, it's just that they're in a meeting."

Why can't they have the fucking meeting after? I think. Then she comes out again and says, "They'll be here any minute, but you might not read. They may just look at you today."

Great. We've been sitting here for over an hour so some asshole producers can look at us, even though they've already seen us on the audition tape. And just as I'm thinking I'm going to tell the lady I can't stay, because "any minute" hasn't come yet, who pops up but Richard Marx himself.

He walks into the room and does a double take, with the fakest look of surprise on his face. "Oh my God, look at all of you!" he says.

Or some bullshit like that. Like, what are we all doing waiting for him? Like he can't figure out that our call was for three and now it's after four, but we've wasted this much time, so we don't want to just leave and blow the whole thing.

Then he goes inside and a whole bunch of producer-looking people follow him.

"See you in a bit," he says, like we're all in love with him or something. Then the lady gives us the order. Even though I haven't been here as long as some of the others, I get called in second or third. That feels like a good sign.

When the first girl comes out I ask her what the deal is. "They don't have you read. Just talk," she says.

I can't tell anything from the way the second one comes out. Then it's my turn.

"Nicky Ferrer," they call.

"Hi," I say with a big smile.

But nobody says anything back. They just look at me.

"Hi, guys," I try again.

"You are?" Richard Marx says.

"I am Nicky Ferrer. Didn't you just ask me to come in?"

"Uh, yeah. It's just that you're much prettier in person than you were on the tape."

And I'm wondering, how am I supposed to take that? Aren't I going to be on tape if I get this thing?

"Thanks, I think," I say, again smiling. Again getting no response. "Well," I try to break the enormously awkward silence, "did you want me to read for you?" I just say so somebody will be saying something.

"No," one of the producers says. "We just want to look at you today."

And then again silence. I hate this. It's so rude. I mean, couldn't they just pretend to be interested in me and ask me some questions while they're looking at me? Why make it so humiliating for us all? So I spread my arms out to the sides and do a very slow and deliberate turn. "Well, look away," I say. Somebody sort of laughs, but mostly I think it's my imagination. And then when nobody says anything else, I again make the effort. "Will that be all?" I say.

"Yes. Thank you," somebody says.

"Oh, no, thank you," I say. *Thank you for reminding me that I don't have to take this fucking bullshit.*

CHAPTER 4

I'VE BEEN HERE for months, but it feels like a lot longer than that since the day I came in looking for a job.

I walked in and wasn't sure whom to speak to. It's always like that, but he was staring at me—the long-haired guy with the ponytail behind the bar. "What can I do for you?" he said, his eyes all over my breasts.

They tell you in bartending school (not that I went, but I've heard) that you should wear a white shirt and black slacks when you're out hunting for a bar job. And if you have one, a tie is a nice touch. I was wearing a long green, purple and black floral dress. Not a frilly floral, but a floral down to the floor that hugged my curves and let go at the top where my cleavage might catch your eye—if it was open. Your eye, that is.

It was a tough call, because I wanted to be professional, but I couldn't overlook the profession I was applying for. The Bartending School Theory was a good one. Most bars implement a uniform in some variation of black and white. So they figure if you show up for your interview in a uniform, it looks like one of three things. One: you're coming from another bar where you work, making the point that you've done this before, that someone else has trusted you to do this in their bar. Two: you can look presentable. They can envision you working in their establishment because you practically fit in already. Three: you have a uniform and can start immediately because you're prepared.

I understood the theory, but I'd found that it wasn't as effective as looking as good as I could. Any assortment of blacks and whites always ends up baggy on me. The truth is, I look better in fitted clothing. I'm not tall, and my breasts are on the large side. They're not as big now as they were when I was younger, though. After years of obsessing over whether or not I should get a breast reduction, I realized that by working out to excess, I could shrink them without the operation.

It was strange because one year my breasts just ballooned, like someone had taken five or six minutes and blown them up. It wasn't a gradual thing. I guess it was the year I got my period. I was eleven. Before that, boys used to say I was too flat, and I didn't even know, too flat for what? So the year I went from too flat to voluptuous, I became very self-conscious about my chest. It's funny to have that, because people act like they have a right to say anything they want to about it. As though having these two big mounds on your chest is, of course, their business, and you know it is. And they also make you feel as if you've done something that maybe you haven't. Like they're thinking, *with tits like that, you know she's been fucked.*

But after a long time of wearing big bulky sweaters and loose work shirts for camouflage, and thinking up good comebacks to lewd comments, I pretty much got over it. I guess I was about twenty, because I'm twenty-nine now and I'm okay with them. Sometimes I even like them, maybe because I shrunk them a little, or maybe because when I became a woman, I began to understand their value.

So when the pony-tailed guy said, "What can I do for you?" maybe thinking about getting a mouthful as his eyes bounced back and forth from my chest to my face, I didn't really care, because there *was* something he could do for me.

"I could use a job," I said with a big smile.

"Do you have a resume?" he said in a patronizing tone.

"Sure do," I said pulling it out of my large carry-all. *We sure do,* I felt like saying, *me and my big tits.* At least in California resumes mean something. In New York you don't need a resume for a bartending gig. In fact, if I had broken one out when I lived there, I think I would've been laughed out of most places. But California is so serious. Seriously ridiculous. So he looked it up and down, attempting to wield his power over me. And then he came out from behind the bar. Apparently he was just standing in for the bartender, who had gone to the bathroom.

"I'm the bar manager," he said.

He said it the way they used to teach the vowels in school, enunciating each one so exaggeratedly, making a much bigger deal of it than it was.

"Let me see if the owner is around. I want you to meet him," he said. And he walked off toward the back. I sat on one of the empty bar stools. They were all empty. Well, it was only about four in the afternoon, and this was more of a nighttime bar.

A long bar, maybe forty feet, it was made of wood, but the edges were finished with brass. The same brass extended all the way to the wait station, where it became a pipe looping up into an arc above the bar, dividing the wait station from the patrons. I imagined customers hanging on the twisted pipe and over it for balance as the crowds pressed them against it and their drunkenness tipped them off center. The floors were slate squares, the kind high heels can make a clicking sound on.

The bartender the manager had been standing in for was now back in her spot behind the bar, polishing bottles. There were three long stations of them and she pulled them down one at a time, taking their pour spouts out and scrubbing the goo off their sides. Every now and then she glanced at herself in the mirrors behind her shiny bottles and pushed her long curly hair out of her face. I didn't bother looking at myself. I knew my hair was falling down. I'd put it up to offset the outfit—professional and sexy, but not let-your-hair-down sexy.

Big paintings hung on the walls. Each one was a painting of a large, bug-eyed bug. The ponytailed guy came out of the back.

"I'm Sonny, by the way. We change the artwork every month," he told me with pride.

"That's nice," I said.

"Yeah," he said, "Listen, can you stick around for a little while? Trevor wants to meet you."

"Sure." It's not like I had a job to run off to.

"The thing about us is, we like New Yorkers. Most of us here are from New York, or we've lived there. You know, Fioreca's is like a New York–style bar."

"That's what I like about it," I said.

"Well, the other thing is, we're the highest-grossing club in Hollywood."

He said Hollywood even though we were in Beverly Hills.

"So we make money and you'll make money. You see up those stairs there? There's another bar up there, too. It's for the restaurant, which is really high-end gourmet stuff."

I looked at the staircase. The carpeting made me feel like it led up to a big living room. It was a deep burgundy with gold borders.

"Great," I said.

I wondered why he was trying to sell me on it when I was the desperate one. He had hazel eyes, and his ponytail was a blondish brown. He was about six feet tall and nice-looking. But the other bartender didn't seem to notice, and it gave me the feeling his looks were the kind that fade and don't mean anything once you get to know the person.

When Trevor came out he was very businesslike. He walked fast and he didn't look me directly in the eye. He had a military crew-style haircut and a big build. He talked fast, too. He told me that they would be opening two more stores in a short time and so if it didn't work out here and now, it might down the road.

"How long did you work for Perry Stone?"

"Almost two years."

"How was business there?"

"Pretty jamming," I admitted.

"But is Perry still on the 'thrifty' side?"

I got the feeling he didn't like Perry, and it made me like him. "That's a nice way of putting it," I said.

He grinned ever so slightly and continued looking at my resume. "Why so short a time in each place?" he asked.

I didn't think two years was a short time to work in a bar. That was the longest I'd spent in any one bar. Phil (who, did I mention, encouraged my choice of outfit for the interview) was the same way working as a cook. Two years seemed very settled in this business. I decided to push the envelope a little with the animosity Trevor seemed to feel for Perry. "Two years was overtime working for my last boss."

This time I got a chuckle, and then he shook my hand and said to make a pest of myself by calling regularly to see if anything had opened up.

I couldn't detect what the ponytailed guy, Sonny, had said to Trevor about me. But later, when they hired me, I discovered that my big tits were a big part of the conversation.

The freshness of the first day wore off in about a minute because it was really the millionth day, only in a different place. The old faces blur as the new ones drift in.

But some of my customers I like more than others. I liked Steve right away. My first week, I bumped into him on the street and he recognized me. A lot of times people don't recognize me when I'm out of uniform. Too out of context.

"Hey, how about some service?" he'll say, banging his fist on the bar, announcing his arrival officially.

I enjoy him because he's entertaining and he always seems happy to see me, but sometimes I really don't need to hear what he's got to say. Today he comes in, takes a long sip of his Absolut and Cranberry, looking a little tired around the eyes, and says, "I like her, but she can only get off one way."

I wonder if he's having the same unexplainable eye ailment that I've been having. I went to the doctor about the swelling, but so far he hasn't a clue. "Stress—it's the stress," they always say.

Half of me hopes Steve will tell me the one way; the other half of me hopes he'll bump into someone he knows and tell them instead. Hope being beside the point, I just nod my head slowly as I replace the old soggy straws with crisp new ones. But there's a plump guy with a comb-over next to Steve who looks like he's just been goosed, and he starts making a stab at guessing.

"She can only do it when you've got her on her hands and knees?" he asks.

"No," Steve says, "it's not like that." And then to me, "Nicky, man, she's driving me crazy."

"Well, she is a little weird," I say. "But have you told her this one way that she, you know, does it, bothers you?"

"I just don't think that's a fair thing to do. You know, maybe she won't get off at all if I get her tensed up thinking about it," he says.

"Yeah," I say. I can appreciate his concern.

"Yeah," he says. "I just try different ways to make her do it, you know, and see if she goes for it. And then I try to keep things new. I've even been buying her flowers. And you know I don't have a lot of money right now. She likes lilies. So every day this week I've been slipping a couple into her purse, her cosmetic bag, her panties, even." He smiles at me kind of nastily. Then he just sits there looking depressed.

"But the thing is, she always ends up in the same place. I made her dinner the other night at my place. Ya know, the whole nine yawds." Sometimes his New York accent really kicks in. "Champagne, these little crab appetizers, a Dijon chicken dish—I got the recipe from my roommate's Julia Child cookbook—and chocolate-covered strawber-ries for dessert with whipped cream; you know, trying to shake things up, throw her off her course, send a little romance her way."

Steve's roommate is in his late forties. Divorced. (And apparently has a thing for Julia Childs.)

"Well that's a good idea. That's nice," I tell him.

"Yeah, and I hardly drank that night. Speaking of which, can you freshen this one? But it doesn't make a difference. I think it has to do with what she used to do, you know?"

"You think?" I ask. I know what she used to do, but I can't say it out loud because the nosy guy next to Steve, who looks like a Larry to me—I've never seen him before—is still trying to guess the one way. I think he wouldn't be able to contain himself if he found out Janine used to work in a massage parlor that wasn't just a massage parlor.

"Is it that she has to be tied up?" Larry asks.

"No," Steve says to the guy and I can tell he's getting annoyed. And "Yeah," he says to me. "I think it's like a control thing."

"Are you at least in her when she comes? Just tell me that much," Larry says, holding up his hand. "I think I can get it if I know that much."

Steve ignores the guy, and I withdraw, leaning back and resting my elbows on the back bar. I glance around, and when my radar doesn't pick up an empty glass or a finger rising to wave me down, I just gaze up at the ceiling, pretending to think deep thoughts.

Everyone asks about the ceiling, because it's so high and has those steel-bolted rafters that crisscross like in an old hangar. "Hey, did this used to be a hangar before?" they ask. They hope it was. They like the idea of sitting in a place that used to be full of old airplanes. I wish it was a hangar and that it had never converted. Then, right now, I could climb into one of those little two-seaters and *whiissh* right out of here. Maybe I'd grab a bottle of McCallan's Eighteen for when I touched down.

Steve asks me for some change for cigarettes. On his way to the machine, he calls me over. As if the change is wrong, he says, "It's three dollars, isn't it?" That's for Larry's benefit. And then he leans over and whispers, "It's the kind of thing that I don't feel so great when she does it, you know?"

When Steve comes back, Larry is in the men's room and I make my own guess.

"Is it that she has to touch herself no matter what you're doing to her?" I whisper into his ear. It's the kind of thing that wouldn't surprise me about her, now that I know her a little.

"You got it, baby," he says, not even surprised. "It's such a drag. I mean, why can't she let me do it? I feel like she could just plug herself into the wall for how much it has to do with me."

It's a creepy thought, because when I think of *anyone* plugged into a wall, I think of electrocution. Janine dyes her hair this really white, white, blonde. I see these stiff white springs of hair boinging out of her head as her body contorts itself into a four-legged creature, the plug coming out of her behind like a tail: an electrified porcupine sprayed white for Christmas.

Whenever Janine comes in, she follows Steve around like a puppy dog. She drinks what he drinks, sits where he sits, calls the waitstaff the same nicknames he calls them, even tries to be my buddy the way Steve is. But on her, there's something wrong with it; something sinister; something familiar that I haven't quite been able to put my finger on.

"Hi, Nicky," she'll say, oh, so sweetly. "Can I have a Chardonnay, please?"

Her mouth seems to quiver her requests at me, her lips popping open and closed, accentuated by the wet sheen her lipstick holds even in the dim lighting of the bar.

"Hey, Jonie," she'll call to our cocktail waitress, "you want a piece of gum?"

"Mel," she'll say to Melissa who's working right alongside me, "don't bother with a new pack, just smoke mine."

It's odd the way she sucks up to everybody while at the same time acting like she's the Queen of Sheba. She's a totally different person than the one Steve first described. But tonight, coupled with her masturbation problem, it starts to make perfect sense. It clicks: she reminds me of Eve in *All About Eve*.

Because she doesn't want to be with Steve, she wants to *be* Steve— the regular we all like, who gets drinks comped and receives phone calls at the bar. She may even be *using* Steve to attain this lofty status, but one of the problems is she's too high profile. She carries a beeper and runs to the pay phone whenever it goes off. But that's not the only problem.

The main one is, nobody likes her but Steve. And a lot of the time he doesn't even like her.

One day, Sonny takes me aside and asks me, "Do you think Janine is a pro?"

"No," I say. "I mean, I can understand why you ask. But no—not out of here, anyway."

My answer doesn't satisfy Sonny. He wants her to be a hooker so he can exert some authority over the situation. He loves drama and he loves control. He likes to know what nobody knows, even if the information is inaccurate. That's why, that same day when Steve comes in, Sonny takes Steve aside and tells him, "I know the score with Janine. She's 86'd."

Steve says, "What are you talking about?" She's always getting into some kind of trouble, it could be anything.

Sonny says, "I know she's a hooker. I've seen her working it in here."

Steve tells Sonny, "She's not a hooker. Believe me, I'm fucking her. I know."

Sonny says, "I'm sorry, man. Maybe you think you know, but she can't come in here anymore. And listen, buddy, if I see you in here with her, I'm going to have to 86 you, too."

I hear the whole thing, because it's during the day and it's just the three of us. But they both tell me the story of what happened, each version a little different.

I tell Steve, "I told Sonny he was wrong. I know she's not."

Now I'm not so sure. Does Sonny hear her on the pay phone outside his office, returning beeper calls, talking to a john? Or does he know from personal experience? In any case, she can't come here anymore.

So the next time she does, Sonny takes her aside, but I can only imagine this conversation. And I can only imagine how hot and hard he is after he's completed his mission. On her way out, she calls to me, "Hi, Nicky! Listen, I can't stay now, I'll see you later."

What's she thinking? Does she think I don't know Sonny just called her a hooker? Does she think I didn't notice that she didn't spit all over his shoes or scream and yell at him? If anybody called me a hooker, and I wasn't, I'd kill him. Or at least kick him.

I told Steve from the start she was trouble. She's like the perfume they spray on you in department stores as you walk by—a tester. The way she talks, her mouth opening wide, her teeth grinding between words, loud, twitchy and fidgety in her tight minis and high heels, waving her long manicured fingernails around; always looking around to see who was watching her, always making sure someone was.

Larry comes back from the bathroom and says, "I got it! I was sitting on the can and it came to me," waving his finger around like he's Newton and he's just discovered this thing called gravity.

"Good," Steve says, closing the subject. I just smile at Larry like he's really sharp. Then I walk down to the other end.

There's this guy Shell down there. He drinks beer, sometimes vodka. His hair grows long on the sides of his head as it slips further and further away from his forehead. And he's very pale. Anemic. He's coming from work and describes an incident to his Mexican friend that must have happened at work. As he speaks he develops a Hispanic dialect, as if he thinks his friend will understand him better this way. He drops his S's and rolls his R's. "He say he don't do it. I leave the twenty dollar and come back, pick up change. I go do my ten report and it still open. He send me message. He fuck with me. I don' b'leeeve it," he says, stressing the "e" like my bar back, Ricky from Zacatecas would.

I ask Ricky about it. "You ever notice that he does that?"

Ricky says, "Yeah. Why the fuck he do it?"

We both shake our heads in disapproval. Ricky says, "He's loco. Crazy."

I love Ricky. He helps me pass the time because he's always noticing something funny or strange. He's been telling me for weeks now that he thinks Shell is going a little crazy.

"Watch how he always buy his boss from the hotel drinks. He's fucking up over there and I hear he give his boss head, just to keep his job."

"No," I say.

He nods.

"I tink so, honey," he says kind of sing songy. Ricky has just had a baby. Everyone runs around the restaurant saying, "Ricky had a baby!" as if he has given birth to it himself.

"What did you name her?" I ask him.

"Montserrat," he says. One of the waiters, Lonnie, is in earshot. He's fair-skinned, with strawberry blond hair, and he's gay. Ricky and some of the busboys like to make fun of him. They make fun of everything, every chance they get, but Lonnie is a good target because he can be dictatorial at times. They don't have any bright ideas about how to get his goat, so they just bring Santa Monica Boulevard into their taunts in as effeminate a way as they can, and figure they're on the right track.

So now Lonnie says, "Oh, Montserrat, after the opera singer. Is that why you named her that, Ricardo, after the famous soprano?"

"What he say?" Ricky asks me as Lonnie walks away with more deliberate sway in his hips than usual.

"There's a famous opera singer called Montserrat, and he wanted to know if you named your daughter after her," I tell him.

"No." He smiles.

"Well, how did you come up with that name? It's a beautiful one."

"My wife pick it," he says.

"Oh. Well, maybe she named her after the singer," I say.

"No, I don't think so," he laughs.

"Well, the next time somebody asks, tell them, 'I named her after the loveliest soprano I've ever heard.'"

Shell is still telling his story Hispanic style. He claims that Hector, the bartender over at the hotel where he works, has intentionally messed up the last transaction between them to make him look bad. At the hotel, the bartender is the cashier for all the waiters. Shell claims he gave the bartender a twenty for a customer's check, received change, and returned it to the customer. Then when he went to close his bank and create a report two minutes later, he had an outstanding check show up as not paid. He thinks Hector pocketed the twenty, taking the change for the customer out of his own tips, just to teach Shell a lesson. I can't tell if he himself pocketed the twenty, or if maybe he screwed up somewhere else in the night and he's making this story up, or why Hector would want to teach him a lesson. For what?

Because Shell's a blank to me. A blank nothing.

"How you doing?" I ask him.

"Blah, blah, fine. Blah, blah, nothing."

Nothing to talk about. Nothing to think about. Nothing between us. Nothing. I guess there's nothing wrong with that, except that I need something because it's the nothingness that drives me insane.

When I was first introduced to Shell, he couldn't stop staring at me. Eyeing my body up and down, examining my face, looking for something. He'd sit, glance, drink. Sit, stare, drink. Drink, drink, drink, stare, stare, stare, to see if I was looking at him, until I was. And then it was because his vacant eyes made me think he needed a drink or a beer. I couldn't help myself, because that's what I'm here for. To see to what they need. I wasn't sure if he wanted me, or wanted me to want him. But I was sure that he wanted a drink or a beer, always. And now he's just always here, sitting and drinking, with nothing to share.

Steve heads for the door. "I gotta get outta here," he calls out to me, tilting his head in the direction of the Larry guy. "What do I owe you?" He tosses me a ten.

"That's good," I say. "See you."

I mosey down the bar to my register. Five for me. Five for the house. He's a regular. He only had two, but I have to buy him one.

At the register, looking in the mirror, I notice that the Larry guy, the one that's been guessing how Janine gets off, looks really sad. His jowls hang down below his chin as he stares into his drink.

"Let me freshen that for you," I say, scooping his glass up and adding nice new rocks and a splash of soda.

"Thanks," he says with a shy smile.

"What's your name?" I ask.

"My name? Oh, my name's Bill."

"Oh. You look more like a Larry to me. Anyway, nice to meet you officially, Bill," I say, extending my hand. But I still think of him as that Larry guy and I always will.

"Thanks. And you're Nicky, right?"

"That's me."

"Thanks for the freshener, Nicky," he says.

"You're welcome. If you need a refill, just yell."

I can see why he's disappointed. He's like a kid who tried to play a guessing game, but no one would give him any hints or tell him if he was getting warmer. He looks better with his full drink and dry napkin. It gives him something to do, anyway.

Something to do. Something we, too, long for at the moment because it's so quiet. I wonder how Casey's night is going at Halle's two weeks post surgery and right back at it. We kill the slow time by talking about our real lives. Jonie agonizes over a movie pitch she's working on.

"I just can't get it down to that one-sentence summary. It never sounds right."

"Oh, come on. You're such a fast talker. Make it zippy. It's just to get you in the door."

"I know. I'm trying. I think I gotta put it out there in prayer more," she says, grabbing her tray.

Jonie prays a lot. She's a true believer. It's hard to complain around her because she'll just make you feel like it's all a part of God's plan.

Sandy, another waitress, tries to memorize material for her law presentation at UCLA. Every now and then she gets me to quiz her on torts. I like the law, but every lawyer who comes in here seems to hate it.

And Alex, one of the bartenders, sails in on his long actor legs to collect his paycheck, talking about a day player gig he did today and a part he's waiting to hear on tomorrow; each of us in hopeful anticipation of getting out of this place, definitely including me. But instead of continuing the conversation in the same vein and complaining about this audition or that audition, I start a new subject.

"Phil's coming home tonight," I volunteer to Jonie.

"Are you excited to see him, or has it been a nice vacation for you?"

"Well, I've been aware of his absence, but I wouldn't call what I'm feeling excited. Unless you mean anxious."

"That's too bad," she says. "Sometimes the first days when they get back there's a niceness, though."

"Yeah, sometimes," I say.

We're talking in code. She doesn't want to say what she's thinking, and I don't want to think what I'm thinking. I wouldn't count on the niceness lasting a few days, but I am curious to find out how his family's doing. He's usually excited just by having gotten away, so maybe there could be a nice day or two. He's better when he's happy.

The conversations fragment between orders.

"But he said to me, I could seal the deal if, oh, I need two Chardonnays," Jonie says.

When she returns, "If I just change one little aspect of the premise. But do you know what that aspect was? Wait. I'll tell you after I get 28's order."

When she comes back, "Hey, by the way, how did that audition go, Nick?"

"Well, I didn't get the music video, but the one after that went great. Still I haven't heard, so . . ."

"Yeah, I know."

The busboys chatter among themselves. It's difficult to understand their fluent Spanish, but sometimes I pick up a few words. Like they say *hijo* a lot. It means son, but they're not talking about their children, of which they have many. They refer to each other this way. "Mi hijo," they start the rhythm, usually ending up in boisterous giggles.

They make the sign to me that they've created to mean "I want you." It's the heel of the hand held upright with the fingers curled under. I respond with the sign that indicates, "Yeah, take me," by extending my arms out in front of me and then pulling them into my sides, with one smooth motion, clenched fists, and a slight thrust of the pelvis. They've taught me this. *Mis hijos.*

Sometimes I'm a part of the conversations. Sometimes I just watch them carrying on. The waitresses stand lined up against the wall, giving the appearance of full attention while conversing amidst themselves. Sandy leaves her place to pick up a drink and tell me that she doesn't know whether to leave her boyfriend or marry him.

After I empty five or six ashtrays three or four times in a half an hour, I mention to Ricky that I would not be offended if he emptied an ashtray once in a while.

"And what do you do?" he says. "All you do is make drinks."

The night creeps along in slow motion, the clock proof of this as I stare at it and watch its big hand crawl toward ten.

Most nights it's two bartenders and a bar back, but on Mondays, like tonight, the only night Ricky and me work together, it's just the two of us. I do make him work hard, but that's because he has a tendency to be lazy. They push me around, I push him around, and that's how it works. He knows it's just my way. I think he prefers it to someone making polite requests of him.

"Which night you work hard? Wednesday? Friday? Or every night the same, you do nothing," he says, walking away like I've really irritated him. He's probably going to the kitchen to find something to eat. He loves to eat.

A Marvin Gaye song comes on and everyone at the bar starts to sway a little. It's that "Brother, Brother" song that nobody can resist singing even when they don't know the words. A very pretty light-skinned black woman lets it out full throttle. She grabs hold of the man standing on her left; she's dancing and she wants a partner. The tall man, self-conscious, looks around as if he might actually find a hole to crawl into. The pretty dancing lady has to reel him into her power.

"Come on," she says rubbing her hip into his thigh, forcing him to bend his knees and move.

"Don't be shy," she says, taking his hands and rolling her shoulders down and around until he's moving with her. They dance well together, and her girlfriend sits at the bar singing and shaking it on her stool until she can't restrain herself any longer and she's up and dragging some other poor fool man onto the floor. And one by one, people are swaying on the floor or shaking it on their stools, in and out of the bathrooms, and up to dinner. They all smile and laugh, and I think, this is what it should be like all the time: people singing and dancing and laughing in a bar. I wiggle along with them to the beat behind the bar, groovin' right up to my customers.

The dancing and fever of the music make the flames of the candles flicker in their holders. Jonie catches some of the rhythm as she picks up empties and stops to take orders. Her toes move to the beat, and soon her tray is towering above everyone's head as her own head lifts out of her long and graceful neck like a ballerina's.

It reminds me of this artist that used to come into a cafe I worked in in New York. He always came in wearing a wonderful hat. A hamburger hat, or an ice cream sundae, or an animal—he made every kind of hat you could possibly imagine. And some days he'd sit there, watch us working, and draw, cut and paste. One day, on his way out, he handed me a beautiful collage. It was me, wearing my work shirt above my waist and a ballerina's outfit below. My legs extended strong and long right down to pointed pink toe shoes, and my arms were outstretched, juggling drinks. He had used the white lace from our doilies and some pink tissue to create my ballerina costume.

"I see you all as dancers," he said in a beautiful accent whose origin I couldn't quite figure out, and smiled as he made his way to the door.

I start to feel hopeful that this night may happen after all. Maybe a high roller will step through that door and shower me with twenties.

Ludwig steps up to the bar. Definitely not the high roller I had in mind.

"All right, I'll take one," he says, as if I'm pushing it on him.

"Delighted," I say as he reaches for the Beck's I put on the bar, testing it for coldness.

"Does your boyfriend like cigars?" he asks.

"Yeah, actually, he does," I laugh. I don't know how he even knows I have a boyfriend.

"So, take a couple," he says dropping a few in front of me on the lip of the bar. "Beck's. It's the best," he says, grabbing his beer. "The best beer in the world." He always says this.

"Isn't it time for you to go home?" I ask.

"Time? What's the difference?" he says, shrugging, as if he doesn't go home at the same time every day.

As he shuffles back to his familiar little corner of the bar, there's a little bebop in his step. It seems even he has picked up the rhythm dancing through the room.

Everybody remembers when it's like this. The thought of the people laughing and drinking and dancing brings them back again and again. Then, even when it's not like this and they're disappointed, when it's dreary and dark and cold and empty, the hope of what it could be like keeps them coming back. It's that love/hate thing. Even my worst night doesn't seem to erase my best, and I keep coming back, too.

I usually work only three nights a week, but this week I'm picking up extra shifts, paying back favors for the road trip with Casey, earning a little extra, making this my fifth night in a row. I cruise up and down, focusing on every detail: soft white napkins under each glass, ice cold beers paired with frosty mugs, fresh-cut lemons and limes stacked to the rim, and not one loose pimiento in the tray that holds the extra-large olives. I cling to these moments that move.

"Are you still working here?" I ask Ricky when he returns from wherever he disappeared to. "I thought you went home."

"What's wrong with you?" he says. "Are you sick? I was talking to some customers. They say you are the worst bartender. Nicky, she's so slow and bossy, what's wrong with her?"

"Shut up, you idiot, and go set up those two guys on the far end for dinner," I say.

"For dinner? The kitchen's closed," he says, making me panic a little.

I look at my watch. "You're not funny," I say, even though he kind of is.

"Idiot," he says.

This is one of my pet names for him. He's picked up on it as a new word in his vocabulary, using it whenever he can.

"Which ones?" he says.

"The two funny-looking ones on the far end," I say.

"Oh, them," he says. "What are they having?"

"The salmon pesto with capers and the filet mignon with gorgonzola." It's fun to make his mouth water.

"Go. Look, incoming," I say, pointing to the people on their way in and pushing him along.

"Nervous, nervous," he says, meaning me. But he picks up his pace.

Shell calls me over. He looks bad tonight. His skin is not just pale, but yellowish, too. Last night when I was getting into my car, I saw him with guys I've never seen him with before. They all walked fast towards a big, ugly, garish something, not a limo. I didn't want to stare. He's jittery, talking fast, saying nothing as usual.

"Are you mad at me, Nicky?" he asks.

"No."

"Are you sure?"

"Yeah. Why would I be?" I say.

"I don't know. You're not, though, right?" he says.

"No, Shell. You need anything?"

"Not just yet, thank you," he says.

"Okay," I smile. I walk away. He watches me as I get the order of the five or six people that have just come in. He waves me over.

"I'll have another beer," he says when I get to him, as if to reward me. The beer he drinks is stocked on the other side of the bar, where I just was. He knows it. A simple wave of the bottle or "one more" with his index finger would've been sufficient, but he likes to control me. For a regular he's not very cool. He's not very cool, period.

So I walk down to the other end, grab him a beer and an ice-cold glass, then back to his end, and as I'm putting the glass up, he says, "Can I have a cold glass, please?" I always give him one. Then he throws a twenty at me and says, "Here, take this, Nicky."

I'm not sure what he wants me to do with it. Do I throw it in my cup, or will I have to use it for his drinks? Twice more he asks me if I'm mad at him. Maybe because I can't buy him every drink he orders. I can't afford it. I mean, I don't own the place. If I didn't charge everybody who told me not to, I'd never make a cent for the house and I'd be out of a job. I know. I've seen guys try it. It's not right.

But Shell gets offended when I ring his drinks up, even if I do it on my own check.

He tells Ricky, "What is she doing ringing my drinks up? None of the other bartenders ring anything I drink."

I hope no one hears him, because it would make the other bartenders look bad. He's glued to my every move, wanting me to break the rules for him just to prove how important he is.

Now he orders a drink for his friend and tells me to put it on his tab. I feel his eyes on me as I go to the register, and this time I put it on his tab. If he's not paying for his drinks, and their drinks are on him, and I don't charge him for their drinks, who the hell is paying for drinks at my bar?

At the register, I think I see Casey in the mirror. I turn around and it *is* her, walking through the door.

CHAPTER 5

"**Y**OU'RE OFF ALREADY?" I blurt out.

"Hey, what do you want from me? It was dead," Casey barks back.

"You make anything?" I ask.

She just looks at me with one eyebrow cocked as she breaks out a cigarette. I light her up.

Her dark brown hair stands out so strikingly against her white, white skin. Her lipstick is rich like blood in the middle of all that white. Usually I can't help but stare at her because of whatever funky, cool get-up she's wearing, but tonight she's still in her black and whites, lipstick still blood, but faded.

"Well then, what'll you have, sweetheart?"

"Well then, that's more like it," she smiles. "How about a Cab?"

"Seriously?" I say.

"Seriously," she says back, staring me down. "Doctor's orders."

I take a big bowl-shaped red wineglass off the shelf behind me and place it on the lip of the bar in front of her. I uncork a bottle of Ravenswood Cabernet, the best we're pouring by the glass tonight, and we both watch as the deep purple liquid falls into the belly of the glass like a waterfall. I put it in front of her on a clean white cocktail nap and the wine swishes around a little, leaving fine legs dripping down the sides of her glass.

"Cheers," I say breaking the awkward silence. "Next time, bring a note." She looks confused. "From your doctor," I add.

She grins, and I grab one of her Marlboro Lights for myself.

"So what's going on?" I say, blowing mediocre smoke rings and trying to act cool.

"Lisa wants to know if we want to go dancing tomorrow night. I didn't know if Phil was back, so I told her I'd have to check with my wife."

"He'll be back tonight, but he's going to have to work tomorrow and probably every day for the rest of his life to start paying off the car. How're you doing, uh, feeling?" I ask.

I ask it casually, or at least I try to. I want it to be casual, I want it to be light, I want it to be the opposite of what our hellish journey from San Francisco through surgery has been.

Because now, weeks after the surgery, Casey's leg is healing nicely, and there is no evidence that the cancer has spread. She still has to go in for an MRI every three months and whatever other kinds of watchful waiting things they do, but basically it looks good.

So I don't know what it was exactly that threw me when she asked for the wine, or why it still feels odd to see her sitting in front of me sipping it. It's not like she's going to live the rest of her life like a monk just because this happened to her. I mean, she hasn't even quit smoking, so far. Still, I'm confused as to how she should proceed. How should I? What are the guidelines? Is it okay to act normal? What should be normal for her?

"You want to go?" I ask.

"Yeah, I feel fine," she says. "She said Luann and Gigi want to go, too, so I thought it would be a kick."

We'd worked with Luann and Gigi at Halle's, but I didn't figure on them both lasting so long. They were always late, weren't particularly good waitresses, and smoked and drank on the sly. But me, who was always on time, rang a fortune in sales, and was clean as a whistle, got the boot all the way downtown.

"Gigi just got fired."

"For what?"

"They said for being late."

"But she was always late. She probably thought it was okay to be late."

"I think that's just what they do. Look at you. They're assholes."

"Tell Lisa your wife said yes."

"Okay, sweetheart," she says with a mock smile.

They call us the husband and wife team because when we used to work together, Casey waitressing, me bartending, we were inseparable, but we'd bicker a lot.

"Were you smoking out back?" I might say when she'd come to the bar to collect her order.

"In the bathroom," she'd reply.

"That is sooo gross. Can't you go like half an hour without one?"

"That *was* half an hour."

"You smell like an ashtray."

"You smell, period," she'd say, making off with her drinks, a grimace of pungency on her face.

Even though we don't work together any more, we've maintained that solid matrimonial bond.

"Was Gigi really late?"

"Yeah. But I'm late every other day, and nobody bothers me."

"Well, maybe that's because Murph doesn't have a crush on Gigi. Is she upset?"

"She's pissed. She says if they don't give her unemployment benefits, she's gonna sue. And you know them, they might not."

Ricky comes by and grabs Casey's hand, giving it a little peck.

"*Hola, mi amor. Como estas?*" he says.

"Well, she's just fine," I say. "Quit flirting with her. Eeewwh," I say making a "yuck" face.

"Hey, Ricky. How's the baby?" Casey says.

"*Que bueno,*" he smiles, "Thank you. How was tonight?"

"Not very, Ricky," she says.

"I'm sorry, honey. Nicky's not making us much tonight either. But you know how slow she is," he says, shaking his head and looking down to the ground as though he feels genuinely sorry for me.

Casey laughs as I give Ricky a big squeeze around the shoulders and pat him down the bar and back to work.

"This is good," Casey says taking another sip of her wine.

"Yeah. We don't usually have it by the glass, but Sonny wanted us all to taste it, which I thought was kind of cool."

"Very cool, for him," Casey nods. "Why do you think it's so quiet?"

"Not a clue," I say pointing an index-finger-and-thumb gun to my head. "I'm glad you popped up, though. No offense, but what are you doing here? You could've called to ask me out."

"Yes, darling, but I had something to tell you."

"Good or bad?"

"I'm not sure how you'll feel about it. You might think it's funny."

"Funny would be good."

"It's about last night."

"Oh, the party! How was it?"

"It was pretty good," she says, trying not to smile, or something weird is going on with her face. In fact, she's acting kind of weird in general. She tells me a little more about the party, but she's just bullshitting me along.

"What's *wrong* with you?" I interrupt.

"Nothing. Why?"

"Who'd you sleep with?"

She takes out another smoke, lights it from the old one, a sip of her wine, and finally she speaks.

"Jay."

Jay is our friend. He works with us. He's worked with us for years, and Casey and he have always seemed to have a sibling-type relationship. He's got sandy brown hair, a really cute smile. He's our friend.

She studies my face, searching for a reaction. But I don't know how to react. She said I might think it was funny, and I know what she means, but it's not ha, ha funny, so I just wind up smiling what I imagine is a really dirty grin.

"Okay, so now you know."

"Okay, so now tell me."

"One minute we were at the party, the next we were at my house."

"Were you drunk?"

"I had one glass, doc."

"Did you like it?"

"Yeah."

"Do you like him?"

"Yeah."

"You *like* him, like him?" I say, like we're in the third grade.

"I think so."

Now that I think about it, I think they'd make one of the great quirky couples of all time. They're both kind of off-center. His side jobs include radio and carpentry, hers, design. She has great taste and big style, and he dresses funny, in a good way. I don't want to discourage her.

"So you think this might be a thing?"

"It might."

"Well, that's cool. Jay is great."

"You think?"

"I love Jay. I just never would've pegged it, because you're always fixing him up with someone else."

"I know. That's what makes it kind of funny, though, right?"

"That, and just the whole thing of you and Jay makes it funny."

"Yeah," she admits.

I light up another one of her smokes and take a sip of her Cab.

"So how'd you leave it?

"I told him I'd see him at work."

"He worked today, too?"

"Yeah. I went in before he did, so I just left him the key to lock up and he came in when his shift started, at six."

"So you were with him all day?"

"Yeah."

Then, fuck it—I'm too immature and can't resist.

"Ooooh. And then he came to work and you were giving each other googly eyes all night?"

"Do you know that you're an idiot?"

"Sometimes," I say, following a wagging finger down the bar to its empty glass.

As things go from slow to slow motion, a guy comes in sticking his forefinger and thumb into each eye socket as though he is trying to dig his eyeballs out.

"Rough day?" I ask as he slumps onto a stool.

"The roughest," he sighs.

"Can I get you anything to make it better?"

"A double Bloody Mary," he says, in what sounds like a Jersey accent.

After several he's ready to talk. My name is printed on his receipts and so he begins to feel familiar with me.

"Nick," he says, "It's my brother-in-law, my stupid fucking brother-in-law."

"Ho! Excuse me for a moment," I say.

"Sure, Nick" he says, "And how about another double on your way back?"

A double Bloody Mary—strange drink to order a double of (Can I carry you home, sir? 'Cause I'm thinking I might have to), but he isn't really slurring yet.

I make my way back over to Casey.

"I think I've got a long story coming my way. You gonna hang for a while, or are you outta here?"

"Out," she says, throwing down some cash and gathering her stuff. "Hey Nick, don't say anything about Jay. We want to keep it low profile till we know what the fuck is up."

"I gotcha," I say, throwing my hands up to indicate *I* will not be guilty of spilling the beans. "Can I let on that I know with Jay, though?"

"Yeah. He knows I'd tell you."

"Can I make fun of him a little?"

"No, you idiot."

"Well, okay. Thanks for coming by, lover. I'll see you tomorrow."

"See you tomorrow."

"Hey, leave me a smoke, would you?"

"Sure thing, pumpkin," she says, dropping a couple on the lip of the bar.

"Mañana," she says pinching Ricky's butt on her way out.

I deliver Jersey's double to him, and light up as he continues his story.

"Where yuh from, Nick?" he asks.

"I'm from New York."

"No kiddin'. I'm from Jersey."

"Oh yeah?" I say.

Those few wonderful moments dancing to Marvin, now dead. My back hurts and so does my head. I choke on the smoke as it enters my mouth, my ears, my fingers and clothes from every direction. The alcohol runs down the sides of the liquor bottles after I pour from them. To protect my back, I lean against the well, but as I reach for used napkins and ashtrays with the chewed up-gum stuck to their sides, the sticky liquid saturates my thighs. It soaks through my black pant legs.

My stomach is torn between what it really feels and what it wants to feel. The smell of the food, hot, wafts by me and I'm envious of the people who get to eat it. Something hot would be good right now. It's cold here. It always is. I can't get warm. My uniform is too light and doesn't protect me. Even when they turn off the air, I'm cold.

A couple of people flag me down to close out their checks. A few are sucking that last bit of hope out of their glasses, while one or two look like they're ready to settle in for a sleepover.

"Hey, Nicky," Sonny calls out.

He waits for me to get to him so the trivia he's about to lay on me will feel as important as he wishes it was.

"Tomorrow night is inventory, so make sure you really marry the bottles well tonight," he says.

"Okay," I say. "Can I get started now?"

He looks around. "Yeah, go ahead."

There are only a few stragglers now, the last survivors. A few men that have already been in are back, empty-handed. They walk up and down the bar pretending to look for someone they know, when really they're just looking for someone. Some have already spent hundreds for dinner and drinks on women who have eaten heartily and are now on their way home, alone.

And poor Jersey sits slumped over his double Bloody, dragging out his story so he won't have to go home to his wife and his brother-in-law crashing out on their couch. Apparently his brother-in-law has been kicked out of his own house by his *pregnant* wife who has just been informed by an intern in Grenada that her husband has been fucking her, which apparently is not the only thing the wife and the girlfriend have in common, 'cause it sounds like the girlfriend is pregnant too.

I want to look at my watch. Every night we all tease each other by looking at the clock on the credit card machine and feigning amazement at how quickly the time has flown.

"Wow, twelve o'clock already," Jonie will say after glancing.

I'll jerk my head to look and, tragically, it's only ten.

So, now, I hesitate before I look at my watch, hoping it's time for last call. It is two long minutes away. I busy myself by scraping the black gunge out of the soda gun and throwing the cherries and olives back in their tremendous jars.

I smoke another cigarette, though I don't smoke (well, only when I'm here). I want a drink. No, I want ten. I don't have one, because I don't think it will help. Maybe tomorrow, when I'm refreshed, I'll drink to excess. For now, I sit here clocking the minutes, and then finally I bellow it out in my loudest bar voice: LAST CALL!

I count the bottles as Sonny, playing bouncer and enjoying it, ushers the last few hangers-on out the door.

"Let's go, people," he says, gathering them and shuffling them along. In the daytime he looks like a janitor in coveralls and grease, but at night, he slicks his ponytail back and struts through the place in expensive-looking Italian suits—Day Manager/Night Manager.

The staff quietly sings, "You don't have to go home, you just have to go."

I scrub the brass clean and close my bank. It hurts to stand. I tip Ricky 40 percent of my take. He's only supposed to get twenty, but after a whole night's work the twenty from tonight's crappy take would be cruel. But when I do well, I can afford to tip him forty. So I tip him forty anyway. He's got a baby and a wife.

Phil is waiting out front to give me a ride home. My car is in the shop and he's got the new used one. It looks like it's red.

I can see him sitting out there. His hair looks shaggy hanging over the back of his turtleneck, like in these few days it's grown. His eyes are hazel and big and his frame is on the small side. His looks are more scholarly than jockish, and so is he, but he looks sweet and handsome, relaxed, while he waits for me. I have to remind myself he's like a volcano: beautiful to look at from afar, painful to be near when it explodes.

"Well, hello there, good-looking. Nice wheels," I say, climbing in.

"Pretty cool, huh?" he grins.

"Verrry. You're sporting, man. Did you get a good deal on it?"

"I think so. Four thousand with forty thousand miles on it."

"That sounds pretty good," I say, sliding my hand across the black upholstery, then back behind Phil's neck, pulling him close for a welcome-home kiss.

He whispers "I missed you" into my hair.

"I bet you did," I say, stealing another kiss, then sliding back over to my new copilot seat.

"Wow, a red sports car. You better mind your speed, now. They're watching you, ya know."

"I know," he says with a devilish grin crossing his face. "Fasten your seatbelt, this baby rocks."

Flying down the side streets, Philip reminds me of a kid at a video arcade with one of those pretend cars and pretend driving courses, the kind of kid that's good at it and likes to play for a long time. He's got his window wide open, and his dirty-blond hair is blowing wildly through it.

"Uh, Mario Andretti, let's not get carried away," I say, having a momentary anxiety attack as Phil really seems to be simultaneously test-driving the speedometer and playing chicken with the quietly parked cars.

"Relax," he grinds his teeth, annoyed, continuing to accelerate, as though my warning forces him to prove how much faster he can still go without crashing.

When we get to our front stoop, he slows, pulls effortlessly into the last spot on our block, and asks, "What do you think?"

"I think you're right. This car rocks," I say, letting his bad attitude slide.

Then I hand over the cigars from Ludwig. He lights one up right away and gets a happy smile on his face.

"This is a really good cigar, honey. Thank your friend for me."

When we get inside, I run to the bathroom. I leave my pants down at my ankles when I'm through, too tired to pull them up only to pull them off.

"Will you help me get my shoes off?" I ask.

"Sure, little sleepyhead," he says, sitting me down on the bed and bending down over my long Doc Marten laces.

"How was it tonight, anyway?"

"Not horrible. I managed to scrape together a little over a hundred."

"Not horrible," he agrees.

"Were your mom and dad able to get down there and visit with you?"

"Yes and no," he says.

"What do you mean?"

"They made it down okay, but they were mostly dealing with tying up the loose ends of the old house. They want to make Florida their permanent home."

"Oh. Well, Florida's not a bad place to visit, anyway."

"Yeah," he says. "It's just that we'd be visiting them."

"Was it that bad?"

"Not really. It's just my Dad. He can be a real asshole."

"So it was kind of horrible, huh?"

"Kind of."

"Well, I'm particularly glad that you're home, then," I say, giving him a big bear hug.

Then both of us, closing in on exhaustion, start peeling our clothes off. So much to do to get undressed. Buttons to unbutton, sleeves to unroll, ties to untie. I can't wait to be naked.

My body snuggles against his warmth in our soft new flannel sheets and I feel my breathing slow as my eyes grow heavy.

I'm walking out to an old shed behind some house that I live in. I'm going to clean out some old things that have been in storage for a long time. It's way out back. It's getting dark out and the sky is very gray, like a storm is about to hit. As I approach the shed, four men are coming towards me. At first I'm frightened that they will bother me, but then I think I'm being paranoid. Just as I think again, the threat becomes real.

One of the men grabs my arm and says, "Not so fast, girlie." At the same moment, the others huddle around me, forming a barricade, as one of them starts to undress. All I can think is how they're going to take my soul and destroy it. If only I could have gotten to the shed sooner. "Get out, get out, get out," the voice in my head screams, though my own vocal cords can create no sound to call for help. One of the men holds a bar up to my neck, like a crowbar. He presses it against my throat as if he has read my mind and knows I want to scream.

I awaken to gooey mucus on my pillow and the fuzz of our black flannel sheets clinging to the sticky wetness of my sweat. As I reach up to touch my neck I can still feel the bar pressing against it, suffocating me like a noose.

CHAPTER 6

"**W**HAT'S THE MATTER?" I hear Phil say.

"Had a nightmare."

"You look it," he says.

"Thanks," I say.

"No. It's just, you're all wet."

"I know. It was a nightmare."

"I'm sorry," he says, wiping a piece of black fuzz off my face. "You want to talk about it?"

One of the things I like most about Philip is that he likes to talk. He likes to talk about everything and in detail. There is never a time when I go to him with something I really want to talk about that he won't.

We talk about people and places and plays and science and sex. Talk, talk, talk and more talk. Maybe it's because he's a writer. And when he isn't writing he feels like talking because he isn't writing, which I sometimes think is just another form/way of talking.

Sometimes he can talk your head off, though. He can wear me down so much with his talk that I sometimes forget what my point is. And I'm a person who likes to talk.

But right now, I don't feel like talking about my dream at all. I feel like talking about Phil's trip. I want to know how he's really doing, because I know he tries to make light of his feelings about going home to his Dad when there's very little light about it.

He's an army brat, so the truth is, home can be anywhere. Wherever his parents are is home. The last place was North Carolina; that's where this family reunion took place. But it wasn't really a reunion. His Mom and Dad were there selling their house—the house that they had spent the most time in since Phil can remember, which was not an enormous amount of time because in the army that's just not the way it goes. And while they were there selling their house, their nephew turned up selling his red 1989 Toyota Supra, and they got word to Phil that if he wanted a car, he should come down and check it out and they could all get to visit each other as a bonus. Or, as it turns out, not.

"Tell me more about your trip."

"I got to see Ally and the baby."

"Cool."

"Gilly's almost walking already."

"Falling on his head a lot?"

"Basically."

"Was Matty around?"

"Of course not. He was on a *special project*."

Phil's sister, Alyssa, is married to a military man, Matty. I guess if your father is one, you kind of get used to it. Or maybe those are the only guys she ever met growing up. I can't imagine it myself. All I know is that it's a world so foreign to me that I'm terrified to meet Phil's father. Yes, sir.

"It's too bad about Matty."

"It really is. Especially for Gilly. That kid needs positive role models, you know? He's surrounded by all that military shit. The comings and goings, constantly moving around."

"It takes you back, huh?"

"Yeah."

"How old were you the first time you moved?"

"It seems like the minute I was born we were moving."

"Do you have any early memories? Maybe a special bed you had or a kitchen you loved to eat in or anything that reminds you of what you felt like as kid?"

"The earliest memory I have is of this open grassy courtyard that all of us kids played in. I must have been two, or maybe three. We were all outside kicking a ball around, and I was having a hard time connecting. I was kind of scrawny as a kid, too, so that didn't help my self-confidence any. But this time I'm thinking of, a lot of the kids were older and bigger, and they were cheering me on. We had soda bottles lined up as goal posts, or bowling pins, whichever worked for you. And after several tries where I missed the ball completely, or just nicked it so it plopped down a half an inch in front of me, finally I nailed it. I kicked it dead on, and it really went, right through the goal, and I was so happy I must have had one of those ear-to-ear grins spread across my face, and the other kids were psyched, too, saying 'Way to go Philly!' and 'Whoah!' and whistling, and everyone's eyes were on that ball because it just kept going until, boom, it smacked right into my Dad's shin.

"He started yelling and screaming, and then he took the ball and smashed it in half—it was only a cheap plastic ball—and then nobody said anything. Then my Dad went inside to get another beer or whatever he was drinking, and I climbed under the stairs of our bungalow and cried there, where nobody could see me. I remember under those stairs, though. They were redwood. One of them was badly cracked, with fungus eating it away, and a nail was sticking out of it. And there was a ton of dirt and weedy grass under the house, too. But it was so nice and dark under there, cool, and really private, like my own little house."

"That's a sad story, honey."

"I know. We should visit Ally more."

"Was your dad always doing shit like that, or was he sometimes nice?"

"I guess he was nice to some people."

"Did he ever play ball with you?"

"Sometimes baseball. He'd always pitch it really fast, or sometimes he'd pretend to pitch it, but hold onto the ball to see what I'd do. Then he'd say, 'Don't flinch. Don't flinch. Stay in there.' Then if I flinched even when he didn't throw it, he'd say, 'If you're gonna play like that, I might as well be pitching it to your sister. Why don't you go get her out here?'"

"Sounds like a big bully."

"He wasn't that bad."

"You're hardly able to tell me any good stories about him."

"Well, what do you want me to do? Agree with you and say, yeah, my Dad's a real dick?"

"No. I'm sure he has redeeming qualities; it's just that in those moments he was acting like a dick. And you were just a kid then. I don't think it's so bad if you admit he was kind of mean."

"I just don't see it like you do. He was what he was. He is what he is. He's not the nicest guy, but there are good things about him. I don't run and tell you every good thing about him, you know. I mean, not everyone can be Joe fucking sensitive like your dad."

"Oh, here we go."

"Well, you seem to feel free to criticize my dad."

"So you have to attack mine?"

"Well, not everybody has a dad that will bend over backwards and do flips for them like you, you know?"

"Yeah, and it's a fucking shame, don't you think? I'm not saying your dad is a vicious murderer. I'm just feeling for you that he wasn't always the nicest guy to you, like you yourself said. Anyhow, we're having a conversation about you and your dad, and you're trying to turn it into a fight about mine."

I've had to work through a lot of stuff with my dad, too. But I'm close to my dad, and I know it makes Phil sick. I don't know exactly why— if he's jealous, or he just doesn't understand how any dad could be so nice to his child when his wasn't. And he acts meaner when my dad's around than other times.

When we're with my dad and my dad's being really nice to me, nurturing me, getting things for me, giving things to me, listening to me, hanging out, Phil's putting me down, criticizing me, telling me I don't know how to do whatever it is and I always do it wrong, as if to counteract my dad's effect on me. And I know it really hurts my dad. And I hate that. I hate seeing my dad hurt. I think it hurts me more than it should, actually.

It's got something to do with the fact that my mom hurt him so badly. Or at least, that's how it looked. No matter what he may have been at fault for, she definitely came off as the villainess, and I feel like I was a part of the secret that blew up in everybody's face. And my dad was wounded. So somehow, though I know I'm a little confused, I feel like I hurt him, too. I wounded him. Because I love my mom so much, and I love to see her happy, and I'm so much like her that I feel like I divorced him, too, even though I love my dad, and I know I'm not my mom. Still, though, I feel guilty and bad just like she does. And this one way that I'm like her worries me. The way that my dad was so hurt by her makes me feel like I have a huge capacity for inflicting pain on another person. And I'm afraid of it like an explosion. Like it's sure to happen, I just don't know what, exactly, will set it off.

"I just don't want to be figured out and analyzed. It's like you're trying to get to the root of some big problem you think I have, through my paternal history," Phil says.

"Well, why not? Isn't that a good way in? I'm just interested in you. I'm sorry, but it's my feeble way of getting to know you more. I don't know why, but I want that."

"Well, that's sort of a good segue into what I've been trying to tell you. Matty's trying to get stationed in Florida next. And if he does, my dad wants us to try to come for a visit then."

"And how is that a good segue?"

"My dad, you, me."

"Is it really so bad of me to ask you questions that might end up revealing intimate answers?"

"No."

"I mean, I've told you shit about my parents that isn't always the nicest. It doesn't mean I love them any less."

"I know."

"Then why do you have to talk shit about my dad? What do you have against him, anyway?"

"Nothing. I shouldn't have said anything."

"Is that the truth? Why do you act so mean around him?"

"Well, anything's gonna seem mean compared to him."

"What, are you in competition with him or something?"

"Fuck. I'm sorry. No. Your dad's a nice man."

He drags his suitcase around to the foot of the bed and starts unpacking.

"Well, why should I go to Florida with you? I don't think I want to meet your dad. I'm pretty sure he would hate me."

"Well, my mom and dad both want to meet you. And Tracey and Ally would love to see you."

"But why do you want me to go with you?"

"I don't know," he says.

"You wouldn't want to see your dad for a while, anyway. Would you?"

"I'd like to see where they settle in Florida. I'd go whenever they get there, if you promised to come with me."

"Let's just talk about it later, okay?"

"I'm sorry I got sarcastic about your dad. I just feel like there are good things about my dad, too. I just don't always get around to telling you about them, because he *can* be a big asshole."

"Well, I'm not committing to visiting the big asshole."

Then he brushes the hair out of my face and kisses me.

So even though he likes to talk, he doesn't like to talk about his dad. I guess he'd rather let me see for myself. And even though I'm scared, there's a part of me that needs to see for myself. Not meeting Phil's parents is in some ways even scarier than meeting them.

"Do you have to work tonight?" I ask.

"I have to work as much as possible until I can pay off that car," he says.

"That's what I figured. I think I'm going to go dancing with Casey and some of the girls from Halle's Place, okay?"

"It's fine with me. It would just be nice if you two tried to steer clear of trouble instead of looking for it," he says in an authoritative tone that weirds me out.

"Oh. Well, okay," I say, as though I'm carefully considering it.

CHAPTER 7

"**C**AN I WEAR this one?"

"Yeah, that one looks really good on you," Casey approves the olive-colored hat I've just pulled down off its hook.

"Where are we going, anyway?"

"We're going to meet at Pink's, and then I don't know."

"Where'd you get those shoes?"

"Melrose."

"They're cool."

They're these really cool, chunky brown boot/shoes, with a thick heel and a big old toe. She's wearing them with lightish-brown trousers that look like men's and a dark-brown vest with the faintest baby-blue pinstripes. Her hat is cream-colored and velvety. Design, it makes sense; costumes, props, sets, she's got a real knack for it.

"You look great, by the way," I say.

"Thanks," she says. "Hey, how did your audition go?"

"Oh, they loved me. Thought I was great, really liked my voice, didn't give it to me. Said I was too young."

"How old's she supposed to be?"

"Late thirties."

"Late thirties? Hel*lo*?"

"I know."

"Well, at least they didn't think you were too old."

They don't make us wait outside when we get there, which makes me happy. I get enough rejection on a daily basis I don't get any thrill from waiting to be chosen on my social time.

Lisa, Gigi, and Luann are across the dance floor close to the bar. Casey and I make our way over to them in an exaggerated version of the bump. Mutually impressed with each other's finessing, we take turns adding other popular Seventies steps: a few hand rolls for me, a few chin juts for her, a team squat down to the ground and a spin out of it. We grab hands as we come up, pulling our left shoulders into a rendezvous and then switching sides so our right shoulders meet. Whirling around each other like partners in a disco dance class, we struggle to keep straight faces until one of us can't. Then we fall down on the couch, giggling.

When the blaring music takes a break, so do we, stepping up to the bar for refreshments.

"What're you drinking?" I ask Casey. "I think I want a beer."

"That sounds good. Get me an Amstel." She tries to shove a twenty into my hand. I shove it back.

"Two Amstels," I signal to the bartender.

While I wait, I'm conscious of the bottles banging back down into the wells, the shaking and the pouring, the silent *cha-ching* of the register, the pulling, the twisting, the pure physicality of being back there. And I don't have to imagine myself back there, because I already am. My hands collecting money, my feet sticky on the mats, my heart racing as the crowd thickens and I thin it with sheer speed.

"Eight dollars, please," the bartender leans the price into my ear, competing with the music.

I leave ten. Casey and I take a few sips and then drop our drinks on a table next to the dance floor with the rest of our stuff. It's hot and smoky in the bar, but not so much on the floor. It's "Hits of the Seventies and Eighties Night," with strobe lights flashing and songs we all know the words to. It's been a long while since we've been out dancing, and we're both very aware of it. We're giving ourselves to it, just doing what feels good.

"This is a pisser," Casey yells into my ear.

"I know. Let's make some really groovy requests."

"Yeah, come on," she says, racing me to the DJ booth.

When we get there we point out Lisa, Gigi, and Luann, insisting that they are "YMCA" freaks.

"They'll really get the room rocking if you play that," we agree.

From there we move on to "Shame," "Backstabbers," and whatever they have of Diana Ross. They start the set with "Ain't No Mountain High Enough," and soon we're dancing our way over to the bar for another cold one.

"Hey, Gigi," I call.

"Hey, Gig," Casey yells louder.

"What do you want to drink?" I say, once we've got her attention.

"A Cosmo," she yells through cupped hands.

"Come with," I motion her.

We get Stoli Cosmos, three of them, in big up glasses. Having made a little space for ourselves at the bar, Casey and I throw some money together and pile it up in front of us.

"Here's to you getting out of that place," Case says, lifting her glass.

"And to finding a better place," I say, lifting mine.

"Thanks, you guys," Gigi says, smiling. "Cheers!" She clinks our glasses as Casey and I echo her.

The cold, slightly sweet, slightly tart taste feels good in my mouth, and I don't hesitate to gulp my next sip down to its finish. It burns a little going down, but mostly it's warm and comforting. It all feels so back to normal, and I keep struggling with whether or not that's possible. But there's Casey, drinking and laughing, smoking and dancing, hanging out with me, just like always. Just like before she discovered that ugly black mole on the inside of her thigh.

We decide not to go to any other bars to dance because Gigi is a little hammered.

"I can't believe I'm really unemployed," she keeps saying. "I could dance all night. I don't have to get up for work or anything, you know? Hey, maybe I'll get a job dancing, huh?" she says, gyrating.

And I bet she'd do quite well, too. Gigi is tall and lean, with short curly black hair and long, muscular arms. She's exotic looking. Casey and I dance with her a little, and when she seems to be swaying a little more than dancing, we encourage her to take a ride home from us.

"Oh!!! Don't you guys want to keep dancing? Let's dance," she sort of pleads.

I don't know how she got this drunk in so short a time, but I think the longer she stays out, the worse she'll feel in the morning when she wakes up jobless. So I grab her bag and Casey and I edge her over to the door and out it, waving night-night to Lisa and Luann, who are flirting ferociously with a couple of studly-looking guys while never seeming to skip a beat in "partying like it's 1999."

After Casey and I get Gigi home safe and somewhat sound, we pass by our favorite ice cream place, hankering for a frozen yogurt, but unfortunately the lights are out.

"Wow, it's later than I thought," I say looking at my watch.

"Yeah, it is late," Casey says. "You better get home before you get in trouble."

"What do you mean, trouble?"

"You know. Trouble like when someone kicks your ass."

When I get in, the light over his computer is on and Phil's in front of it. Our place is basically a living room, one bedroom, and a tiny little kitchen. Phil's made a semi-office out of the living room, and I have to cut through to get to the bedroom.

"Hey, how was work?" I say, leaning over him for a kiss.

He doesn't look up and he doesn't answer.

"Where were you?" he asks solemnly.

"At Pink's. Gigi got canned and we were all out dancing. I told you we were going."

"Oh, yeah. Did you have fun?"

"Kind of. But Gigi got a little toasted so we gave her a ride home. I didn't realize it was so late."

"Who's we?"

"Casey."

"How's she doing?"

"Really good. She seems fine."

"Well, that's good. Work sucked."

"Oh, I'm sorry, honey."

"Well, as long as you had a good time," he says, but obviously means something else.

"What's the matter with you?" I say.

"Nothing I want to talk about at two o'clock in the morning."

"I'm sorry, I really lost track of time. Is that what's bugging you?"

"You're bugging me. Just you in general. You come and go as you fucking please, and you act like you don't give a shit."

"I really don't want to fight with you, Phil. Especially about not giving a shit. What am I supposed to do? Apologize profusely for going out with friends and not noticing the time? If I didn't give a shit, I wouldn't come home at all."

This last seems to press that button that I know is there but try to deny. He gets up out of his chair and takes me by the shoulders, turning me towards the bedroom with forceful fingers that push me out of his sight.

"What? Now I'm banished? Am I supposed to be thinking of how bad I am and feeling guilty?" I say from behind the closed door.

The door swings open and I'm in front of it. "Oww!" I yelp as it slams into my knee.

"Oh, boo-hoo. So sorry. Should I feel bad for that? Or maybe for this?" he says, grabbing my throat and giving it a tight squeeze, seeming to feel better as he sustains it. Then he loosens and walks away.

I get into bed, hoping he won't, and thinking how I can't help getting into trouble, no matter how old I get. Doing the wrong thing even when I know there will be consequences.

But tonight I wasn't aware of any wrongdoing. Maybe I should have called, but it really didn't cross my mind. Maybe I really don't care. I know I don't care when someone tells me I have to. And I wonder what caring has to do with coming home late.

Anyhow, I wasn't doing anything bad enough to get into trouble— why should I get in trouble for dancing? Trouble wouldn't even have crossed my mind if Casey hadn't brought it up. And I guess she brought it up because she knows Phil and knows what he's like, and there is definitely something wrong with that. More wrong is that she was right.

In the morning, he tries to gloss over it. He makes me breakfast and acts all polite.

"Good morning," he smiles sweetly.

"Hi," I say back.

"I've got some oatmeal cooking and I was thinking of putting up some eggs. Would you care for some?"

I'm not sure which persona I like less, the mean one or the polite one. Both make me uncomfortable.

"Sure, thanks," I say.

"I'm not going in until the lunch shift, and I was thinking maybe we could take a walk after breakfast."

"Okay," I say.

We have a nice civilized breakfast and then go for our walk. He holds my hand.

"I'm sorry about last night," he says. I don't know what to say. "I spoke to my Dad last night while you were out," he says and then pauses.

"And?"

"He thinks they're going to be moving to Florida soon."

"Well, good for them."

"Probably in a few weeks."

"That *is* soon," I say, trying to understand the connection between last night's abuse and the move to Florida.

He takes us over to a bus stop bench and sits us down.

"Will you come with me to visit?"

The oatmeal and eggs start to feel heavy in my stomach.

"I'm not so sure that's a good idea."

"I know why you're saying that, and I really am sorry about last night, but I think it would be good for us. We've never even taken a vacation together, you know? It would be fun."

"Maybe."

"Nick. It would be. Come on," he says rubbing my hand with his. The bus comes and he waves it on. "It *is* Florida we're talking about."

"Not really."

"Are you saying that you never want to meet my family?"

"No. I'm just not sure if we need a vacation away together or a vacation away from each other."

CHAPTER 8

WHEN I WAS seven I went to sleep-away camp, and we had three hours of specialization that we could choose from any area of interest offered. I chose drama and dance as two of my hours, and if I was allowed to I'd double up on drama. I wasn't even very good when I first started. In fact, I only wanted little parts because I was scared. Two lines were a major production for me.

My first year at camp I auditioned for *Oliver* and got the part of a boy who runs across the stage warning the female lead, Nancy, to protect Oliver because the villain, Sykes, is coming to kill him. I was **Boy Number One.**

I can remember standing backstage and getting psyched up for my two lines, repeating them to myself over and over again, while the girl playing Oliver scrambled around trying to make a costume change. She changed so fast she looked like a dryer on high, and I couldn't take my eyes off her. Something was going terribly wrong, and I remember her ripping off her shirt in a complete frenzy, exposing her bare chest. That day she became my hero.

I guess she was supposed to have somebody there to help her (I couldn't, because I was just about to go on and had to be on constant alert for my cue), but when they didn't show, she did what she had to do, pulling her shirt off, allowing her little pink nipples to fly out, and determinedly throwing on her new shirt for her next scene. I don't know what I would've done. I mean, I was completely flat back then, but still, it would have been a crucial moment of decision—there were boys backstage. But she was a he in the show, an orphan boy living on the streets, and so it hardly seemed to occur to her/him.

So I ran across the stage (with **Boy Number Two**), and I said in my best Cockney accent, "He's coming, he's coming," and then off to the wings, where I watched Oliver slip onto the stage.

She smoothed her hair as she stepped out of the shadow. She walked slowly, gracefully, almost pointing her toes. Dancing on in the dark, finding her marked place on the floor, and sinking into it, her legs curling sideways beneath her, the spotlight illuminating her.

She sat there quietly, the light looking like the zoom of a camera as its brilliance grew and defined every little part of her. Her hair fell over her left eye as she looked down, and every other eye in the theater was transfixed on her. She looked like a magnificent bird in her turquoise turtleneck, in her little world, so peaceful, so all her own.

When she opened her mouth and sang a song questioning where love is in her sweet soprano voice, I cried. (It didn't matter that my makeup ran, because my part was finished for the night. My part was really just to buy time for Oliver's costume change.) The song was so beautiful, and so was she: a little boy with no parents, alone and scared and wondering which way to turn. She had entered a different world.

(I rented the movie *Oliver* the other day and it made me cry again. But this time I cried when Nancy got knocked to the ground by her boyfriend, Sykes, and then sang a song called "As Long As He Needs Me." I cried, which made my eyes swell a little more than their new normal red, puffy look, and then I felt like I was going to throw up.)

The first play in which I felt I had entered a different world was the one I did in my senior year of high school. I had never been in a play at school before, too cool to become a member of the drama club.

I auditioned with a monologue that I had worked on with my mom. Having graduated Salutatorian from the High School of Performing Arts herself, she was a great coach.

I climbed onto the big stage and walked out to the edge. I said my name, the name of the piece I was going to do, and the character's name, Doris, a regular kind of gal, close to my age and funny. I was glad I had to introduce myself, because it gave me a chance to test my projection and feel what it would take to reach the director, the new guy, out there in the middle of the empty auditorium.

The director said "Thank you," and "Whenever you're ready."

I started talking to the imaginary person I had placed just behind him, and once I started, everything else disappeared. It was just me sharing a story with my friend. When I was finished I said "Thank you" and went home.

The new guy said, "Thank you, Nicky," and I had no idea I had just landed the lead in a play by Paul Zindel called *The Effect of Gamma Rays on Man-in-the-Moon Marigolds*.

It was basically a three-person play, with a fourth who was really old and didn't say anything. There had been some controversy over doing a play with so few characters in high school, where they wanted everybody to get a part. But the new guy said there'd be plenty of parts in the musical; this was a drama, and this was the drama he was going to do.

I was to play Beatrice, an alcoholic single mother of two in her mid-forties. How he got that I could pull that off from my sweet little monologue I don't know, but I wish the directors of today had as much imagination.

Beatrice was a bitter, depressed woman who prized one of her children and virtually abused the other. She was obsessed with the loss of her youth, ashamed of her youngest daughter and her daughter's brainy science projects, and Beatrice was drowning herself in alcohol. Maybe that was where my affinity for drunks really began. But, alas, I believe it was earlier.

Even though neither of my parents is a drinker, I've always been fascinated with drinking and the people who do it to excess. I'm drawn to them. Drawn to all that boundarylessness: the lack of concern over what time they start, how much they consume, what time they stop, and all those reckless moments in between and after. In fact, if I ever get so depressed I want to die, I think I would like to just drink myself into oblivion.

As Beatrice, I had to wear really funny suits with boas around my neck, housecoats and curlers, and smoke and drink like a fiend. We rehearsed every weekday for six weeks, and Mr. Arlink, my director, brought that character to life inside me. By the time we went into performance, there was nothing that could happen to Beatrice on stage that she couldn't handle. I remember one night my housecoat got caught on a nail sticking up on the stage, and Beatrice just yanked at it until it broke free, with the same considerable irritation she felt toward most of life.

She walked and talked, laughed and smoked, cried, and showed the ugliest sides of herself to a whole theater full of people. It was one of the greatest parts I've ever played, and I think it's because I found it particularly freeing to be so ugly: Ugly inside and out. Ugly in how you felt about yourself and others. Ugly in how you treated people and shamed them, even the ones you loved—a license for ugliness. So ugly that it almost became a thing of pride. Something to carry around and use against people, powerfully, as it cloaked the deep wounds, the missed opportunities, the wasted talents, the life you desperately wanted but were never able to have.

It was a turning point for the school to pull off so serious a project—a four-person cast in a play about love and loss, abuse and the effect of gamma rays on marigolds and people.

My mom and her Performing Arts buddies came, and the response was tremendous. My dad came, and after all the time and worry he'd spent warning me that an actress was not the thing to be, he said to go ahead and be an actress. Everyone was so proud of me, but mostly I was proud of myself. It was the first time I admitted out loud that I wanted to be an actress, that it was the dream I actually wanted to pursue. I had been afraid to admit it because of my mother's struggle with it: the sacrifices she had made for it, the people that had gotten hurt along the way, and the rejection she had suffered through so many failures. It seemed foolish for me to broadcast to the world that this was the path I was choosing.

And now, as I mosey into my thirties, I wonder if I won't wind up a bitter alcoholic, mourning the loss of my youth, throwing "Why, just yesterday"s across the bar and damning myself for never getting out from under it—the bar. It would almost be worth it if only somebody would discover me and typecast me in that role again.

At some point during the show, I felt my talent filling that high school auditorium. It was a huge feeling. Powerful. Mostly the presence I felt. And I think now, if only I could've taken a piece of it home with me to call upon when I was feeling down, to remind myself what I was capable of, life would be so much easier. It was that moment when I found myself alone on the stage, commanding the attention of so many people, but instead of losing focus and drifting off into fantasies of fame and fortune, I noticed that the audience and I were united. Focused on the same thing: the details and nuances of the life I'd come to know and love, in spite of its flaws, or maybe because of them; the person I'd created and for a short while become.

I guess that's part of why it's so hard to give it up. It seems pitiful to give up now, when I've invested so much time, have nothing else I'm good at, and nothing but old reviews and age to show for my efforts. That and those moments when I've found myself there in that special place, inhabiting the life of that person that I never even knew was a part of me.

CHAPTER 9

I N MY LIFE, sometimes I wish I had nowhere to go and nowhere
to be.

Nowhere at all.

I wish it a lot. Like I wish I didn't have to wake up in the morning at
all. Didn't have to leave my bed or talk to anyone. Didn't have to be anywhere and had no time I had to be there. I long for that feeling of endless
time just to think and rest; I believe that not having to be anywhere
would give me plenty of time to go somewhere special. Somewhere I
didn't have to go, but just went because I wanted to.

And every now and then, I don't have to be anywhere. I don't have
to be there at any special time. I've got nothing but time. And I feel no
better than I do now.

With nowhere to go and nothing to do, sometimes I do nothing.
Sometimes I don't leave my bed or talk to anyone, at least not until I
have to. And then sometimes by the time I get to the bar, I feel better.

I have to be there, and it compels me to come alive. It forces me to
engage with people. To talk with them, maybe laugh with them, serve
them, share time with them, the kind of people who wished that they
didn't have to get up in the morning and go to their jobs. People like
me, who wished they never *had* to be anywhere at any particular time.

And once forced out of bed and through their workday, then there they are, right in front of me, just because they want to be. Or maybe they wanted to be when they first started showing up, but then it became a habit. Anyway, it makes me want to talk to them. Talk with them like they're my best friends. Find out everything about them.

"How you doing?" I'll ask. "What do you do? Do you like it? What kind of law do you practice? That must be hard work. Is it worth it? What makes it worth it?"

The busboys light the candles. They're in thick glass holders and they light up the bar all around me, their flames dancing on the edge—libations and laughter, music and hors d'oeuvres. I welcome the guests to the bar as the night begins—hostess.

A tall man with sandy brown hair and blue eyes sits at the bar.

"Where you from?" I ask as soon as he sits down, because he looks so stunningly out of this world.

"I'm from Alaska. I fish," he says, smiling.

An Alaskan fisherman! We get to talking about fish. He describes their changing colors.

"First they're white," he says. "Then they turn to silver. But when they die, they turn black. They all die," he says.

"Why?" I ask. "Why do they all die?"

"After they spawn, they're spent from the process. It's too difficult for them to survive."

The way he says it makes me think he knows the fish. Not at all like he's a fish killer, but rather someone who knows their life process and helps them to fulfill it. I guess everybody knows this about spawning—everyone except me. But I want to.

In the morning I go to the library and look up salmon in *National Geographic*. I find a huge article on Pacific salmon. I don't know why, but suddenly I'm fascinated by the fish and their life cycle. I need something to focus on. Something other than the next shitty script I might be lucky enough to get a crack at.

There are such pretty photographs of them. One shows an orange one with a silver head sweeping its tail along a streambed amidst deep blue-green water. In another one, you can see just the tips of what look like millions of fins, all swarming around this swimmer's head in white choppy waves.

When the man from Alaska told me about the fish dying, I realized he was trying to simplify their cycle for me. At work there's hardly ever a time when I don't have to excuse myself or there isn't some kind of interruption. And usually I hate anything remotely scientific. Maybe he sensed that. But when he said they all die, I forgot why I've always hated science. Because lately, I'm extremely interested in exploring other life forms, dead or alive. What do they do, how do they survive, what makes them feel alive?

I discovered that there are seven different species of salmon, and spawning salmon stop eating in fresh water even if their river journey is a thousand miles. They travel up the river, finding their birthplace by the smell of the home stream and other ways that even scientists don't understand yet. When they find where they themselves were hatched, that's where they begin to spawn.

I knew "spawn" meant to create life, but I knew nothing about how the salmon did it. *National Geographic* explained it in detail. This is what it said:

When a hen salmon finally gets home, she begins digging a nest in a riverbed, thrashing with her whole body to make a hollow. Two or three males hover nearby, fighting for breeding rights until the nest is finished. The hen, now accompanied by the strongest male, shudders and releases her eggs, dropping them into a nest. Simultaneously, the male shudders too, releasing a milky cloud of sperm to fertilize the eggs. With her tail the female sweeps a protective cover of gravel over the nest, at the same time scooping out another for more eggs.

Not long after the spawning is done, both the parents die, spent from the process, from the weeks of fasting, from the territorial fights, from the nest building. They become food for the eagles and bears. Their decomposed bodies add nutrients to the water, which in time will nourish their progeny.

Then the cycle restarts: From the eggs hatch alevins, translucent fish carrying pouches of food on their bellies, which feed them for weeks. Alevins become fry, fry become smolts, and smolts are salmon headed to sea.

Most never make it home again. If a female lays 3,000 eggs, no more than 300 or so survive as fry; of that 300, no more than four or five reach maturity and fewer still return to spawn. The survivors beat the odds, traveling as much as 10,000 miles in the ocean, eluding predators, fishermen, pollution. Given the natural and man-made perils faced by a salmon, the amazing thing is that any survive at all.

What a life. They don't even get to have sexual intercourse to make the baby fish. At the top of one of the pages the whole cycle is illustrated in cartoon form, and it says in bold print, **"A perilous life cycle."**

Beautiful and resourceful, they spend their whole lives struggling and fighting obstacles, just to end up in exactly the same place they started from and die. Which is, I guess, the exact thing that I'm afraid of. Struggling, struggling, struggling, fighting desperately to achieve a special goal, but then, whether you've gotten anywhere or not, when your time's up, you die.

I mean, I've heard people say "You look like a fish swimming upstream" when they're trying to make an analogy for struggle. But it's one thing to struggle for a glorious end, and, I think, another to struggle for a glorious end and wind up in exactly the same place.

I once saw a nature program on the same topic, and the narrator said, "You may think it sounds like a sad existence, but when the salmon dies, she dies triumphantly, having achieved her lifelong goal." I guess. I wish there was more to it, though. Her goal. Her life.

CHAPTER 10

THIS ISN'T ONE of those times when I don't have anywhere I have to go or be. This is one of those times when I have to go and I don't know who I'll be talking to when I get there.

Matty, Ally's husband, Philip's brother-in-law, is getting that transfer to Florida, after all. Our opportunity to spend some time with Phil's whole family in sunny Florida is now officially upon us.

To be fair, I try not to dread it, and am surprised to find I don't entirely. I've met his sisters before and they seem very nice, and Florida is (if nothing else) relaxing, and if nothing else, I can finally find out how curiosity killed that cat.

So I arrange for some time off from work, and Phil works out something with his parents to help him get there, because the timing is bad for him, what with the new car and all.

Then we're off to Florida. When we step off the plane, I'm struck immediately by how tropical it is here. Everything is so bright. And there's that warm breeze, and palm trees wherever you look, and the people are friendly, even though it's a kind of superficial friendly, saying "Howdy" or "Hey there" every time you turn around, but still, it's cheerful. And I'm kind of excited about being on vacation with Philip, after all. It is the first one we've ever taken together, and even though things haven't been going too well, it's forced us to talk.

That's why it's hard for me to understand the black cloud that hangs itself over my head almost the minute we exit the airport.

As soon as we step into his father's house, almost like a mutant cell, Phil seems to split off from me. It's as if I'm watching him go through a typical day with his family as a boy of twelve or thirteen: quiet and off on his own, not really talking to anyone, yet somehow very much a part of the clan.

As I look around trying to find my place in this new family, I find everyone quietly involved in their own things, or maybe it's uninvolved, talking only when necessary and expressing emotion only when it's anger, and then flaring up with such a fiery crackling that it breaks the common silence with a boisterousness hard to ignore.

And even though Phil likes to talk (or at least he did before we got here), it's strange because his family never talks. I mean, his father always talks, in fact he talks incessantly, but never about anything. He talks so much about so much nothingness that I get confused: am I missing some crucial points in his conversation, or can he really be that successful at sustaining the chatter of empty words?

"Well, the weather's beautiful, but what'd you expect? The shops are all down there, one right next to the other, expensive, too. Because nobody wants to work more than half a day, they have to make it with every purchase. We don't go down much, unless we need to, which we don't very often..." Blah, blah, blah. I'm lost, because he speaks quickly, continuing to say nothing.

The rest of the family seems to have reserved the floor for Dad, keeping their own conversation to a bare minimum and feeling kind of depressed about it.

Ally chases her fourteen-month-old, Gilly, around making sure he doesn't destroy anything precious, looking worn and tired from it, but not asking for help or complaining about the lack of help being offered. Gilly takes a porcelain turtle off the bookshelf, and Ally puts it back. She turns around to clean some string cheese off the brown carpet and Gilly grabs the turtle again, this time dropping it on the carpet beside the string cheese and stepping on Ally's hand as he attempts to retrieve it.

"Goddamn it!" she yells, grabbing the turtle and putting it up high out of Gilly's reach, then plopping him, screaming, into the corner to face a wall while she storms out the door for a smoke.

"That special assignment Matty's on better be over soon," Phil's older sister, Tracey, calls out from the kitchen, where she's playing checkers and having a beer with her boyfriend.

Phil has been away long enough, it seems, to have maintained the desire to talk and speak his mind. Every now and again, when he's feeling secure enough to snap out of his regression, he tries to contribute intelligently to his father's conversation. Unfortunately, his contributions are not received well, are in fact belittled whenever possible, and his resolve seems to weaken as the day wears on.

"Dad, funny you should mention that," he'll say, trying to pick up on his dad's conversation and lend his own spin to it. "Because I'm working on this play about this town where nobody works. Well, people work, but, there are no stores, so everyone is a salesman, and you can only buy things from the different salespeople, who won't just sell to anybody. It makes for a very hungry society, where the people turn savagely against each other—"

"Son, it sounds like you're trying to get out of working a real job, sitting around making up crap like that," his father reclaims center stage.

The look on Phil's face, though fleeting, makes me gasp inside. It's like the look on a child's face when he's shared some wonderful new accomplishment with his mom or dad and they are so lost in their own world that they fail to acknowledge the achievement and instead berate the child for the intrusion. But the look is only there for a moment, because Phil quickly changes gears by scooping up the still hysterical Gilly and turning him into an airplane, whooshing him through the air and transforming his screams into giggles. They come in for a landing, and Gilly takes turns between riding Phil like a horsey and running away from Phil the monster, both of them rosy-cheeked and breathless, stirring up the stale, repressed stuffiness of the house. Until, of course,

Phil's dad, irritated by the noise factor, stifles the obvious emergence of joy with, "That's enough of that, now," as though "that" were a bad thing.

I go outside to see how Ally is doing. I'm thinking maybe a smoke would be good, too.

"Can I have one?" I ask her.

She unfolds her Marlboro box and hands me one, followed by her lighter. I'm not really a Marlboro girl, but somehow it seems right to be out here smoking with Ally. More right than being inside, anyway.

"So how do you like your boyfriend's asshole family?" she asks.

"I don't know yet," I admit. "Can I be of any help to you with Gilly?"

"Not really. I have to take him to the dentist in a little bit, and he'd freak if I wasn't by his side every second. Thanks, anyway."

"Sure," I say, not knowing what else to say.

As the day wears on, I feel more and more somber. I decide a shower might revive me, but both Ally and Tracey urge me to make it a quick one unless I want to freeze my butt off. Something about Dad not keeping the water heater on. Each moment seems to come wrapped in heavy gloom. Fun is just not something the Steele family understands you're entitled to have.

Everyone is doing something that doesn't allow him or her to engage with one another, but nothing seems like an important activity. Even Ally, who should be preparing to take Gilly to the dentist, seems to be walking around idly. Tracey and her boyfriend keep drinking their beer and playing cards, but in a kind of silence that does not make it inviting to join them, and Phil keeps combing through his family's bookshelves as though he's taking inventory, while never taking any of them down to look at or read. Phil's mom is in the kitchen, but we're not planning on eating at home and I can't smell anything foodlike wafting by, so I wonder if she's just hiding in there until Phil's dad calls her.

Every now and then someone (even Phil) storms out the door screaming, "I can't stand this house," throws a little tantrum in the driveway, and then returns more somber than before.

But there's a moment when Phil and I are in the back seat of his sister's convertible (and that alone makes me feel kind of happy) and we're laughing. Tracey is driving, and her boyfriend, who turns out to be her fiancé, is next to her, and Phil and I are in the back seat. I think it's the first time I've laughed all day, and I'm very grateful for the opportunity. I don't even know what we're laughing at, but we're really laughing, all of us, and the wind is blowing through our hair and Philip has his arms around me and, and the sun is shining and I think, oh yeah. Philip's back, the playful Gilly-Philip, and he knows fun and it's going to be okay. But when we pull into the parking lot near the beach and his Dad gets out of his car and comes over to ours, something goes wrong.

I'm still not sure what, his Dad says something and then we say something and then he says something and starts to walk away and then I say something like "Well, I'm glad we got that established," and then we're laughing again. Next thing I know, Phil's Mom is by the car telling us that she and his dad and Ally and Gilly (who are now back from the dentist) are all going home.

And this bit of news plummets us all back into somberness.

Phil says, "What's going on Mom, is Dad okay?"

She says, "He's fine, he just wants to go home."

Everybody seems to be fidgeting with extreme discomfort, which forces me to blurt out, "Is it something I did?"

Phil's Mom says "No," but this seems really to mean yes. Tracey says, "Come on, Mom, tell Dad we'll meet you at the other parking lot, over at the beach. Don't go home."

Phil's mom is quiet for a minute and then she says, "I'll see what I can do," and heads back to Phil's sulking dad in the other car.

On our way to the other parking lot, I ask everybody what's up. I can't help feeling that they really think it is something I did.

"Does he think I was making fun of him?" I ask. Was I making fun of him?

"No . . . I don't know," they grumble.

But at the next stop sign, Phil's mom is back.

"Your father wants to go home," she says.

And so I ask again, "Mrs. Steele, is it something I might've done?"

She gets very quiet and then says, "Well, he is upset."

So now I feel like I have to get to the bottom of it, and I get out of the convertible and go over to their car, with Phil's mom kind of racing me over there. She beats me to it and gets into the driver's seat, mumbles something to Phil's dad, and he sits there in the passenger seat looking straight ahead.

He can see I'm just standing there like a fool, but he doesn't roll down the window, so I knock on it to let him know I'm not going away.

"Excuse me, Mr. Steele, did I do something to upset you?" I ask.

First he doesn't answer. Doesn't say anything at all, just sits there as if I don't exist. But when I don't move, he finally says, "Just forget it," dismissing me with a wave of his hand.

"No, I'd like to apologize if I did anything that offended you. But I'd like to understand what I did," I say.

And that's when he looks at me, rolls down his window a crack and says, "Get back in the car, Nicky."

He doesn't say it nicely, and his face has turned to stone. One of his eyes is squinting and the other is wide open; his mouth is very tight around the edges. And when I realize he's threatening me, I say, "Well, I'm really sorry for whatever it is I may have done," even though I don't feel sorry at all.

He says, "Get back in the car, now."

And so I go back to the convertible and relay our conversation. I'm beginning to put the pieces together—the morning's events with some of the problems I've had with Philip and the ways he reminds me of his dad—and that's when I feel it click: this will be the first and last trip Philip and I will ever take together.

My mood goes from somber to sad. Not just for me, but because I know how hard it must be for Philip to exorcise his father from deep inside himself, and I know how far he's come.

He was an army brat, moving from place to place, leaving the people he'd gotten to know and love every time his father got reassigned. And despite his father's gruff and paranoid ways, or perhaps because of them, he's become a sensitive man, who writes eloquent prose and beautiful, tender poetry, and who likes to talk, except when he's around his father.

He has a very playful side (which makes him a child magnet), loves video games, literature, film, theater, and me.

It's just those times when he can't erase his past . . . like that time a few months ago when we were playing cards and I was winning and gloating about it, and he couldn't repress the urge (the urge that I now think really belonged to his father) to pull my head back and pour beer in my face.

I would have thought getting hit would be worse than getting beer in the face if I'd ever actually considered those two things and compared them. But I would have been wrong.

The cold bubbles burning in my eyes and the surprise attack of the liquid going into my mouth and down the wrong pipe, gagging me, as my hair bunched into sticky little clumps, had a far more humiliating impact than I ever could have known.

My efforts to clean myself up, driving home the reality of the moment, did not help matters, and probably hurt. Phil must have perceived my caring for myself as a way of sticking the guilt to him; perhaps it was this that brought on the next attack.

So why I bothered comparing beer in the face to a punch in the face I don't know, since I would inevitably end up with both.

Being back home doesn't feel so bad compared to being there. I left a few days early so Phil could have some alone time with his family, which I think he really needed. The day of the fight with Phil's dad, I wasn't allowed back in the house. Phil stuck up for me that day. He told his Mom if I wasn't allowed in, he wasn't going in either. Then he said, "And Mom, you better tell Dad to get some therapy, because he needs it big time."

I thought that was pretty brave, but his mom seemed flustered by the suggestion.

"What are you talking about?" she said. "Your father isn't going to get any therapy. That's your father. That's the way he is. He's not gonna change."

Now, as I get up out of my big empty bed, I'm happy for the space. I brush my hair and wash my face. Once I smooth the make-up over my eyelids and lips, I begin to feel differently about having to be somewhere. I still don't want to have to be somewhere, but I have to. And once I get to the bar, it's somewhere I know, and it's a relief.

The gorgeous fisherman is back tonight. Maybe he's staying at a hotel nearby.

"Hey, there, Alaska," I say.

"Hey there yourself, pretty," he says.

"How you doing?" I ask as I set his ale down.

"Good," he says smiling right into me. "What about you?"

"What about me?" I ask.

"How you doing?" he says and his eyes haven't veered from mine.

"I'm fine, thank you," I say.

We don't say anything else for a while, but I stay right there in front of him, a comfortable/uncomfortable quiet between us.

Then he says, "What do you like to do when you're not here?"

I want to say, "Fuck men that look like you"—mostly to shock him, partly because I'm shy and I want to cover.

"I'm getting into rollerblading lately," I tell him.

"Oh yeah? I used to play a little hockey," he says.

"You any good?"

"Not bad. You like to hit it around sometime?"

"With you?" I say, just making sure I'm getting him right.

"Yeah, with me, if that's not too awful a thought for you."

I just look at him. I walk down the bar. I feel his eyes on my body. The farther I walk away, the more of me he can see. When I come back, he says he has to get going.

And then he says, "What do you say? Want to play sometime?"

I hand him a Fioreca's business card and ask him to write his number on it. His face looks a little wary, wondering why I take his number instead of giving him mine, but I cut off any possible question about it by answering his.

"I think I would like to play sometime," I say. "But I don't know about the hockey."

He smiles at me. His name is Beau. Nice long legs that I imagine are hard at the top. I can imagine my hand on his thigh. As he turns to leave, I notice just below his frayed Levi pockets the material is a faded white.

I'm trying to understand how he's worn them out that way when I hear somebody say, "See something you like, Ms. Ferrer?" It's Steve.

"Very much," I say as unabashedly as I can.

"How you doing, sweetheart?" he laughs.

"Not bad. How's tricks with you?"

"I'm gonna die if I don't get a job soon, Nick."

"What about that guy you were talking to last week? I thought he was going to hook you up."

"I thought so, too. But it's all commission. It's bullshit," he says.

"Is your unemployment still coming in?"

"Yeah, but only for another two weeks."

"Can I buy you a drink?" I say.

"Thanks, Nick. The usual, but easy on the cranberry, please."

He's not saying my drinks are weak. He just wants this one particularly strong. I don't think anyone could honestly say my drinks are weak. Every one of the bartenders here pours a good drink. But every now and then some smartass will ask us to pour more liquor into his drink. I don't know if it's because I feel like they're calling me a wimp, or saying I'm trying to cheat them, or assuming I don't know what I'm doing because I'm a woman, but I take it very personally. We all do.

Last night it happened to me at the bar. I was really busy. This cocky guy at the bar had a shot. He told Ricky to get me.

"This isn't a shot," he said.

I took his glass and held it up to the light, the candlelight.

"You know, you're right," I said. "This actually looks like more than a shot."

"Oh, come on," he said. "You're whacked," holding it up in disgust.

Frankly, I don't think people should throw "whacked" and "crazy" around as much as they do. Especially since I've been feeling a little crazy lately. But while he was calling me names, I went over to the glass-ware and grabbed a shot glass. His shot was in a rocks glass because I find most people prefer it that way, or in a snifter.

So I took his rocks glass and the shot glass and I set them down side by side, with a pretty good glass-to-bar slam. Then I tilted his rocks glass and started to fill the shot glass with the shot I'd poured him. When I got to the top of the shot glass, I stopped before it overflowed. I picked up his rocks glass and peered into it, dramatically comparing it with the now full shot glass. Then I froze, as if playing statues, to emphasize my obvious victory, but he didn't acknowledge that I'd won. So I lifted his rocks glass to my lips and downed the remainder of the generous shot I'd poured him.

I licked my lips as I lowered his glass and let out a refreshed "Aaaah-hh." Then I smiled at him and his friend and, just to show them that it was the principle of the thing, said, "Your next one's on me. Let me know when you're ready."

But so far tonight nobody at the bar is that into drinking, except Steve, who doesn't have any money.

Not having any money means different things to different people. To me it's having five or ten dollars. To some people it's the few coins they can scrape out of their linty pocket. But in college I had a couple of roommates who, when they said they had no money, meant it. None. Not a dime.

That's one of the things about this job. You always have cash flow. You can feel so rich, even when you're really poor. You always have money in your pocket. There's something to be said for that.

CHAPTER 11

E VER SINCE HE'S back, there's something unspoken that lingers. It hangs around the room like cobwebs gathering on a window that won't open. If there was a test in the trip to Florida, we definitely failed it. Or at least I did.

As long as the conversation steers clear of anything real, it's okay. But if, for instance, I touch on some family irritant, there's a small volcanic eruption. Even when it's *my* family I'm talking about.

"My mom called. She's thinking about coming out for a visit."

"Oh. Do you want me to stay at a hotel?" he says out of the corner of his mouth.

(Yeah, kind of.) "No. But if you think it's bad timing, then I'll tell her not to come. That's why I'm asking."

"You're not asking."

"Forget it," I say.

"Yeah. Why don't you?" he says, grabbing a pencil off his desk and throwing it against the wall as he leans back in his chair with his hands behind his head.

I really want my Mom to come out. I need her. But I don't need her to see this shit. It's not good for *anyone* to be near Phil when he's like this.

I go into the bedroom and start sorting out some scripts that are piling up. Scripts are a pain in the ass to keep around unless you have a great filing system. They always look so messy. I should probably bind them in pretty jackets and make them keepsakes, or else get rid of them altogether. They're hard for me to part with. Some I could use for scenes, some friends of mine wrote, and some never got made but still might.

"What are you doing?" he says, casually coming up behind me.

"Just trying to clean these up a little," I say.

"About fucking time," he says, sitting down, making himself comfortable.

I ignore him. Maybe I could find some milk crates and stack them in those. I put my shoes on.

"Where are you going?" he says.

"I'm thinking milk crates."

"Where are you going to put them?"

"I haven't gotten that far."

"Why don't you just throw that stuff out? You don't need it."

"I don't want to."

"Well, they're never going to look neat, and I guarantee you won't ever bother with them."

"Thanks for the advice, Mr. Clean."

"*My* stuff sits, neatly, on my hard drive."

"Oh, like you don't have any scripts lying around?" I say, indicating his desk and the area surrounding it, littered with scripts, candy wrappers, rolling papers, and clothes.

"A few, but I'm working on those."

"Well, why don't you throw that stuff out? I guarantee you'll never do anything with it."

"You're a real bitch," he says pulling my head into the crook of his elbow and squeezing it like in a vise.

I pull his arm off me and back away from him.

"Can you leave me alone?"

"That's all you really want isn't it? To be left alone," he says, curling his lower lip out in mocking baby talk.

"Top of the list, right now," I say.

"Well, I certainly wouldn't want to stand in the way of your solitude," he says. "Speaking of which, make sure you call your mom and tell her not to come."

He leaves the room, but not before he kicks a big pile of my scripts across it.

CHAPTER 12

I OPEN MY EYES. Pitch black. Still, I can tell these aren't the walls in my bedroom. They're lower to the floor and closer together, confining. I lie frozen, afraid to make a move that will stir him awake.

My eyes start to adjust to the darkness, and I can see my bra dangling from a chair. It's one of those office chairs—an old, dirty green one, on wheels. The mattress is right on the floor. Close enough for me to make a subtle roll and retrieve the necessary clothing to make a run for it.

Watching his chest rise and fall I can see he's breathing quietly, and yet it seems like thunder with each exhalation. *I* can't breathe at all. Sitting on the beach earlier in the evening, just talking to him, I couldn't stop thinking about having sex with him, and I couldn't understand it, because his talk didn't impress me. He didn't have much to say, and *I* felt like an interpreter, trying to explain everything I meant, feeling embarrassed by my own strong opinions.

He seemed to have no opinion of anything I brought up, and as the conversation (or lack of it) progressed, I felt like I needed to translate even the simplest things to him. Like "That's a play, you know," which he obviously didn't. "It's from that wonderful book," or "Did you see the movie?" Granted, he was from Alaska, so certain things he didn't know were understandable. But even that part of him—Alaska, being a fisherman, the great outdoors, the fish knowledge, the whole experience that made him interesting—seemed to have disappeared completely. I began to feel like Lenny from *Of Mice and Men*. Instead of "Tell me about the rabbits, George," it was "Tell me about the fish, Beau." Tell me about anything, but please tell me something.

Yet when he did say or do something, every word, and every move of every part of him, felt like a subtle hint of what the sex might be like. The circles his fingers drew in the sand, the way he wrapped his arms and legs around me, shielding me from the wind.

Even when he responded to what I was saying with "Yeah" and a nod of his head, the grin that would cover his face made me feel as though we were both agreeing to something other than the conversation we were supposedly having.

So after a while I figured the best thing to do was just to go with what was working for us, which was, without a doubt, the sex and the anticipation of it. So I stopped trying to have a conversation. But just in case I was overlooking something, I made one more try to talk to him on a level that I thought he would understand.

"So, Beau, what do you like to do besides fuck?" I said.

He smiled this sexy, animal smirk, but said nothing.

So I said, "C'mon, what?"

He reached across our beach picnic and took my head in his hands and whispered into my ear, "Lick you while rubbing my cock between your tits."

I wasn't even sure if this was, in fact, possible—he was quite a bit taller than me—but it didn't matter because it didn't turn me on, right then, when I was really trying my best to see if he had any other thoughts in his head. Even so, I did follow him home.

Even if he had said much, though, I couldn't have heard what he was saying. I had no idea what it would be like to interact with him normally, without this sex thing in between us and crawling all over me. There was something almost frightening about the sex pouring out of him and into me, so infectiously, while I sat there wondering if he was quiet and smart or just quiet. It made me feel out of control and out of myself. Like I wasn't there anymore and instead, in my place, was this sexual urge dressed up in my jeans and my bra, smiling, thirsty, waiting and wanting like some kind of panther about to pounce.

But then I thought, what's wrong with getting a little lost in the heat? What's so wrong with feeling a strong desire for someone, but not much of anything else?

After the beach we took a drive, and when he pulled off to the side of the road, I let myself feel like a teenager parking. We sat there just staring at the moon.

"Wow, it's unbelievable," he said, staring more at me than at it, as he tickled the inside of my arm by swirling his fingers around in little twirls. Then, without removing his eyes from mine, he said, "Is the chemistry between us just too hot?"

I wondered if he said this to all his dates, and if he was maybe laughing at me, but unable to deny it, I said, "Yes."

Then we started kissing like it was our first and last time ever. Touching each other everywhere, hard and soft and hot.

The moon chuckled down at us, cartoonishly close to full, and I thought it would be all over right there in the car. But it was cold and ridiculous trying to get comfortable, bumping into door handles and arm rests, sticking to the upholstery and trying to avoid the stick shift. Somewhere along the way, we both realized we weren't teenagers and opted for his apartment.

But then, in the warmth of his apartment, I slowed down. Testing myself to see if it was worth it, I tried to hold onto my shorts for defense, only sometimes letting him work around them. No matter how close I'd get to giving in, I kept thinking I should like him if I'm going to do it with him. Otherwise, I know I won't be able to stop worrying about whether or not he's sleeping with other women. I'll think about it every time I see him, with each layer of clothing I remove, terrified of picking up whatever disease any of his girlfriends might have.

There's a slickness about him—a slickness I don't really blame him for, but don't really like. I saw him in the grocery store once when he didn't know I was there. I overheard a conversation he had with the checkout girl, and then her enthusiastic analysis of it after he left.

I was in the line directly beside his on the right, and he was talking to the checkout girl in the next lane to his left.

I heard him say to her, "You look nice today," though I assume she wore the same smock everyday.

"Thank you," she fluttered.

"How you doing?" he asked.

"Fine," she giggled. "How about you?"

"Good," he said, in a slithery, caressing voice which sounded as if he was praising a dog. And then he said, as if he couldn't find words, what with all that beauty behind the counter, "Well," just simply like that, "Well," but then, as if he'd just remembered what day it was, "Happy Valentine's Day."

Then he went on his merry way. The checkout lady gasped, "He's so cute! Susie, what do you think?" she yelled to the other cashier. "Do you think he's too young for me?"

"I don't think so," Susie placated her.

"I wonder if he has a girlfriend. He probably does," the smitten cashier said gloomily.

I wish I could go back and tell her not to worry about it. If he did have a girlfriend, it sure didn't stop him from trying to rip my clothes off, and I'm sure he wouldn't think twice about doing the same to her.

The fact is, I have almost nothing in common with him except for this chemical overreaction. And what I do have in common with him doesn't work for me.

He's a model, now. A model. What happened to the fishing gig? Well, on his visit here, he says, someone met him on the street and handed him their card and he's been getting calls for jobs ever since, so he thought he'd hang around for a little while. Of course, this bugs me, because when was the last time that happened to me? Never. But okay.

Except that his main goal in life, now, instead of catching fish, is looking good. And I, on the other hand, am trying desperately to hone my craft, to work the subtle nuance, to be a real person living in a real place, so that it won't matter how good I look. Because I would like to be recognized for my good work, knowing only too well that I'm never going to be called upon for how good I look. And I guess that's part of what bothers me: that when you look that good, you don't have to have too much else going on. And he doesn't seem to.

But that didn't stop me from wanting him, from that first time he came into the bar and we started talking about the salmon and every time after. I wanted to touch him and wrap myself around him and get dirty with him. He's really tall, and he's got these scars all over his face, and I was right about his legs. Hard.

So tonight, when I got to his place, I tried to strike a happy medium, attempting to slow down the voracious hunger while at the same time getting a taste. But this approach only created a delicious cat-and-mouse affect, making me hungrier and more frustrated.

Because when I felt his tongue enter my mouth, I felt like it was entering me. He brought my nipples to attention and they saluted him before he took them into his mouth (this was one of those times when I fully appreciated the worth of having these illustrious mounds of womanhood spread across my chest), turning their mass into silly putty while transforming the reddish-brown tips from declarative periods into bold exclamation points.

And when he made his way down my belly and beyond, I found it difficult to think of how to form the sounds that would say *no* out loud, leaving only my thin cotton shorts, wet panties, and whispers as a shield. So we touched and sucked and explored, getting wet and sticky and breathless, while we played tug of war with my clothes, until I couldn't stand it any longer and I let him in—over and over again.

And now I slither to the edge of the mattress. I poke around in the dark with my bra and sweatshirt slung over my arm and my shoes bumping the walls as I try to find the living room. I find it and turn the light on dim with its dimmer. I slide my bra on without clipping it and toss my sweatshirt over my head. A clock strikes, and every chime forces me to come up with an excuse for sneaking out in the middle of the night. Fortunately, there are only three chimes, and he doesn't stir. No excuse necessary.

I just don't want to wake him. Or talk to him, because now that we've done it, his sexiness has turned into humiliating repulsion. The whole thing reminds me of cotton candy. The way it starts out light, fluffy and sweet, but after I eat it, I'm sick.

Something snaps inside me. It's like a trick—the sexier he seemed, the more he doesn't now. As if those moments of intimacy, touching, sucking, licking, squeezing, rubbing, thrusting, and pounding, opened up a door, letting me see inside him, and now I just want that door shut, effective immediately. It's none of my business, end of story. But maybe he's also unleashed something in me, exposed something, uncovered something, so raw and personal that's it's really none of *his* business. I guess with Beau it's all about sex, and that makes it kind of unsexy, after all.

I click the lock on the door handle behind me as I pull the door shut. My car is parked right behind his in his carport, because I'd asked if he wouldn't mind meeting me at the beach instead of picking me up. In just a few minutes I'm home. I turn my key in the lock to our apartment and close the door quietly. I pull my sweatshirt and bra off, my shorts, jump into the shower and then climb into bed next to Philip. Threeish, he must assume I'm just getting home from work, as he rolls over without any significant notice of me.

CHAPTER 13

I N THE MORNING when we kiss I sense he's looking for a fight. Not because he knows what I've done, but because he inherently hates me. Three and a half years and I'm just beginning to understand what keeps him tied to me. It isn't that he likes me so much. And now, back from the fiasco in Florida, he surely has new reasons for hating me. No, it's more of a sick thing, a sick connective tissue that we share— some dynamic force that ties together my fear of being mean and destroying another person with Phil's ability to be mean and destructive. For me, it's reassuring to know that I'm not destroying him. And for him, it must be liberating to be with someone he can attack regularly and then make amends by simply saying I'm sorry, it's my problem, I have to get better at this.

We met in New York. I was bartending and he got hired later as a cook.

He used to come to the bar after his shift ended and have a beer or a margarita. He liked them straight up with lots of salt. He used to take some of the salt off with his finger and then lick it. His fingernails were very short, like maybe he was a biter.

It was a small bar, all wood, light like oak. Small and square, it was easy to whip around and give everybody lots of attention. What I lost in volume I made up for in good service, regulars and turnover. It had one of those old-fashioned manual cash registers, whose keys were fun to bang away on.

One night, Philip offered to walk me home. I lived six blocks from the bar, which was on Lafayette Street, but I never walked that late at night if I was going by myself. When we got to my place we talked on the front stoop for a while. He was good to talk to. He reminded me of my dad, because he seemed good, like I would be bad for him.

My immediate thought was that I would destroy him. It hadn't even started and already I sensed it would never last.

Then he kissed me. It was different from what I would have expected, though I can't really describe what I expected. His lips were forceful as they pressed against mine, and yet his hands were gentle as they pulled me into him, sliding around my waist before I could object. And there was this innocent intimacy about the whole thing, like he'd done it with me before and knew what I liked. I didn't want it to mean anything, but I wanted to try it again.

He lived in Brooklyn at the time, because the rent was cheaper. He was a writer, struggling. I liked that. It was romantic. All of us in the business of serving others, really artists en route to our dreams.

I was particularly fascinated by the fact that he was a writer. And when I had the opportunity to read his stuff, it was a little like reading his mind, getting to know all his secrets without having to ask a single question.

I liked his poetry the best. It was very forceful and clear. It provoked thought, not confusion, and it was straightforward. I loved his short stories, too, but he was actually more of a playwright. That's what he liked the best. For me, though, his plays were kind of Beckett-like or Pinteresque. I think I would have understood them better watching them, rather than reading them, but maybe plays are like that.

Sometimes I fantasized about switching places with him. Staying home and clicking away on the computer, sitting quietly and alone, putting my most personal thoughts down, without anyone interrupting or criticizing but me. Enjoying solitude, instead of banging on casting directors' doors begging them to let me in.

By the time he kissed me it was very late, and he had to work brunch in the morning, and I couldn't stand to send him onto that cold, dark subway at four in the morning after he'd walked me home, so I invited him to stay.

Nothing happened that night, though we did sleep together in my tiny single bed. Two strangers, we more grazed each other's skin, trying to determine boundaries rather than exceed them. Little by little, though, that's how our relationship started. He'd walk me home. We'd talk. We'd kiss. We'd touch. Pretty soon he was living with me, even though I was still sure it was never going to work out, and I'd told him so a million times. But he could be very sweet and he was persistent.

But this morning he is only persistent in picking away at me. Pushing on me till I feel pressed against the walls. Making me crazy mad—the kind where you just don't care what the consequences of your fury will be. You've got to let it out. It's the kind of mad that you just have to scream your loudest scream, or simply, and perhaps calmly, say the meanest thing you can conjure up. The meanest and most specific thing about that person you're mad at, the thing that will drive them crazy. He makes me mad like that a lot.

But his crazy mad is that physical thing. At first it was really subtle, but it isn't anymore. And since Florida it seems to have escalated. He shoves me a little. Or sort of pulls my hair. It's too obvious to make excuses for now.

So this morning we sit down to have breakfast together and even though he's not anywhere near crazy mad, he starts right in blaming me for anything.

"You know, this kitchen is a fucking mess," he says to me.

Which is not my fault anymore than it is his, but he says it like it is. So I just say, "Yeah, well, we're busy."

To which he says, "Well, you sure are."

I don't know what to say. I'm not sure what he means and I didn't get enough sleep last night, so I'm not too interested in getting into it.

That's when he comes up behind me and makes like he's going to put his arms around me, but instead presses me up against the counter and says, "What are you doing tonight?"

It's not a sexy press, it's more like I'm kind of scared. But I tell him anyway, "I'm going out with Casey."

"Casey? What about me?" he says. "Why is it always you going here and there and never with me?"

"Phil, we go places together, it's just that I'm always the one making the plan," I tell him. "You want to take me somewhere, how about you make the plan and I'll make sure we go? Besides, I thought you were working tonight."

"How am I supposed to make a plan when you always have something planned?" He seems to be getting into a panic.

"Well, sometimes I have something planned for you and me, right?" I say.

"Right. Which never gives me a chance to make a plan on my own."

I can see that this is going down I-can't-win-lane, and I suddenly feel hung over.

"Why can't you just relax once in a while?" I say. And as soon as I say it, I know I said it wrong. I should have said, "Let's just relax," sort of friendly, like we're in it together, but I can't.

"Oh, I guess I should be more like you. So relaxed I won't commit to anything but my own impulses."

And this is where I get confused, because did he start it or did I? It shouldn't matter, but it does. Maybe in my own sad way I am destroying him.

"What the fuck is that supposed to mean?" I ask.

"Do you really fucking care?"

"No. Not fucking really," I say.

"Well, that's relaxed."

He's right. I can't relax either. Not long enough for the conversation to finish. I want the shades up and the windows open before I jump through one of them.

I go to get my sneakers and he stops me. He takes hold of my arm and twists it. I can feel the skin turning purple and it makes me want to get out even more, but I can't seem to show fear. Instead, I tell him to get off me like he's a real asshole for touching me like that. It makes him madder. He grabs hold of both my arms and pins them behind my back. Then he pushes me down on the bed and sits on me. I try to fight back, no match for his strength, but behaving as if I truly believe I can kick his ass. I laugh at him as I squirm and push, as though he's no match for me—laugh right in his face. Because I can't stand even one glimmer of a second where he thinks his brute force has intimidated me.

Then I start to scream at the top of my lungs, "GET THE FUCK OFF ME."

That's when he puts his hand over my mouth and starts to choke me and the neighbor from downstairs comes up and tells us we're so busy trying to kill each other that we left the faucet running and he's having a small flood in his apartment. Philip gets off me and I get my sneakers. I grab my gym bag and snap the shades open on my way out.

When I get to the gym, I feel more sane. Everybody working on their bodies and their health, it feels safer.

It's so weird how there're no visible marks on me, and yet my neck and just above it where the bottom of my cheek is feels bruised. And one of my arms feels strained. Is he conscious of planning just the right attacks that leave no obvious trace?

I get on a StairMaster because it's too early for class. I turn up the tension and set the timer for thirty. Pressing through the balls of my feet and my quads, I feel the sweat come slowly but steadily as my body starts to get hot. I watch the people below, lifting weights and spotting each other. I enjoy seeing people's bodies move. The flexing of their biceps and triceps, the different lines of definition that ripple with the movements, the sweat and the concentration. No matter how good or bad their bodies, they're all so different. Some people laugh, some talk casually. Others compare routines, assisting each other with tips on the perfect circuit.

My pace becomes more feverish, my own concentration intensifying. People look at me like it's strange to be working so hard. But I think it's stranger to see people on the machines barely moving their feet or their arms.

I don't know whether I've heard this advice in the movies or in real life, but I know I've heard women give it a million times, and it keeps echoing in my mind.

"The first time a man hits you, it's time to walk."

It always sounded so stupid to me. Like some guy punches you in the face and you have to be told to walk away? But it wasn't until recently that he actually hit me.

He was like a nightmare, the way he snuck up on me. A nightmare because you don't know how bad it's going to get until it gets so bad that it forces you awake, and only then do you know how really bad it's gotten. And then you wake up and boom you're this stupid, abused woman.

I've moved on to the Versaclimber so I can work my arms and legs at the same time. My arm reaches, my leg extends, and I feel the stretch all the way up the sides of my abs and deep into my lats. It only burns a little on the right side from this morning's wrestle.

Now I'm ready for class, and it's time. The music starts and we all stand lined up in various stages of leotard dress. Though I teach aerobics a few times a week (a complete contrast to my night job, and maybe that's the point), today I don't teach. Today I'm just here for me. I like taking other instructors' classes because it gives me ideas for my own, but it also allows me to be one of the pack.

After the warm-up, we leap into the carefully woven combinations, and it makes me feel stronger to be dancing along with everyone to the insistent beat, kicking and turning in rows, letting the endorphins seep through our pores. I wonder where my suitcase is.

CHAPTER 14

A COUPLE COMES IN and the guy keeps calling the woman "dear." It sounds like Deearrah.

"No, Deearrah, I didn't know, but you're pretty impressed by that."

"No, not impressed. Just making mention of it," she says neutrally.

"Oh, yaw're impressed, all right. You don't fool me," he says, raising his Boston-sounding voice.

"Please don't yell," she says quietly. "You really don't have to yell."

"Oh, I don't?!" he says a decibel louder. "I don't have to yell even though you're impressed with some bullshit wine salesman and ramming it down my throat, baby."

Now he starts calling her baby.

"I wasn't ramming anything," she says. "Anyway, I looked into your trip and you still have time if you want to make that stop in Cleveland," she says, clearly trying to change the subject.

"You mean you never made the calls and the reservations?" he practically screams.

"You asked me not to until you knew more about your timetable, remember?"

And I'm thinking, why doesn't she just tell him to make his own damn calls? What is she, his secretary? But then I think maybe she is.

"Yeah, I re-mem-ber," he says, enunciating each syllable like he's talking to a two year old. "I remember faxing you a complete schedule yesterday."

"Well, I'll go ahead and make the calls, then."

"Make the calls? No, it's too late to make the calls. You can't make the calls now, baby," he slurs and probably spits, but I'm not close enough to see.

I want to call *him* baby. Big, brooding, nasty baby, but before I know it he's up and out the door, leaving the secretary/woman his watered-down gin and unpaid tab.

She pretends not to notice, as if he said, I just need some night air. So I ask her if she needs anything, as though I've heard nothing.

"Just the check, please," she smiles.

So I get it and she pays, tipping generously, and then I imagine her wandering through the streets, looking for him, not sure why.

And Steve comes in and I'm happy to see him even though he looks kind of sad, or very hung over.

"Hit me, please," he says.

And I do.

"You, know, Nick, sometimes I wonder if Sonny isn't right?"

"You mean about Janine?" I ask.

"Yup," he says taking a gulp.

"Why?"

"I had to bail her out of jail last night."

"No way. What for?"

"She got a DWI, but she was flying on coke."

"Steve. Where'd you get the money?"

"The unemployment office."

"Two words for you, my man: dump her. You're in over your head," I say, thinking of the Boston guy and his woman, and then of Philip and me, and then how Steve really isn't any more in over his head than the rest of us—or any less.

"I don't know," he says, shaking his head, rubbing his eyes.

A few hours and several Absolut and Cranberries later, Janine walks in, fully manicured, hair shellacked, lips glossy.

"Hi," she says, smearing her wet lips on Steve's cheek. "How you doing, sweetie?" she asks him in a high, squeaky, happy voice.

"How are *you* doing?" he says, looking her over, possibly trying to figure out the same thing I am: Is her cheerful demeanor a new buzz freshly caught, or is this just time-release from last night's escapades? And isn't she 86'd?

My feet feel flat in my shoes, like there's nothing supporting the arches, and my soles stick to the beer-splattered mats. My legs are heavy as they pull me up and down the bar, surveying people's glasses.

I wonder, when they say "There's someone for everyone," if they don't mean someone bad who will torture us our whole lives.

I look up and Beau the Fisherman is standing in front of me.

"Hey, how about a quick one?" he says, grinning. It's the first time I've seen him since I snuck out of his apartment.

"Sure," I say smiling back. Then we just stare at each other.

"What'll you have?" I ask.

He leans in closer to me and half-whispers, "Well, I would say you, but since I've already done that, how about a beer?"

I smile again as if I've heard nothing that might disturb me, and I say, "You're funny. A beer sounds good, what kind?"

"A cold, wet one," he says, but this time he's not smiling.

"Sounds better and better," I say, even though he's beginning to make me nervous, especially because Phil's supposed to come by tonight.

Then he doesn't tell me what kind of beer to get him, so I lean in and make like I'm going to whisper in his ear, but instead I say louder than I need to, "When you say a quick one, do you mean like you the other night?"

To which he says, "Now, that's funny." Which I have to admit it is, because he was anything but quick.

"Well, we're just a couple of funny people, I guess. Now, if you tell me what kind of beer you'd like I'd be happy to get it for you, but if you keep up the comedy show, then," and now I do whisper in his ear, "I'm just going to let everybody at the bar know that your dick bears a striking resemblance to a frozen pea."

"You really are funny," he says.

"Thank you," I say.

"Bass Ale," he says.

When I place it on the bar in front of him I say, "It's on me. And, funny man, sorry if there's anything I may have said or done to offend you."

"Oh, you can offend me anytime," he says, sliding onto a stool and taking a big swig of his beer while looking me up and down.

I climb out from behind the bar for a pee, a stretch, and an excuse to escape, because I realize that didn't go so smoothly and perhaps isn't the end of it.

When I step back into my spot behind the bar, Ludwig steps up to the bar, an empty Beck's bottle in hand.

"One more, Nicky," he says with his sun-spotted finger. I go to fetch it, wondering if he's going to say, "Beck's. It's the best. The best beer in the world." He always says it like he's some kind of an authority, and I guess, being from Germany, in a way he is.

When he first started coming in, his skinny little legs poking through his Bermuda shorts as he paced back and forth, he reminded me of my grandfather. They both always had a smoke stuck between their lips, my grandfather a cigarette, Ludwig a cigar.

In the early hours we usually have a nice chat, or he'll remind me of something I forgot to put out on the bar.

"Napkins," he'll say grinning. "I know, I know, you forget, you slipping, Nicky."

But today he doesn't say anything. He's been sitting in a dark corner with his beer and his tiny, tanned bald head, alone, not talking to anyone, not even trying to bark or annoy someone as he usually does.

Beau is now hitting on a small blonde at the other end of the bar, so before Ludwig goes back to his corner I say, "Hey, Ludwig, my friend had a nice smoke the other night."

His yellow teeth shine as he beams at me; I can just about see the gold-capped one far back, sparkling. He must see this as his opening to pry into the particulars of Philip, because he starts to nose around a little.

"Is he Jewish?" he asks.

"No. He's not."

"But he's good to you?"

No, he's not. "He's okay," I say, and make my way down the bar.

"If he's okay, why you mumble?" Ludwig says as he shuffles back to his corner.

I ignore him, hiding behind a smile.

Steve calls me over to settle his check and, of course, crazy Janine's. It's still early, but they seem to be headed home together. I can't help thinking she must be really something in bed, even with the way she gets off.

"Nicky, Nicky, Nicky," sounds the annoying gnat that won't go away. It's Ludwig, calling out as if he's got a matter of great urgency. And as he slips a carefully folded dollar bill into my palm, I realize he does.

"You tired today?" he says. "You look tired."

"Oh, be quiet, you crazy," I say.

"You crazy," he says.

"Hey, you didn't touch your beer. What are you doing?" I say, really stopping to take a good look at him. *He* looks a little tired.

"I don't feel like it," he says.

"Whaddya order it for, then?" I say as though he's failed to take his medicine.

"I don't know," he says.

"Because you crazy, that's why."

"No, you," he says pointing.

"Don't come back tomorrow, then," I say.

"Okay, I won't," he says.

"Good," I say. "See you then."

"See you then," he says, waving his hand, walking his walk, smoke trailing out the door.

CHAPTER 15

T HE HEAT OF his thumbs deep in my arches makes me want to cry out right now, but I'm afraid he'll stop. I do anyway. He doesn't stop. He takes his time. Slowly he lingers there, smoothing out the tops, unjamming my crunched toes, pushing and pressing the pain away from the rest of my body and my thoughts, so much so that I can stop thinking about what will come next and just enjoy what does.

He doesn't dwell on my ankles, but instead digs into the meat of my calves. And as he makes his way up my leg, kissing my neck and ear as he goes, I grab hold of his hand trying to slow my own pleasure down, get control of it. I press his hand back on the bed, and as I touch it, I wonder how this generous hand could be the same one to hurt me.

I can't imagine it, and so I let go. We merge into each other for what feels like a long time. Then he gets a story he's written and reads it to me. It's about me.

It's called "The Ropelight." It's all about this little girl and this Ropelight that she discovers one day is a part of her. It connects her to other people and guides her to act in particular ways. It's kind of written in a child's voice, which contributes to the simplicity of it, and in some places it's very flowery, like a *Father Knows Best* episode, but that's intentional, to make you want to be there, back in your childhood, or somebody's childhood, and because fairy tales are like that.

Then the girl grows up, and the ropelight gets dimmer and brighter along the way, until one day it's so brilliant it's practically burning a hole in her chest, and that's the day when she becomes whole.

That's the day when all those temptations tugging her in different directions, making the ropelight fade in and out, disappear, and she's left knowing what she wants and not being afraid to go out and get it. And wouldn't you know it, the same day there's this man across the river with a ropelight burning a hole through his chest, too, and like magic the two lights come together and live happily ever after. But the funny thing is, the man across the river isn't Philip. It's somebody else she's never even met yet.

It makes me cry. And he tells me this story has been running around in his head for a while now, and that we'll always have our own ropelight connecting us, even if we end up on different sides of the world.

I love the story, I'm a sucker for a good fairy tale, but I can't help thinking I'm not ready for a ropelight to burn a hole in my chest. If I met a guy with a ropelight coming out of his chest I'd probably run the other way. It's just too scary.

He gives me a kiss and goes back to his computer, and I fall asleep. When I wake up, I sink into the only comfortable chair in our place, feet naked and up, my hair still a just-fucked mess. Pressing PLAY on the answering machine, I cringe at the sound of Sonny's pleading voice.

Nicky, you got to help me out—four o'clock, Alex can't make it, he's sick as a dog.

As the digital clock clicks from 2:59 to 3:00, I wonder if Alex's sickness has anything to do with a callback. Afraid that any attempt to relax will be interrupted by more phone calls and a relentless effort to get me behind the bar, I save Sonny the trouble and call him back.

I take my time getting ready, because he's lucky to get me at all. When I arrive, hair still wet, shirt untucked, the happy hour crowd is just starting to trickle in, and Ludwig is left over from lunch.

"You look good today," he says, surprised.

"Probably 'cause she took her sweet time getting ready," Sonny says, adjusting his watch with attitude.

"Oh, I guess I should've hustled, what with you back here all by yourself and this jumping crowd to manage," I say, looking around at the empty bar stools.

"Nicky, Nicky," Sonny says, coming behind me and digging his fingertips into my shoulders with a grin. "I'm just messing with you. I really appreciate you coming in and covering for Alex, helping me out."

"Good to know," I say, looking for the limes, beginning to wonder where all the set-up stock is and just how long Sonny's been back here.

"Hey, did you work the whole day back here?" I ask.

"Some back here, some on the floor," he says.

"Because I can't find anything. You got any fruit cut or what?"

"Oh, no. I didn't get a chance. I'll go get you some," he says climbing under the bar.

"Gee, thanks, Sonny. I really appreciate you helping me out," I say.

So I'm forced to regress back to the chores of the dreaded day shift, even though I'm working the night. The days when Ludwig and I first got to know each other; the same sequence of events, only now I have to get it all done in an hour instead of seven because by five o' clock it might actually be rocking.

First a big bucket of limes—they come from the kitchen along with the other members of their citrus family, the lemons and the oranges. I line up the buckets alongside my cutting board, grab my trusty knife, and watch the rich greens of the limes' skin as each incision makes a dent in their rough exterior, revealing their pale insides. I cut them into perfect little chunks that will later have the life squeezed out of them, and I pile each piece on top of the others until they're so crammed into their new home that some of them fall over the sides, trying, I think, to grab a space all their own.

"Nick, a Beck's," Ludwig says, pointing to his empty. A little break in the rhythm as I advance to the lemons and oranges, it's just like old times.

That's how it used to go. One at a time they'd come in. A beer or a smoke, or sometimes all they needed was a light, and yet it snapped me out of my solo assembly line at the fruit-cutting factory long enough to marvel at the fact that this was an actual job. Doing inventory, polishing bottles, stocking dry goods and glassware, and mostly just waiting, waiting. It was hard to believe. Seven hours of setup for one hour of potential payoff: the happy hour, the hour when I was just happy to have people around me, to be finally making drinks and conversation, a break in the dead, depressing silence. A refreshing change from the hours spent reflecting on what a loser I must be to cut fruit all day, polish mirrors, and fritter away my time in a bar filled with smoke, misery, and drunken illusions of hope.

The day shift, before I graduated to nights. The shift I always thought I was going to die in. One at a time they'd drift in, but sometimes they didn't, and then it was just Ludwig and me.

He would come in at noon, yelling, "You closed?! You fired."

I'd bark at him. Make fun of him. I'd yell at him, like he yelled at everybody else. We'd talk about the bar, if I had set it up to his liking, what I missed. He'd get all choked up telling me how great Beck's beer was, so I couldn't always understand what he was saying. Something about how expensive it was, in Germany or here, but he never pays for it here. Sonny told me one day not to charge him. Said he did a lot of work with us.

I'd ask him about his business but he'd never tell me. Did he work with us/for us? I don't know, but he laughs as if I do.

Every day around four o'clock he used to ask for a Coke in a cup for his men—for his man? For some guy working out there that I never saw? After a while he wouldn't actually ask, just put his hands together pantomiming a cup and say, "Nicky, Coke," pointing towards the door with his head. So I'd give him the Coke and he'd take it outside and I'd never see it again.

He was intentionally loud. Yelling. He was as obnoxious as he was embarrassing and he knew it. At noon the doors were just opening and he'd yell a hello to the owners, which embarrassed them because lunch was being served in our posh Beverly Hills dining room, just above the brass staircase. During the day, the long stretch of bar was so empty and he was so loud that his voice echoed as if he were calling out from a tunnel. Late in the day when people started coming in and he was still there, carrying on, I'd just tell them not to mind him, he was a little crazy. He'd hear me and just smile a little smile, shaking his head. Or sometimes he'd yell, "*You* crazy."

But he was my friend and a good thing, because sometimes it was just the two of us for hours at a time, Ludwig smoking cigars and me cutting fruit. Once he told me how beautiful Germany was. As he spoke, I could see both the love and the hate in his eyes. He said it was green and also clean.

"Very, very clean," he said, "The most beautiful country in the world." Then he got very quiet, pensive.

"But it's bad what happened there. I was in a concentration camp, you know."

I had been struck by the Auschwitz branding on his tiny forearm from the first time I met him, but I just said, "You were?"

"Of course," he shouted at me. "You know!"

"Yeah," I said.

He shook his head from side to side.

"Terrible, terrible things. Craziness. Such craziness."

I went about my business, not wanting to intrude on his thoughts and also not knowing what to say. I could only imagine the terrible things he had been thinking of. I thought of all the movies on the Holocaust I'd seen, with the emaciated, shaved-headed, and lifeless characters robotically moving through their non-lives in the prison camps. He sat there quietly and I thought that no matter how beautiful Germany was, I didn't want to go there.

His loud voice broke the silence: "Before the war I worked with wood. Carving things. I made clubhouses, tree houses, bird houses, doll houses."

As he spoke, his fingers caressed the wood of the bar. He touched the smooth parts and examined the corroded parts. He wore glasses, but through the thick lenses I could see into parts of his past.

"My father teach me everything. He had a little cabinetry shop. He teach me the best kind of wood to work with and how to work with it."

"Always work *with* the grain," he said mimicking his father.

"He'd work late into the night and get up early in the morning. Sometimes I'd help him. I liked to sand the wood. I'd sand it until it was soft, like velvet. He'd make cabinets and shelves, chests and boxes. If you could make it with wood, my father would."

Was he trying to slip a joke in on me with the "wood/would" thing? I wasn't sure and I didn't laugh. Maybe it was just his choppy English. He kept right on talking.

"I'd help him with the measuring and the cutting and later on, the hammering. At first, he wouldn't let me hammer because he said I was too noisy."

"I don't blame him, you troublemaker," I chimed in.

"Oh, shut up, you crazy," he'd yell. And then, "I know *you* think it's strange, but the thing I liked best to make were music boxes. I liked the little tiny pieces of metal—piecing them all together; smoothing out the wood and then shining it with shellac—different shapes and sizes, but mostly small and sometimes thick red, green or black velvet in the bottom so the ladies could use it for jewelry, too. Not the cheap stuff, though. Always the best quality."

It was funny how he bragged about the littlest things.

I pictured the day when the Nazis became a force and stormed the world. I wondered if Ludwig and his father had been at work. Ludwig's father whistling and working, Ludwig hammering away, and boom, the Gestapo comes into their little shop, grabs the hammer out of his hand and one by one smashes all their precious wood sculptures.

One morning I read an article about new Nazi groups sprouting in Germany, trying to recreate Hitler's dream by burning down Jews' homes. A photo showed a sweet, smiling little girl whose legs were so badly burned in a fire started by one of the groups they said she might never walk again.

I told him I didn't ever want to go there.

He said, "But it's so beautiful, and it's different now."

"Really?" I told him about the article.

He said that for the most part it was different. But he had heard about a few isolated incidents like the one I had described in certain parts of Rostock and Solingen.

I envisioned going there, ducking around corners, tiptoeing, trying to figure out which parts of town to avoid because I'm Jewish, too. I asked him if he thought "it" could ever happen again.

He said, "The people are so ashamed of what happened. They carry so much guilt." He shook his head. "No. The people would never let it happen again." He was yelling again.

"Just the same," I said, "I don't ever want to go there."

"My son lives there. He's a lawyer. He makes a lot of money. Do you know how much? A lot," he barked.

Ludwig also talked about being a very wealthy man. But this seemed incongruent with his tipping tendencies. He always tipped me, but not a lot.

Sometimes he'd say, "Don't worry. Wait, wait, I'll be back with you tip."

Then he'd leave for a while and go to the bank. Or at least that's where he said he was going. When he returned he'd bestow it upon me. A dollar. Not a bad tip in itself, but when someone had been sitting there all day long, drinking for free, it wasn't particularly good, either.

He'd always make a big deal of it, too. "Nicky," he'd yell out, no matter what he was interrupting, "Here. I don't forget."

"Thank you very much," I'd say, as if it was a big deal.

But he helped me get through the days stuck in the day shift while I waited for somebody to drop dead or get pregnant, making room at the top. That's when I really got to know him, and it made some of that drudgery worth it.

And as it turns out, he knows a lot about survival—my Jewish friend Ludwig, who hangs around bars a lot.

Now a few more thirsties come in and the hot, hot water feels good on my citrusy fingers. And here Ludwig is calling me over, folding a dollar bill into my hand, saying, "See, I don't forget. I don't forget."

I don't forget either. I don't forget sharing those moments in the long idle hours of the day shift. And now when I see him it really is like a visit with my Grandpa. We don't always talk a lot, sometimes it's just a few words here and there, and sometimes I get him to tell me his stories, but there he is, this guy that I sort of know, pacing and smoking.

Several million limes later, nearly seven, it's starting to pick up. I put the cherry and olive jars away, all stations overflowing with both, making a colorful array amidst the lemons and limes. The oranges stand alone in their own container, accented only by the shiny pearl onions.

A guy comes in and sits down.

"How you doing?" I say, throwing a cocktail napkin down in front of him.

"Vodka/tonic," he says.

"No, no, no," I say, "I asked you how you were doing."

"Oh," he says, "Thanks," he says, "not bad, a little stressed, but for the most—"

"Okay. What'll you have?" I say, cutting him off with a smile.

I swirl my glass mixing cup around in the palm of my hand, watching the speed of its spin. I'm not traditionally a spinner, but I know how. I stop the spin in my left hand by grabbing it with my right hand, and tossing it upside down into a quick flip and then back into my left hand, down low. I stake my claim to the power I've earned with this demonstration of finesse and remind myself that even the slowest nights feel good compared with the days.

Slowly they trickle in. At first, I'm making one or two at a time. Kind of dragging the orders out just to keep busy. But suddenly I start getting three or four at a time, and soon I'm getting into the groove. It's the beginning of that long-awaited rush.

It's like waking up. Everything becomes more precise. I slide the beer cooler open, toss the beers out and catch them, flipping their tops off and flinging the cooler top shut with a flick of my wrist and a loud "thunk." Even the way I hold the money has new purpose.

I get a twenty, hold it up and call, "Out of twenty." Over at the register my fingers dance on the keys, and as I pull the change, I rip the computer receipt off the machine and in the same motion tear it in half, proof that the transaction is complete.

The more I take on, the hungrier I am to take on more. Seven or eight tasks at once, still that smile on my face, I amaze myself. Here I am at the glorious top. But soon people start saying "Excuse me," as if they need to ask me a quick question, and when I acknowledge them, they run off a mile-long order of cocktails.

Sometimes I challenge myself and say, "Yeah, sure," and see if I remember. Sometimes I do. But sometimes just as I say "Yeah, sure," I notice the cocktail waitress has lined up ten glasses, chock full of ice and ready for the pouring, right on my spill mat. She makes task number nine or ten, but she's not going away. I have to get rid of her, whatever it takes.

I pour her drinks while I pour mine, if she fucks up her order she's fucked. One chance for her, or I'm off and running, catch me on the next ticket. Amidst the chaos of strangers calling out drinks and fumbling for money when I line them up, regulars pop in.

"Nicky, what's up? Can you set me up?"

"Sure, no problem."

I set their glass up with the round I'm making, set it on the bar, ring it, and I'll catch the cash later.

And so I get a rhythm going. The music starts to jam, and this helps to fuel my speed. Sometimes I even get cocky.

"Who needs a drink?" I call out. "Who needs something?"

Sometimes a group will wave me down, but when I ask them what I can get for them, they become tongue-tied. One guy will start to order, and then, as if I'm watching a cartoon that keeps repeating certain frames, his face turns into the back of his head as he consults his friends again and again, and I'm left standing there with the one drink he ordered and everyone else's stinging eyes on me, wondering why I've gone to sleep on the job.

Then Sandy, my cocktail waitress, comes along, and her ticket says eighteen shots of orgasms. Eighteen. This is the third time she's had an order like this, and I'm beginning to wonder who the hell is drinking them. I pull the Kahlua, Bailey's, and Amaretto off the shelf and fill the shakers with ice. I try to figure a way to go easy on the alcohol and heavier on the mixer, to help the house out, because this drink is just not economically sound, but there is no mixer, so I don't have a lot of options.

I think they're all ready to go, so I can finish them off and then get back to the six other things I'm doing, but shit, no shot glasses. I can use other glasses, but it looks like they're getting less, and they're really getting more, and with eighteen shots of premium, precision is difficult enough, so I yell out, "I NEED SHOT GLASSES!"

While I'm waiting, I take care of someone else who insists on getting my attention, and Sandy stands there panicking. Out of nowhere, Sonny, who is actually the back of the house manager but sometimes gets a little power-hungry, has slipped behind the bar with me. Though he's a workhorse, he doesn't go to help me, but instead starts flipping through some checks I've set aside so that when I need them I'll know exactly where they are and in what order. I ask him what he's doing.

His response is, "Nicky, in my day, I could've run circles around you. I was awesome, I was like lightning."

This response has nothing to do with what I've asked him, and I realize that I should probably ignore him. I've got shots to fill, more tickets shooting out of the printer, and people stacked four deep, oblivious to any of this and getting hostile because they haven't gotten what they want yet. But he persists, swinging his dick around my bar, telling me he's the best there ever was.

Most of the staff think Sonny's a prick. But he's kind of like a brother to me. Sometimes I hate him and sometimes we're pals. Right now I agree with the rest of the staff.

So I turn to him and say, "Yeah, but you know what you are now? You're a big fucking asshole. And if there's nothing I can help you with, I'd like you to step out from behind the bar, before I leave you back here by yourself and you have to prove how big and bad you really are."

Now I'm having a little problem. I feel distracted by this encounter and I think it would be fun to walk out right now. I'd like to see Sonny freak. The only thing I know about his famous bartending skills is that he doesn't have any. Apparently Trevor, the owner, had him behind the bar for about four months when they first opened. Rumor has it that not only was he turtle slow, but none of the customers could stand him. But he's a workhorse. That's why they pulled him and made him *back* of the house manager.

I know it's not worth it, so I stay put. I'll tell Trevor later and he'll understand what wiped the smile off my face. Unfortunately, I run out of change. I make the mistake of calling out for it, like I did with the shot glasses. Trevor doesn't like this.

He comes up to me with the change and says, "Nicky, a good bartender doesn't panic and always keeps smiling." Then he says this is not Vegas and I should call for change quietly and discreetly.

Maybe he's right, but I don't like that part about what a *good* bartender does. He sees the daggers I'm shooting out of my eyes, but doesn't dwell on it.

Sandy sees the whole thing and tries to calm me down with "He wasn't mad. He was just saying."

So now he thinks I'm in the weeds and sends *Sonny* back to help me. I don't want him anywhere near me, but I'll put him to the test. He takes the wait staff and I take the rest. Well, that's *his* idea. But every time I turn around, one of the wait people is jumping up and down begging me to help them.

He's turning red from the stress and at the same time fucking up any rhythm I attempt to establish. I'm knocking them down like they're ducks at a shooting gallery, one at a time, starting on one end and working my way systematically to the other. But every now and then, when Sonny can come up for air, he lifts his head for two seconds, just long enough to see the people directly in front of him, waving him down. Overwhelmed, he arbitrarily grabs whoever is most in his face and attempts to fill their order. However, his skills (or lack thereof) aren't up to it, and when the wait staff reappears with an order, he becomes flustered. Again I pretend he's not there and am only reminded when customers come to me with a drink made incorrectly, or ask to pay for some drinks that the guy bartender never collected for.

When I first started doing this work, struggling to support my acting, I'd always start out having to prove myself, usually to men.

They would often hire me because I was a woman. They thought it would be good for business, not that I'd be good for it. I was regarded as a stupid girl until I got behind the stick. That's where I earned my respect.

The last place I worked in New York was a classic example. It was a fifty-five-foot bar. We were opening it. There were nine of us—five women and four men. At first I got all the shittiest shifts. I wasn't the prettiest woman and I wasn't a guy. But when things started to pick up, people got fired for poor performance or quit because they couldn't take the heat. Within the first six months, the staff changed to eight men and me.

It was a great setup for a bartender. Everything was designed for a busy bar—a huge well of liquor so you'd hardly have to turn around. Big ice bins with room for your juices. Lots of glasses, and later plastic cups because business was good enough to get away with it, and our own homemade tap beer, available in four sizes, one tap by each well. The computer was easy and fast once you got to know it, and there was cranking music that blasted every night, sometimes live.

We'd come in at six and say our hellos. By eight we'd start to move and barely stop right through till four. When things got really hectic, the bartenders would call a time out and meet in the middle for a shot. We took in hundreds and hundreds in tips a night. Sometimes we'd use huge champagne buckets, and sometimes the green lined the back bar as if it were decoration. As for the house, we made them thousands each night. And I personally rang such high sales that I came to be known as "the machine."

There was this one guy I worked with, Pete, who would sometimes go a little crazy when we worked together. I worked the end and he worked the middle on Friday nights. Friday night was the busiest night of the week, and the owner, Russ, would do an incentive thing. Whoever sold the most would get an extra twenty. But it really wasn't the money as much as the pride in being the fastest and the best.

Things would really heat up when the crowds began to flood in. At first we'd each be doing our own thing, making drinks, chatting it up with our regulars. But little by little we'd have to pick it up. We'd watch each other out of the corner of our eyes. How fast were the crowds building up in front of his station and then disappearing? How many drinks could I make in a minute or less? How fast was Pete actually going? Because his bartending style was such that he always *looked* like he was blowing my doors off.

He had big muscular arms from bodybuilding and wore a bandanna around his head, or a ponytail tying back his long rock-and-roll mane. He'd fly around, picking things up with his big hands and clunking them down with a loud BAM. His shirt was always cut to shreds. Each week he'd cut a little more of it up, testing to see how far he could go, so by the time he was done with it, you could see every rippling muscle that surrounded his bellybutton as he worked it around the bar.

Around and around again, swinging his arms and flipping things over, pounding glasses down on the bar, slamming beer taps down and popping them back up, clinking our huge beer mugs together, looking like he might be breaking some world bartending record. But actually, in those moments of elaborate activity, he was stalling. Stalling for time to think. Everything whirred by him too quickly—the people, the money, the pressure, and me.

After several peeks down at my end, and a couple of inquiries as to whether I would share the twenty with him if I won—"Nick, you'd share it with me if you won, right?"— convincing himself that nothing would be lost, he would allow himself to slow down. Then he would stop what he was doing and slowly begin to make his way towards me. Casually come down to my end, as if to borrow a strainer or a bottle of lime juice. But when I looked up and noticed him, he would not-so-casually pick up his pace, and before I could be sure that he was coming for me, not my strainer, he would be on me like a sumo wrestler.

I'd try to break free of his initial attack, as soon as I could tell it was coming at me, by faking right or left, but he was huge, and there wasn't anywhere to run or hide, so he'd corner me. Then he'd turn me around and get behind me. He'd slide his arms through mine, interlock them with his and pin them behind his back. Those big, thick arms that the girls on the other side of the bar would blush at would literally hold me back from making drinks.

I'd yell and kick and sometimes try to bite him, but then the absurdity of how he was restraining me, and why, would come over me, and I would laugh. It would make me too weak to fight and I'd just have to submit, trying to convince him that I *would* slow down, so he'd let go of me.

Russ and my managers weren't usually around when it went down, and on the occasions when they were, they mistook Pete's bondage for flirtation. The customers didn't get pissed that they weren't getting service, either. Pete's body wrapped around mine, my chest thrust out, squeals of laughter mixed with loud "Stop it!" reprimands, big Pete's determination to get his way—we made quite a show.

On the other hand, Pete would get really pissed at customers for slowing him down. In the middle of the night he'd come up to me, sweat dripping down his forehead, and say in his thick New York accent, "We should put signs up, *Have your money ready or you will not be served.*" Then he'd walk away, and I'd hear him yelling at somebody to have it out, up front, or forget it.

I always split the twenty with him anyway.

Both of us would have a similar reaction to customers who seemed to be interested in the other one. He'd always say right to me, "I don't get it. He likes you. He would want to date you. Why?"

It killed him that most of the guys would, for some reason, ask about me. I guess it was that thing where just being behind the bar made you look sexier. If they were his friends, he'd get totally frustrated.

I'd hear him: "You think she's cute? You'd want to go out with her? Why?" Like it wasn't fair that they liked me, and it was only because they didn't know me. I would just laugh because it annoyed him so much.

"Maybe when your hair was long, I would've thought you were kind of hot, too, but not like this," he'd say, pissed off. Always making a comment on how boyish I looked wearing my baseball cap backwards with my short hair, as if I was some kind of lesbian, or what was my point.

But everybody else thought it was just that he was secretly in love with me. And sometimes even I wondered, because when he'd start doing shots with his customers he'd become a little friendlier with me. He'd press up against me even when he wasn't trying to hold me back from making drinks.

And at least once a week he'd say, "We should do it. Just once, come on." I'd just push him off me like he was some kind of aggravating insect, because I couldn't even entertain the thought. Not after the stories he'd come out with about his sex life. Not after the millions of women I'd seen waiting for him after hours. God, he was like the gross-out king. It would make his night to share a story of absolutely disgusting details with the staff. Man, he didn't just make *me* sick, even Russ and the rest of the guys would turn green from his unbelievably explicit and picturesque anecdotes. Talking about eating some girl out and chewing on something that came out of her that turned out to be a big ball of discharge, like a ball of wax that accumulates over time, that he ended up sucking on and then swallowing. He had to be making that shit up.

But I had the same kind of attitude toward girls liking him. Some of them were really nice and pretty, normal, not even slutty-looking like I'd imagined. And I'd feel for them. It would usually start out slowly, and then I'd see them more often, hanging out at the bar after hours, waiting for Pete to get off work. They'd try to grill me for an inside line on Pete. Did he really like them? Was he dating a lot of other women? Was he a good guy? It put me on the spot.

But he was my buddy, and there was some kind of bartender confidentiality in force between us, so I always played it really cool and neutral, trying to make him look as good as possible. But if she was really nice and I could sense he was going to screw her over, I'd threaten him to come clean or I would tell all. I had an obligation to him, but to women I had an inherent sense of loyalty.

It was different there than here. I'd snap my gum and blow big bubbles with it. In my tank top and shorts I'd dance and do shots with my customers and managers. My customers there were mostly kids. Kids banging down shots and swigging on Champagne look a lot different from grown men and women. Full-fledged adults look a lot more alcoholic, because they lack enthusiasm and seem extremely practiced.

But I'm not a kid anymore, either. And when people look at me in my white starched collar and tie, I see the pity in their eyes. Sometimes it takes a lengthy conversation before they realize that I'm educated. I can't figure out a way to squeeze into the conversation that I graduated Magna Cum Laude, so I don't. But their eyes stare through me and their questions tiptoe around my life outside of the bar, and I know they wonder if this is the end of the road for me or if someday I will get out. I know I'll get out. I've known it for almost ten years.

CHAPTER 16

"**I** JUST CAN'T BELIEVE it," I say out loud, this time to Phil instead of over and over to myself.

"Why? Tell me what happened."

"You see? I didn't even tell you about it, because I was going to wait until they called me to tell me I got it, and then I was going to tell you the whole thing minute by minute, stretching out every detail."

"Well, tell me now."

"It's just so humiliating now," I say, sitting down on the bed, hanging my head between my knees.

"Why? You still did the same great job. Just because they didn't give it to you doesn't mean you suddenly suck."

"So why didn't they give it to me, then?"

"C'mon. I'm not going to do that with you. If you want to tell me what happened, I want to hear. But I'm not going to turn it inside out and put it under a magnifying glass so you can dissect yourself into tiny pieces. It's not healthy."

"It was my third callback. There were like seven producers there. I don't know why so many, but there they were. I did the scene, no problem. She's a waitress, for God's sake. It's for *Who's the Boss*, and they're all there, and after I'm done it gets a little quiet and then they're talking to me.

"Where'd you get that voice? Where are you from? Where'd you train? Did you have a special focus in comedy?"

You know, so I'm feeling like, fellas, no more questions, please, where do I sign the contracts? Because it wasn't even one of those situations where I felt I could've done better. I mean, what's to dissect? She's a funny toughie of a waitress that I could do with a broken leg and no fingers."

"So you walked out and you never heard from them again?"

"Actually, no. My agent called a couple of days ago and said they were thinking about it, but they weren't sure how old they wanted her to be so they're not sure."

"But then he called today and said they are and it's not you," he says sitting down next to me, and putting his hand on my knee.

"Yep. But my agent really doesn't care, because his other client was up for it and she's the one that got it."

"Really?"

"Yeah. She's about forty or something. Maybe younger, but not like me. She's always booking jobs. I'm sure he loves her. I mean I don't know why it bothers me so much, but it does. Not so much that she got it, but, yeah, that she got it. I just feel like it was so easy for me and I didn't get it. How do you get it? How does she get it?"

I rip my sweater off and throw it into my closet, suddenly very hot.

"You just keep going for it. And try not to have expectations. It only makes you feel more disappointed," he says in that way that really bothers me.

"How do you keep going for it and not have expectations? That's like me telling you not to have expectations when you send your writing out. But the minute you send something out, you do. Don't you?"

"No."

"Well, that's because you never send anything out."

"Because that's not what's important to me about my work."

"Then how can you even say that about expectations? You don't have to keep yourself from having expectations, because you don't have any to begin with. It doesn't seem normal to me to put yourself in a vulnerable position like that and do your best and know that you're good and not expect anything from it."

"You can expect something from it, just don't expect to get it."

"Great. I'll expect never to get it, and I expect I never will."

"You know, I'm trying to help you and you're giving me attitude. You put too much into it. You put too much on it."

"Because I really want this. I want it more than anything and I can't have it. I don't know how. I'd rather have the expectation and all the disappointment that goes with it than have no hope. Not that I have so much of that at the moment."

"You're living in a box, is why. You only see it in your own little way. You're so determined, you've got blinders on and you can't see where you're going or anything else along the way. Take off the blinders and keep going, you'll get there."

"But when will I fucking get there? When I die?"

"I can't talk to you right now. You're too upset," he says, getting up and walking away, but I'm so frustrated I can't let him. Take the blinders off? What does that mean?

"I'm upset because I don't think you understand. I'm busting my ass out there and losing and you're telling me not to have expectations and take the blinders off, whatever that means. And what's wrong with being upset? Don't I get to be upset, or is that only for you?"

"Quit following me, Nicky, I don't want to be around you right now."

"Why? Because I'm upset? So, I'm upset. I'm very upset. Why can't you be with that? Maybe you're the one living in a box. If your advice doesn't make me feel better, can't you take off *your* blinders and figure out another way to help? How about, 'Come here honey, and let me hold you. It really sucks that you didn't get this one. I understand how you must feel. Why don't you just let it out?' It always makes me feel better."

"Okay. You and your expectations had better get away from me now," he says, pushing me away from the door I just happen to be standing in front of.

"Oh, excuse me. Is it too much of an expectation to expect a little compassion from you?"

"I'm giving you compassion, it's just not how you expect it, god-damn it."

When I don't move, he grabs my arm and bends it behind my back to make me.

"Fine, what's the difference?" I say.

"Obviously, I can't make one," he says storming out and slamming the door behind him.

He's always talking to me about expectations, of him, of acting, of life. But I really can't understand how to carry on without them, because expectations are not only about hope but also about belief. If I can envision myself at the top, maybe I can get there. If I'm not even allowed to envision myself there, to believe that I could actually get there, to convince myself and then to, yeah, *expect* that working hard and being good will reap reward, what is it exactly that will help me through the door? What will even allow me to go for the door in the first place?

I guess he's right that expecting makes me hurt more than if I didn't. But I doubt it makes me hurt that much more. And the truth is, I do expect it. It's not even such a big deal to convince myself. To me, it's like math. There's a right answer, and it's me. When I've done my work, figured out the role a little, brought my ideas to it, the answer should be yes. I believe it. I expect it, and I am confused and, yes, disappointed, by the no that keeps coming up instead.

Okay, I'm not always right for the part. Okay. But why should it matter how old the waitress is? Is it so integral to the plot? Is it such a matter of context in the viewer's mind? Is there anything in the story that will change with this one, inconsequential waitress's age?

I've seen lots of waitresses in my short life. They come old, young, fat, skinny, smart, dumb, pretty, not pretty, etc. This is not a question of math—old or young? There's no right answer. It's a choice they make. It's the choice they make that doesn't include me. And perhaps I shouldn't complain, because the way this is going, I'll be able to play all the old girls in town before I know it. (Of course, by then all the old girls will have to be cast young. It will become a state mandate or something.)

But it's not like Phil's writing at all, so I don't know why I bothered trying to make that analogy. Because even if Phil sent his work out every day (which he would never bother doing), he wouldn't expect to hear something good about it. I can't really imagine him running to the mailbox every day looking for that letter notifying him that the Eugene O'Neill Theater wanted to produce his play.

Though, now that I think about it, I *could* picture him running to the mailbox every day looking for the rejection letter. He'd like nothing better than to run home from a full day of cooking at the restaurant, getting greasy and smelly, and tally his rejections up. He likes to tack them up on his corkboard. How many can I get? How rejecting will they be? That's his whole deal. That's the only reason he would even bother sending anything out, so he could rack up another rejection. Big deal. So far he only has two. Different kind of expectation, but still, it is one.

They're hard not to have. And that's what I think trips me up about the whole expectation thing. Can you really control your expectations? Maybe Phil can. And maybe it's true that if you don't expect too much, nothing will ever disappoint you, but then will anything ever excite you, either? Could you dream of doing the one thing you love more than anything else in this world, and actually pursue it, if you had no expectation that you might actually be able to have a piece of it? I don't know. I don't think I could. But maybe Phil's right. Maybe I expect too much.

I expect Phil to be nice to me, even though he's proven on numerous occasions that he can't.

I expect him to stop pushing me around and he hasn't.

I expect myself to remove myself from this living arrangement in general and Phil in particular if he can't work through his many problems and change, as obviously seems to be the case.

I expect myself to be more successful and less obsessive.

I expect Casey will live forever.

I expect to work at something I really love in this world or I expect I'll die from not.

CHAPTER 17

MY LEGS STAY stuck to the mattress like black tar, hot, sticks to a roof. My hair is tangled around my head, my skin grimy from last night's cigarette smoke. And this is how it will stay all day. Phil's working a day shift and I'm alone.

I phone in sick to my gym, which is ridiculous because there's no way anyone can cover me on such short notice. But I cough into the phone anyway, because as I tell Sheri, the aerobics director, "I can't possibly make it." I simply can't get it up. I can't motivate my leotard-clad enthusiasts to feel good, to work hard, to work hard to feel good, because I just can't see the point. I look better than I've ever looked in my life, and still, nobody gives a shit.

I don't particularly feel better clinging to my sheets, except that now I don't have to be anywhere. From here, no one has any expectations for me, not even me.

Lying here, with my teeth unbrushed and that stale morning breath that will creep into afternoon, I wonder how long I can stay right here before the stagnation creates its own destruction.

I want to read, but I can't make sense of the words. I have to reread each section till it becomes too monotonous to continue. Instead, I stare at the walls. Tiny cracks, chipped paint, blank nothingness.

The phone rings. I don't want to answer it, but I'm not good about letting it ring. It could be my agent calling with that part that will change my sorry life. It could be Casey calling to say her life is about to end.

It is Casey.

"Hey, what are you doing?" she says, without mentioning anything about her life ending.

"I'm glued to my bed."

"You sound like shit."

"Thank you."

"Are you fighting with Phil again?"

"Not at the moment."

"Well, is he there?"

"No."

"Well, I'm coming over."

"No."

"Yes. Get in the shower or I'll throw you in when I get there."

"Why?"

"We have to go check out that old Mustang I told you about."

"Why do I have to take a shower?"

"I don't want you smelling up my new car. Hurry, I'll be right there."

I don't want to hurry. I don't even know what that would look like today. I'm not exactly ready when Casey gets to my place.

"Okay, okay, come on," she says picking clothes out of my closet.

"Oh, I'll just wear this."

"It looks like you slept in that."

"I did."

"Get it off you," she says like it's some kind of spider.

"What's the difference?" I say, pulling off my sweatshirt.

"You didn't shower, either."

"So?"

"So get your ass in there. You smell like ten ashtrays."

"Okay," I say, as she escorts me into the bathroom.

"There, now doesn't that feel better?" she calls into the shower stall like she's my mother.

Actually, it does.

"Where's the Mustang?"

"Over in Burbank."

"Oh, yuck. What's it doing there?"

"I know. But it'll be fun, I'll buy you lunch."

"In Burbank?"

"We'll go to Hollywood."

"You think you're really gonna get it?"

"I have to have Hal check it out, but it sounds really good."

"Good."

"It's good that it's in Burbank because that'll give us some time to work on your crabby attitude."

"I'm not crabby, I'm sick."

"What do you mean?"

"I didn't teach my class. I called in sick."

"Well then, we have to get you better," she says, putting her arm around me and then noogying my toweled head.

I already do feel better. There's just something about Casey that always makes me feel better. I can't stay depressed around her. I feel like a complete ass wallowing in self-pity when she's around. She's never depressed. It doesn't seem to be in her makeup. She's not cheerful, either. She's just busy living. Gotta go here, gotta get there, gotta do this, gotta do that. Somehow it rubs off on me. She says we have to go and I know she's right. We have to go.

"What's Jay doing today?"

"Working."

"Oh."

"So is it Phil or acting?"

"Both. Neither."

"Do you know that you're very strange?" she says.

"Sometimes."

The Mustang is beautiful. It's Forest Green with a cream interior. The guy selling it says it's a '67 and it has 168,000 miles on it, which is a lot, I think. But he claims it's in good condition anyway.

"Who used to own it?"

"This old guy. Took immaculate care of it."

"Oh, that's nice," she says, running her hand along the steering wheel, I guess picturing the old guy driving it. She loves anything old—old cars, old people, old furniture—especially old chairs.

"Can we take it for a test?" she says.

"Sure," the guy selling it says.

His name is Jimmy. He's a young guy—pale and thin with grease all over his hands. He makes me a little nervous.

"Take as long as you like," he says tossing Casey the keys and eyeing her up and down.

We get out of the heavy traffic and cruise up into the hills. The radio sounds pretty good, it's comfortable and, overall, I would have to say a very smooth ride. It's relaxing.

"What do you think?" I ask.

"Feels pretty smooth, don't you think?" she says grinning.

"I do. I'm kind of surprised. How did you hear about it again?"

"Through that grip on the shoot I did last week for the USC film. He knows this guy, Jimmy, the one that's showing it."

"Do you trust him enough to buy it from him?"

"No, but I figure Hal will give me the lowdown."

Case takes her time getting back, just rolling around the sunny streets of Burbank.

"Does he hit you?"

"What?"

"Phil. Does he?"

"He can't stand seeing me upset or disappointed, but instead of helping me through it, he blames me for getting upset in the first place. He lectures me. He gets angry. He *did* hit me once."

"I knew it. That's fucking creepy, Nick."

"He's crazy that way. The more uncomfortable he gets with my upset, the more upset I get. It makes me want to let loose and scream because I can't stand that I'm not allowed to have these fucked up feelings, and I want to show him that this is just the tip of the iceberg, but he only lets me get a little fraction of it out, because he leaves the room with this holier than fucking thou attitude before I've even had a chance to let myself spin out of control."

"Where did he hit you?"

"In the neck."

"That's so sick."

"I know. But it's not Phil, that's not even why I'm like this, I don't think."

She looks at me like she can't figure out why I'm saying that. I can't figure out why I'm saying it.

"It's work. I just really don't want to work tonight—so tired of it."

She's still looking at me with a confused face, some measure of disbelief on it, but then she says, "I know what you mean. Monday was my first day back after the USC shoot. I fucking hated it."

"That's the worst. But at least you've got a little cash for the car, you know?"

"Yeah. That's the thing. That's always the thing," she says, pulling into the garage. But then she slows before we pull up to greasy Jimmy.

"So you never freak out on him before he bails?"

"Not really. Why?"

"Because I just can't picture you sitting there and taking that shit."

"Me neither," I say. And I can't.

CHAPTER 18

I WHIP AROUND THE bottles, yelling, "What do you want?" to all the faces scrambling for drinks on the other side of the bar. My bandanna flips and flops around my messy head. But I don't care how I look. Well, I care, but I can't help it, so. It's hot and crowded and I'm tired. But not so tired that I don't notice the guy at the end. He's dark, both his skin and his hair. Smooth skin that I think will smell good. I know it will. I keep going, but catch his eye a couple of times before I come up in front of him and ask what he wants.

I serve some people, but while I'm serving them I acknowledge him, giving him a little nod that says I'll be right over. I get the next customer but notice he, smooth skin, is still looking at me. I smile. Then I complete the transaction I'm engaged in, drop their change and make my way over to him. I feel like looking right into his dark, sexy eyes and saying, "What do you want?" referring to something completely out of this tiny bar universe. Instead I ask him what he's having. He tells me, politely. I go get it.

"Shall I pay now?" he asks when I return with an ice-cold beer, from way back in the cooler.

"Not necessary," I say. "I'll run you a check." I go to the register and ring him up. It's enough of a courtesy to run him a check, since I've never seen him before. I don't have to pick it up, too. In fact, it would be tacky. This way he's just a customer, no matter what thoughts slither through my hungry head. Because maybe he just seems sweet to me now, because I don't know him. Later, he may end up being just like Phil.

I don't talk to him much, there isn't time, but I do a little, as much as I can. I like to hear his voice—so peaceful amidst the noise. He sits there, tucked away in that corner of the bar, as I fly back and forth, calling out prices, collecting cash, pouring alcohol over ice. Then the night goes on and I get lost in the crowds, and he disappears—so do I, just going about my business like a machine.

"Get me this. Get me that," they say. Get me out of here.

His hair was dark and kind of spiky, sexy, like you want your fingers through it. I wonder if he'd mind. That's the wonderful thing about hair and skin. They're always there to touch. Even when you fight with someone and you can't reach them, you could always reach out and touch their hair or skin, if you had the courage. But even just wanting to touch gives me a good feeling. I wonder what it would feel like to touch him. He touched me, the way he spoke to me. I don't even remember what he said, but I can hear his voice saying it, with that mouth. And how he looked right at me, with those eyes that weren't afraid to grab me—to pull me close to him in the middle of all the chaos.

He comes back another time. I can't remember what he drinks. I can always remember what they drink. But not what *he* drinks. He tells me what he wants. I get it for him. I just want to stare at him. Naked. We talk this time, about the people. How they look. What they might do.

"I bet that guy's a pilot," he says, picking out a tall man with a short buzz cut.

"You think?" I say.

"Yup. And that woman over there, eating the macaroni and cheese," he says indicating with a covert toss of his head, "She's a nurse."

"Was it the mac and cheese that tipped you off?"

"No. The white shoes," he says, smiling.

"See, now," I laugh, "You've got an advantage. I can't see the shoes." I know him. Not really, but somehow.

He comes back again, sometimes beer, sometimes coffee. I look at his fingers around the cup. Thick, strong, slightly scarred, on me. Big knuckles like some of them have been broken before, a wristwatch around his wrist, but I can't see the arms under his shirt. Not well enough. In fact, I'm cut off from anything below the chest. The bar is in my way. I can only imagine. I don't mind. I like to.

I chatter. I say things that aren't important as if they are, but I keep talking. He listens. Sometimes I get him talking, but not that much. Not like me. But he is like me, somehow, something to do with that quiet on the outside that hardly hides how much is going on inside.

Really, he's just a customer. I want him to ask anyway, though. Ask for something more than what I'm giving him. I want to see if I can resist, if I can follow my own rules. The rules that say you shouldn't get involved with the customers. I want to see to what degree I can follow those guidelines. Could I say no to coffee? A drink? A touch of my hand? A kiss on the cheek? Because right now I think I'd like him to own me. Come back here and pull me out from behind the bar, holding my hands behind my back so that I press against him when he takes my lips into his mouth and there's no way I can say anything, like no.

But if he did get me out from behind the bar, I don't think I'd want to come back. I imagine what it would feel like to rest my head on his chest, and I think I could sleep for a long time. Cuddled in his arms, smelling his smell. Now he talks to someone sitting at the bar. What is he saying? I get hold of myself.

I'm the bartender. I give them what they want, they throw me some money, and I go home. But he's even good at that. He throws me good money. Only he doesn't throw it. He slides it under a saucer or an ashtray or a beer bottle. He's gone by the time I notice it.

And I never know when he'll be back. But I will him back. I envision him walking through those glass doors that keep me inside this place. He'll come from the doors to the side of me, not the ones in front of me. I won't see him at first. But then I'll feel his eyes on me and I'll catch a glimpse of him in my peripheral vision. I'll finish the transaction I'm engaged in, and go to the cabinet where we keep our personal belongings. I'll dig through the stuff and grab my leather jacket. I'll swing it over my shoulder and go towards him. When I get to him, we'll just stare at each other. Then we'll turn and walk out the glass doors, slowly, casually, together. I'll never look back.

CHAPTER 19

"**L**IKE ANYONE WOULD look good in this outfit but this model."

"Oh, you would, if you were a little taller and didn't have such big hooters."

We lie around on Casey's white carpet, flipping through the magazines that cover much of it.

"Well, maybe I could wear lifts in my shoes and have my breasts removed. Small price to pay for a nice outfit, you know, Case?"

"Well, it is pretty nice. How did your audition for that play go?"

"It went really well. I love that part. She's from Brooklyn, she's young, she's ballsy and funny and I think she *should* be little, you know, not too tall. I'm perfect for it."

"And?"

"They said they'd let us know by Friday."

"So you still might get it."

"I might. But now I'm thinking they said *by* Friday, so somebody else might've heard by Wednesday, or Thursday."

"You know what? It was stupid of me to ask. You'll know when you know."

The problem is, the first real part I got set me up badly for everything to come. All the way home on that train ride back to Armonk, I kept saying in my head, "I got it. I got it." I remember my heart jumping up and down inside my throat when I walked in our front door and handed the script to my Mom.

She said, "You got it?"

I said, "I really got it. Can you believe it?"

That was the first time I had even said it out loud. I went the whole ride home without saying it because it turned out that the stage manager was from the town next to mine, so we rode home from the city together. I acted happy, but kind of cool about it, just skimming through the pages of my script, like, yup, this is great, another great part to play. Instead of, yup this is great, my first part in the real world, on Forty-Second Street, between Ninth and Tenth Avenue, Theater Row. I got it, I got it, I got it!

Now, every time I go for something, I'm waiting for them to tell me on the spot how I got it. And they never do. Even when I get it they don't. (Not that I've been getting it very often.)

"Yeah, I think I didn't get it if I haven't heard by now."

"You're so tortured," she says, halting on a page in her magazine with lots of deep, dark lipsticks.

"I don't know if I'd say tortured," I say, crouching over her, trying to get a look at the different shades.

"You wouldn't say tortured because you don't like to think about yourself that way. But think about it. As soon as it's over, you assume you didn't get it, but at the same time you're hoping you did, and there's a part of you that thinks you did get it, even though you try not to admit that part. But you won't allow yourself to give up all hope, so you keep replaying the audition over and over in your mind."

"Yeah, obsessive."

"Everything you did, the response, what you would do if you were given another chance, how would it differ from what you did, et cetera. Again, you assume you didn't get it, so you have to convince yourself of all the reasons you might've gotten it, pointing out to yourself all the stuff you did right, even arguing the points, 'that was good, that was

bad, still I would've done exactly the same thing if I could do it again,'
and so on. Like I said, tortured."

"Yeah," I say, grabbing her magazine and falling down next to her. I
relax my head back onto this great big orange pillow she has on the floor.

She shakes her head and grabs the new *Vogue*. Then she says, "And
speaking of tortured, how're things with Phil?"

"I guess you could say they're worse."

She closes her magazine.

"So, Nick, what are you going to do?"

"Well, he can't really afford our place on his own."

"So?"

"My dad's moving out of his place and getting a bigger place, and I
was kind of hoping to set Phil up at my dad's old place. You know how
my dad is friends with his landlord? They play tennis together."

"Well, that's very nice of you, and I just want to mention that there's
a CODA meeting just a few blocks away that you might want to go to
before you start finding him apartments."

"I thought this could cushion the blow, and financially, if I move out,
we both have to move. I can stay at my aunt's for a while and if I don't
find a place by the time she needs hers, I can stay with my dad, but Phil
really has nowhere to go."

"Well, that's all very rational, but how do you fucking feel, Nicky?
It's like you're just going along like some kind of robot, and I have to tell
you it's freaking me out."

I flip over onto my belly. The floor is hard even with the carpeting.
I can't get comfortable.

"That's how I feel. Like I'm just going along with everything. Almost
like I'm standing still. Even though I'm aware of it, I can't seem to make
a move. I'm numb."

"You have to just do it anyway, then."

"I guess there's a little secret part of me that really believes I've done
something wrong to make this happen, and I'm still trying to figure out
what. You know he's not the first guy that's wanted to beat me up. I had
a boyfriend in college who hit me."

"Your boyfriend in college actually hit you?"

"Yeah."

"In the face?"

"In the tit, once."

"Oouch. Why?"

"He was really mad at me."

"Apparently. Did you do something to make him really mad?"

"I'm sure I did. I always do things that make people mad."

"Well, sometimes you're a bit difficult, because you're stubborn and neurotic, but it's not true you always do things to make people mad. I don't know why you think that."

"People get mad at me a lot."

"I don't get mad at you a lot, but I still want to beat you up all the time."

"Yeah, I feel the same way about you, come to think of it."

"But see how we don't do it. We just bicker a little. It's how people deal with it. He shouldn't have hit you."

"I know."

She gathers a few magazines and racks them in the little antique holder she has for them. The wood is old and unfinished, painted beige, and there's a worn black wooden handle at the top.

"Don't think I'm an asshole, but do you find it exciting or something?"

"There's nothing sexy about getting beat up. In the movies they make it look there's all this sexual tension wrapped up in the violence, but in true life, it's just violence."

I'm hungry.

"Do you have anything to eat?" I ask.

"C'mon," she says making her way into the kitchen. Then she takes out a pizza dough and starts piling things on top of it. Her kitchen is small and cozy. The walls are white brick and the window frames are painted black. There's an old rustic wrought-iron café table that sits in the corner by one of the windows, and just above the table is an old black-and-white sign that says, "It's Home."

"I've always been the black sheep in my family, but now I just think of myself as the black sheep, period. Phil didn't seem to think about me that way. But now he does. And now I'm more and more worried about getting in trouble with him."

"Nick, you're not as big and bad as you think you are. You're going through some frustrating times and sometimes you're a little obsessive-compulsive, and that can be annoying, but that's your personality, and unfortunately, we're not allowed to punish you for it. I can't believe I have to tell you this shit."

"Well, thanks, I think. But aside from the qualities you've just mentioned, I can get on a mean streak when I'm upset. And when I'm in that mode, I just don't care about anything else. I know it's never right to hit or push someone around, but I guess there's that sick part of me that thinks I'm responsible. Phil always says I provoke him and I know I do. I can't help it."

The pizza's ready. It's got cheese and all kinds of different greens and olives and a whole bunch of other stuff on it.

"Obviously you bring out the worst in each other, but his is dangerous."

"Yeah."

"Just so you know, I've been mean to people, but nobody's ever laid a hand on me."

"I don't see you that way. I've never seen you be mean. I feel like you're good to everybody. You're overly good."

"Whatever, you weirdo, but that's not the point," she says, making one of her funny faces and rolling her eyes.

She lays a slice on a plate for me and I wait, knowing I'll burn my tongue if I attempt it. Seconds later, I take a bite even though it's still too soon. It only hurts a little.

I ask Casey, "Did you ever feel like you couldn't breathe?"

"Not exactly. I mean I've been winded once or twice."

"No. What about with that Amir guy?"

"We didn't get along at all."

"Yeah, but he didn't even give you a chance to feel conflicted; he suffocated you right away. Don't you remember?" She takes a bite of her pizza but seems to have timed it just right.

"Yeah. I guess you're right. He called me every few minutes just to have a fight."

"And yet, you liked him."

"Yeah. Until I realized."

"Well, Phil used to leave me alone. We used to just do our own thing and be together when we weren't. He never made demands of me. If I wanted to go do my acting stuff, I'd do it. If I wanted to hang around with him, "Yeah, sure, great." We had fun together, but I had so much freedom and I loved that. I think it's the most relaxed a guy's ever been with me. It's only recently that he started freaking on me for the littlest things, and so it really crept up on me, but now that I see it, I'm panicking."

"But that's the good news."

"But he's seeing it, and it's making *him* panic. I was thinking he was becoming his dad, but now I think he *is* his dad."

"You didn't get along too well with his dad."

"No. And now I'm feeling really winded."

When I was in fifth grade, I played fullback on the soccer team. And one game, the championship one, I came up on a ball, trying to block it, and I did, but it hit me right smack in the solar plexus and knocked the wind out of me, and I went down. That's how I've been feeling, lately. I was sitting by myself the other day, feeling like I just couldn't breathe, and I thought of this soccer game. Because when you're in the game, you get so focused. As fullback, you're trying to defend the goal and you keep going and going, fighting to protect it. But when I got knocked down, even before I started breathing again, I struggled to get up and keep playing, trying to win that championship, which I know

now would have been stupid, because I would've been too winded to help win anything.

I know I have to take myself out of this thing with Philip. But now I feel stupid that I had to get the wind knocked out of me to realize it.

Casey is staring at me and my now-empty plate. I realize I've inhaled my slice of pizza and perhaps a couple that would've been hers.

"It's about time," she says, I guess in response to my feeling winded, because she can't mean the pizza.

CHAPTER 20

THIS NAME IS actually Troy, but I just call him T or I don't call him anything. Again and again he comes back. We talk. We talk a lot, just like friends. Sometimes I feel like he's my best friend. I miss him when he's not there. There, on his stool, drinking his favorite beer, talking to me. But still, we just talk.

He did ask me, once, whether I had a boyfriend. I didn't understand if he was just asking out of curiosity or if it maybe meant something. It happened when he was trying to give me some work in a print ad he was doing. Philip must've been the one to answer the phone.

"We might have to shoot this thing in San Francisco," he told me. "Could you work that out?"

I said yes. "I could stay with friends up there," I said.

But right away I had thoughts of the shoot going late and me ending up in his hotel room, in his arms. I couldn't lie about the boyfriend thing, though. At the point when he called, I was still trying so hard to be conscientious and make things work with Phil, even though I knew they never would.

So we had this really nice conversation and that's when he slipped in the question.

"Nicky, do you live with someone?"

He said it so neutrally, like he somehow needed the information for the union paperwork.

So I told him yes. Then I just let go of the whole notion of something happening between us.

Sometimes now, though, he'll say, "Nick, we're going to this party tonight. Why don't you come?"

"We" being his sister and he, or friends of his I've met at the bar. (It turns out that Paul, the neurologist, the really nice guy that helped Casey and me out, is T's best friend. Small world.) I can't tell if he is asking me out. It seems like he's just asking me as a friend. But if so, I should be able to either bring Phil along or at least tell him where I'm going and with whom. I can't do either, so I always say no.

"I can't," I'll say, giving some bogus excuse, because I can't tell him I think I might be in love with him.

His neutrality confuses me. He even brings in a date this one time. I serve them drinks and eavesdrop on their conversation. She's blonde and fair and has curly, thin hair. She treats me politely, like I'm the bartender, and it reminds me that I am and I don't like her. That kind of settles it for me.

But now we've been talking for a while. He's got a real calm to him and I wonder what he thinks about. Tonight he tells me about his job. He's been at the same ad agency for six years.

"It's getting a little old for me," he says. "I may make a move soon, but I don't want to make a move just for the sake of moving, you know? I want to go somewhere else because I'm excited to be there."

I know just what he means. "Well, wherever you go, I'm sure they'll be very happy to have you," I say.

For the first time I see in his face a glimmer of recognition that perhaps the thought of having him has crossed my mind once or twice, too.

"That's nice of you to say," he says shyly. "How's the acting world treating you?" he changes the subject.

"It, too, is getting kind of old," I say. "I'm thinking of moving on, but right now I have no idea where to go."

"I'm sorry it's so hard," he says.

"Yeah, and I guess I've just always thought I'd do this, pursue it until finally, one day, I was working regularly. I think the hardest part is never actually getting a chance to do it. Every day is about struggling just to get a shot at something."

"I know," he says.

I guess it is something he knows about, being in advertising. He's actually a part of the team that keeps me from my goals. To them it's always about money and looks, and I never seem to have the right balance of the latter to get me any of the former.

"I hate to see you suffer through it because I know how little it has to do with your talent. It's all about money. I'm sure you're very good."

"Thanks," I say, and then add, "I am." I am good, and there's a chance, a good chance, that I'll never get to prove it.

He really does seem to feel badly for me, and I think it's because he must be cringing for me as he reflects back on casting sessions he's been a part of. The things they must say about us after they say their thank-yous and send us on our way. I cringe, thinking about my poor breasts and how many times they must have been the focus of the post-discussion.

"You need another?" I say, indicating his almost finished beer.

"Oh, sure, thanks," he says.

I go over to the cooler to get it and I can't help thinking how different he seems. Refreshing. There's an evenness about him. A kind of level-headed intelligence—he's smart and calm and there's a kindness and I find the combination very appealing. I want to just keep talking with him.

"On us," I say as I place his beer down in front of him on a fresh cocktail napkin.

"Thanks a lot," he says, as I make my way down the bar to check on everybody else.

Holly, one of the bartenders that usually works during the day, comes in giggling.

"Hey, Nick, how's it going? Can I have a Shirley Temple, a club soda and a Beck's for my Grandpa, over there?" she says, pointing towards Ludwig over in his corner.

The Shirley Temple is for Holly's daughter, whom Holly must've had when she was ten, because her daughter looks like she's about eleven now and Holly doesn't look much more than twenty-one.

"We practically got kicked out of the pizzeria because Ludwig was so loud. I kept apologizing for him, telling everybody that he's my grandfather and when he forgets to take his pills he gets a little crazy, but Mandy seemed mortified, you know?"

"Uh, Hol, I can't say I blame her," I say.

But Holly is so nice, she just says "I know," and laughs it off. She's got long curly hair and she's usually wearing some kind of cool hat. I can't imagine anyone having anything bad to say about her—I mean, pizza with Ludwig on her day off? She really is nice.

I light a few cigarettes, make a few drinks, and I think I feel T's eyes on me. I resist looking up, going about my work, trying to look good, but when I still feel them moments later, I glance over to where he's sitting.

The eyes are on me and that's where they stay. There is no apology in them for having stared, and they don't veer. He doesn't fidget and he doesn't smile. There are no extraneous movements to dissipate the look.

"The look," the one that my girlfriends and I have talked about, at times compulsively. The look that needs no explanation because it says, I want you. I want you specifically because you are all the things you wish you were. That quintessential look that every person wants to be the recipient of, and that, at this moment, I am.

I look back at him for as long as I can stand, which is really just a brief moment and then I pretend to be needed elsewhere, shifting my gaze as if preoccupied with other things. Moving on as though I'm a businesswoman, busy with the business at hand, mixing, clinking ice, pouring, collecting, always moving, as if I may not even have caught the look, and if I did, I may have to have it again to understand what's really behind it.

But the next time I steal a glance he's gone, only the crisp bill and my thoughts to mark his place. And as I tuck the money into our cup and wipe away all evidence of his presence, I wonder what moving on would really feel like. Could it be as simple as finding something else to be excited about, like moving from one ad agency to the next? But if I was really excited about it, wouldn't I still have to shake margaritas to pay the rent?

Closing time approaching, I start my cleanup now. Climbing out from behind the bar, I collect glasses and plates from appetizers, sparing my back the reach. I find a set of keys on the floor. They look familiar.

We call last call and I get to close out my bank first. I throw on my normal clothes, peeling off the smoky uniform. When I come back downstairs there's a knock on the glass window. I unlock the door and it's T, asking if I've come across a set of keys. I put the ones I've retrieved from the floor into his hand.

"Oh great, I'm saved, " he says, "Are you outta here?"

"Just gotta grab my jacket."

"Would you mind if I walked you to your car?" he says.

"No, I wouldn't mind," I say, semi-teasing, trying to make him wonder if that means I'd like it.

We walk huddled close from the cold, and we confer on how our evenings finished out. He tells me that he ran into an old friend on his way home and was having a drink down the street when he realized his keys were missing.

When we get to my little Datsun 200 SX, he must notice that I'm slipping my fingertips up my sleeves for warmth, and he takes my hands between his, heating them up quite effectively.

"Glad I caught you," he says.

"Yeah, me too," I say. Then I find my hands somehow pulling away from his, digging into my backpack, searching for my keys.

"Thanks for keeping me company tonight," I say.

"It's my pleasure," he says, and then, "Good night."

Protective of my safety in the dark late night, he watches as I lock my door and drive away, and suddenly I feel afraid to go home.

When I get there, Philip and I make love. It's not what I had planned, but it's easier to pretend everything is all right. I want it to alleviate the fear. Make me feel close to him like I used to in the beginning, when we'd stay up late talking and thinking and not being angry. But it doesn't. Because I can't erase the empty truth—the knowledge that not only am I not protected, but I'm going to get hurt.

CHAPTER 21

THE SUN STREAMS into our living room, making it warm and bright, and it's so quiet I can hear myself breathing. The warmth feels good because my clothes are beginning to chill me, wet from my morning run. I notice I'm tiptoeing, because I catch myself in the closet mirror, and it scares me to see this. Because what if he were here, ducking under our bed looking for a shoe, and he saw me tiptoeing around. So even though I've done the walk-through, I check every corner again, just to be sure. Then, quickly, because I'm starting to feel like I'm in a creepy movie, I climb up to the top of our closet and pull my suitcase down. It falls to the floor with a loud *thunk*, and the sound startles me. But that just makes me work faster, grabbing armfuls of clothing and shoveling them in.

"It's no good? It's not right?" he said, last night when I couldn't hold it in any longer. "What's so wrong with it?" he asked, giving me a kiss.

Kissing me sweetly, tenderly, like when we were first together, good friends, liking each other.

"It's not good. It's not right. It's wrong," I tried to say, but this was not a convincing argument since we had just made love.

We went to sleep, unresolved, but I thought he knew that nothing about the evening had changed my mind.

Now I look at my suitcase and run to the bathroom to retrieve just my make-up bag and toothbrush, all replaceable, but they're mine and I feel like I have a right to them. I open the cabinet and get an uneasy feeling when I see his shaving cream and tools piled in his corner.

Then I swear I hear footsteps on the apartment landing, and even though I know they can't be his because he's at work, the sound, just like in those creepy horror movies, makes me look around in suspicion, my eyes taking covert glances around the room, and even though no one is here to see me but me, again the sight of myself in the mirror is unsettling. So I hurry my things into one corner of the bedroom and try to figure out if I should take the suitcase first and come back for my purse and make-up bag, because the stairs are tough and the last thing I need is to trip going down them. I decide this is a good plan because, after all, the suitcase is the incriminating evidence, and so I start to lug it out of the bedroom. I'm unfortunately stopped dead in my tracks by the now unmistakable sound of his voice coming from the open doorway.

"What are you doing?" the voice says, making me drop the suitcase and jump what could quite possibly be a foot in the air. He stands there in his chef coat, staring at my suitcase and me and I'm guessing my pounding heart.

"I've got to go," I say in a monotone. It sounds kind of like people sound when they're in shock.

"No you don't," he says.

"Yes," I say. "Please don't be angry."

"Oh. What should I be?" he says.

"I don't know," I admit.

"What should I be when I see you stealing off like this?"

"Maybe relieved," I say.

"Don't run from me," he says getting close.

"I don't want to," I say, thinking I don't want to run, I want to walk, but since that isn't an option, I say, "I don't understand why you'd want me to stay." Even as I'm saying it, it seems wrong, because I really mean, I don't understand why I'd want to stay, or why I've stayed this long.

"I've told you this before, but I know you don't believe me. You're working through stuff. You're searching and hiding and running, but you won't always."

He says a lot of words, some about my loving, nurturing, side, but none of them make sense to me.

"I wonder if you're thinking I might someday become maternal and want a baby. I wonder if that's what you've been waiting for." I wonder if I *am* in shock because I don't know how that links to what he just said, but then I wonder if I'm just talking while I try to figure out what to do next.

"It's not that. Though I think someday you will. But c'mon, put your suitcase away," he says, moving towards me.

"I don't think I'm good for you," I say, making a subtle move further away from him and closer to my suitcase while calculating our distance from the front door.

"Why? What's so bad about you?"

"I feel like, in your eyes, almost everything," I say, and now I'm crying—damn it.

"That's so not true," he says and moves closer.

"I thought you were working today," I confess.

"I switched with Greg. I wanted to be with you. I know you were trying to say something last night about how we fight, but you have to know I really appreciate you."

"I know you do. But I don't feel it. It's my fault." Saying that it's my fault makes me feel like I'm in a scary movie again, but somehow it seems like a valid tactic.

"You don't 'feel' it?"

So even though I'm trying not to have a discussion, there seems to be no escaping it.

"I feel there's something deep-rooted in me that you hate and despise and wish would disappear."

"Are you getting back to that thing that counselor told us once about your mom and my dad?"

We only went to the counselor once. Maybe if we had gone more.

"Well, don't you think it's true that my mom and your dad would pretty much hate each other?"

"But I'm not my dad and you're not your mom."

"No. But sometimes we are. Sometimes we're just standing there, completely unsuspecting, and without our even knowing it, they climb into our bodies and have a kick-ass fight with each other. And I know in relationships both people have to come a little ways to make it work, but the gap isn't always this great, you know?"

"But why do you have to decide that now? Can't you just put some faith into this?" he says with a question mark, yet it's more of a demand.

"I've thought about this a lot, Phil. I can't put faith in it, because I'm afraid of you. The violence does something and I don't even understand exactly what, but I'm more and more shut down."

"But you can't blame me for that."

And now his reasoning certainly confuses me.

"I'm not. I'm just telling you that I don't want to feel that way anymore." I grab the handle of my suitcase and pick it up off the floor.

"Or maybe it's that you're never satisfied. With anything or anyone. It's not that you don't think you're good for me. It's that you don't feel I'm good for you. I pour my heart and soul into you and it is never enough. Could that be it, Nicky?" he says, staring my suitcase and me down.

"It could be, but I don't feel like you're pouring your heart and soul into me. I don't even know how to respond to you, because I'm not getting what you think you're giving, even though I believe that you love me."

I'm working so hard at remaining calm that any more calm and I'd be dead. But something about *him* is now kicked into gear. It's that panic mode. Instead of pleading with me to stay, he gets more physically and verbally aggressive. He gets closer and closer to my face. And he kisses me hard on the mouth and it hurts and it's scary, and he presses against me, grabbing hold of my wrists, until he unclenches and pushes me away in disgust.

"You always want more, Nicky—more, more, more and fucking more. You're so demanding."

And I remember back to a college boyfriend I had saying the same thing. "You're a very demanding girl, Nicky."

So I start to thinking that maybe it's true. Maybe I'm never satisfied because I'm insatiable. I'm just this hungry, hungry person who never stops wanting more. Maybe I make him feel terribly inadequate and he has to use force just to stay on the same level.

I feel greedy and selfish and hungry—but it's for the door. So instead of going off in a corner and dwelling on my own relentlessness, I make a definitive move for the door as I say, "Maybe I just don't want to get beat up anymore."

And he says, moving between the door and me, "Is that what this is all about? Then stop provoking me, that doesn't help."

It's true I say the exact thing that I know will set him off, all the time now. I want to push him over the edge. I need him to go crazy so I can say, "Fuck you, you're crazy." But why do I need to prove something so obvious? And what if I do provoke him? I provoke a lot of people. I'm provocative. And now I decide that I like that about myself.

"You know, when I was a little kid I remember everybody always saying, 'Don't hit. There's never a good reason to hit.' Didn't people ever say that to you?" I say, walking right up to his face and considerably closer to the door.

"You see. You push, Nicky. Maybe you just don't want to see your part in this. Maybe that's what it's about."

"I don't mind looking at my part in this. I do every day. I analyze and overanalyze, questioning myself, excessively, about how I can be with a person who actually causes me physical bodily harm. I tear myself into little pieces trying to figure out who I am and what I'm doing here and if there's some part of me that gets off on being hurt, or if I just believe I deserve to be treated that way. But now, I think I'd rather look at my part when I'm a little further away from you." I spot my purse back in the bedroom, by the closet, my car keys dangling from the side pocket.

"So you're just going to give up? Throw the towel in on all the hard work we've put into this? Walk away?"

It all sounds so good to me, I don't know what to say. But there aren't a lot of words rushing back at me trying to get out of my mouth. Just one.

"Yeah," I say.

"Well, that's just great, Nicky. Fucking walk away. Kill off success before you've even had a chance to taste it. Like you do with everything else."

"Like I do with everything else? What's that supposed to mean?" I say, walking with confidence towards my purse as if I still live here and we're just having a normal, everyday discussion.

"Oh, Nicky doesn't get a part after three auditions in a row, maybe she should quit trying to be an actress. Nicky's boyfriend throws a few temper tantrums, maybe she needs to find another one."

"If you think your strangling me until I can't breathe is a temper tantrum that I should put up with, you're not thinking clearly. If you think your punching me in the face is just another way of expressing yourself, it's not an appropriate way. I never know what your next tantrum is going to have in store for me, and I can't take responsibility for your outbursts, you really need to. As far as my acting is concerned, I'm busting my ass out there. It's not three auditions. It's three callbacks after three auditions and then nothing and then three more rounds of the same. I do feel discouraged. I do feel like quitting. Part of me just wants to get a real job, so I can be like a real person. But it would be a lot nicer for me if I had a little support at home instead of a hothead boyfriend so tightly wound that I don't even know what's going to set him off. Success? Where's the success in that?"

"That's not what I mean. You know I'm working on that—"

"Do me a favor. You keep working on it, but keep me out of it," I say, purse in hand and swinging by him towards the door.

"Where are you going to go?" he says.

"I'm going to stay at my aunt's place. She's out of town, and I can figure it out better from there."

"I guess this isn't exactly a spur of the moment decision, then, is it?"

"No."

"Well. What can I say?"

"Nothing."

"So it looks like you're going to have the last word, after all, huh, Nick?" he says, looking like he might just give up.

"I don't know, Phil, maybe," I say, trying to shrug him off.

"What do you mean, maybe? Look at you. Walking out the door before you've even given me a chance to defend my case."

"C'mon, Phil, please, can't we just drop it and move on?"

"You obviously can. Drop it. I'm the 'it' to which you refer, right? Drop it. Sure. Just drop it. But you don't want to forget this stuff," he says, gripping me by the arm and dragging me back into our bedroom and over to the closet. Then he starts grabbing my stuff and throwing it at me. "No, you wouldn't want to forget this little number," he says, holding up my black miniskirt. "You'll need that when you're trying to reel in your next lucky catch of the day, isn't that right, Nicky? You just keep movin' on till you find another poor fool you can jerk around till you get bored. Wouldn't want to stay in one place too long. Somebody might get hurt, huh? Or maybe you already have, huh? Maybe you've got your eye on someone already—some hot hunk creeping around the bar? Sure, maybe you've got something lined up already, because we all know how bitchy you can be when you go too long without getting any, right, baby?"

So he's going crazy and he wants me to join him. Then maybe when he hits me, it'll be my fault. I'll have asked for it. He wants me to scream and hiss and give him the fight he's been waiting for. Wants me to let loose, thrash and kick and maybe even bite. Wants to turn me into an animal so I really feel the pain of what it's like to hurt another person.

And there's a part of me that does want to join him. Wants to scream out, "Stop clawing at me, you big fucking asshole," as I knee him in the balls and make my break for the door. But the problem is, he wants this.

He's disappointed with me that I'm not acting it out like he is and so he keeps pushing at me, hoping I'll come around. He wants me to hurt him.

But it feels like a moot point in the face of his obvious hurt. And as his badgering goes on and on, it seems to be having the desired effect after all, and then I think, maybe it should. Because the more brutal the ending, the more final. As he goes on trying to make me out to be some sleazy nympho whore, who stands on street corners begging for it, I start to realize I may have to join him to make my final move. So I respond to his last jab, the one that he's brought up three times in the course of this non-conversation; the one that refers to my having my eye on someone. To having it lined up.

"You know what Phil, you're right. Except that I've more than got it lined up, and I've had more than my eye on him. Yup, I've had my whole hot pussy, wet and pulsing, right across his face, baby."

"Well, big surprise," he says, maintaining composure, surprising me.

"Oh that's right. You'd rather let me fuck every Tom in town than be a man and figure out what about you is so lacking that I'm forced to go elsewhere. You'd much rather walk around feeling sorry for yourself than do something about it. Something besides beating the shit out of me."

"What am I supposed to do about it? I fuck you every day and that still isn't enough."

"Yeah, right, Phil. You *wish* you could fuck me every day." I get right up in his face and spew it out, and I guess that's the one that does it.

Thwack, right across my face. My lip only bleeds a little, but it will be the last time. Having finally achieved his goal, he seems frozen, and I can now make my way past him, through him, away from him, and out the front door. Miraculously, I'm able to carry my make-up bag, purse, and suitcase all at once, and ironically, seeming now to be fueled with superhuman strength, I have room for more, so I grab some pots and pans of mine from the kitchen, banging and clanking and crashing them, while I slam cabinet doors and drawers in true dramatically raging form. This is something I've wanted to do for a long time, and now I wonder if it scares *him*.

CHAPTER 22

MY AUNT SARAH is out of town for a month or two and her place is nice—one bedroom with wood floors and an ocean view. I'm happy to have somewhere to be by myself.

When I get there, I open the windows wide and take in a deep breath of the air. It feels so good to breathe and not worry that I'm doing that wrong too. A simple breakfast of cold cereal with fresh fruit and a glass of milk tastes especially good this morning, or is it afternoon? I listen to my own crunching as it talks to the peace and quiet, and I think I'll sleep a long sleep after breakfast.

Sleep and sleep and sleep. I do, and when I wake up, a huge feeling of relief washes over me, almost like I've slept it all away. I don't have to worry about how he's going to be when I see him next, or what he's going to do, or what I'm going to do. It's over. I'm free.

I call Casey to celebrate.

"Guess where I am?" I say.

"No, I don't want to guess, just tell me."

"I'm waking up from a dreamy nap and looking at the ocean."

"You did it?"

"Yep."

"That's great, Nick. I'm proud of you."

"You wanna celebrate?"

"I'd love to, but I have to go to the doctor."

"Why? I thought you already had your check-up a few days ago."

"I did. But I have a little lump on my leg."

A little fucking what? Did she just say a lump?

"A lump? Like a cancer lump? When did you notice it?"

"Yesterday."

"Did you tell the doctor? Does he think…?"

"Yeah," she says.

"I'll go with you."

"Some celebration."

"Oh, shut up. I'll drive."

Sure enough, it's more cancer.

Only this time it's a little bigger, even. It's only been nine months since the first tumor was removed, and now we're starting all over again. At least this time we're a little more familiar with how things work, or, in certain instances, don't.

She checks into the hospital on Thursday and the surgery is scheduled for Friday. I stay with her as long as I can on Thursday, until I have to go to work. But the doctors and Casey tell me not to bother coming on Friday, unless she calls, because again between pre-op and surgery and post-op it will be better for me to come on Saturday when she's had a good night's rest to recover a little. Well, I come by before work on Friday anyway, just to make sure everything is okay. Jay is out of town, visiting an uncle who is more like a brother to him, who is in stage four of some other sick shit. When I come by, I can't talk to Casey or anything, which is fine, because she's being prepped for surgery.

But when I come by Saturday morning and ask her how it went, she says it didn't.

"What do you mean?"

"Doctor Skeiner had some kind of emergency and had to leave town for the weekend, so he couldn't do the surgery."

"So they never prepped you, after all?"

"No, they did."

"Well, what the fuck is that?"

"Apparently somebody was confused, and the pre-op never knew till it was too late."

"So when's he gonna do it?"

"I still don't know."

"Who does?"

"Nobody seems to, until he gets back or somebody gets in touch with him."

"Do you want me to raise hell at the nurse's station?"

"Don't bother. I already did."

"Can you at least check out till we know what's up?"

"No. There're a couple of doctors that are really nice and they told me to stay put. They're doing everything they can to help me out."

"Well, can you sneak out for some Chinese food or something? Because you could die of starvation if the fungus on that tray is what you're supposed to be eating."

"That sounds great. This food is beyond gross."

So we go across the street for some Chinese. When we come back Case feels a little tired, so she gets back in bed. She nods off a little, I read a book. When she wakes up we play checkers, then cards, then look at more magazines. Nobody comes to tell us when surgery is, and I feel worried, because Monday is a holiday. I know they do surgery on a holiday, but will Skeiner, Casey's surgeon, be back by Monday?

I go home when visiting hours end. I wish I could just curl up next to her. Instead, I come back in the morning.

Now it's Sunday, and rumor has it the great surgeon has returned. I walk up and down the halls asking every nurse, doctor and orderly who Dr. Skeiner is and where he is, until by chance I bump into him and ask him.

"Yes, I'm Doctor Skeiner."

"Well, you have a young woman patient in room 406 who I understand was prepped for surgery on Friday?"

"No, I wasn't here on Friday. I will be performing the surgery on Monday, tomorrow."

"Well, that's very useful information that I'm sure your staff could've used before they prepped her for surgery on Friday, when no surgery took place. Seeing as the patient still has no idea what the new schedule is, (maybe she's still a little foggy from the Valium?), you might want to go down there and fill her in on the details," I say.

At first, he actually says, "I'm too busy at the moment," trying to escape. But I insist, physically impeding his path, standing right in front of him, in his face, pointing out that Casey must be as important as anyone or anything he has to take care of.

Then I say, "She's a scared twenty-three-year-old woman whose cancer is growing by leaps and bounds, and I can't imagine anything more important than the life-and-death situation she's facing and your immediate attention to it."

I say it calmly and directly, without the profanity I feel, because I think that sometimes when people feel superior to you, that's the best way. And a little to my surprise Dr. Skeiner reluctantly goes down the hall to face Casey.

She apparently doesn't share my feeling, because before I even get halfway into the room she's cursing his ass out.

He isn't all that apologetic for the fuck-up. I'm ready to conclude that he's a prick.

"Case, hang on, take it easy," I break into her string of four letter words. "Let's try to be calm," I say, worrying about the ramifications of cursing out the man who will, more than likely, be the one to have a knife over her when she's out cold.

"Well, is there anyone else who can do my surgery?" she asks flat out. "I don't want you."

This is where Skeiner snaps out of his Dr. Dreamworld long enough to recognize that he's dealing with an actual person, not just a patient, and a person that is scared and has been wronged by him on top of it.

He looks right at her. He even takes off his glasses to get a better look, and his eyes lose the glaze. It feels as if he's just removed his mask.

"I'm sorry," he says. "I'm sorry, Casey. I'm sure none of this has been too easy for you, and I'm sorry to have made it more difficult. But we can get started first thing in the morning, and I'll do my best to get every last bit of it."

His whole personality doesn't miraculously transform or anything, but he gets contrite enough that Casey is willing to give him another chance. (Though we both still hate him.)

So she agrees to let him do the surgery, and they sort of make up, and he promises her no more fuck-ups.

When he leaves the room, she says, "What a fucking asshole."

"Total fucking dick," I agree.

But as it turns out, he's a good surgeon in spite of his lack of humanity, and a short while later we're going back to get the stitches out.

We have to wait a long time to be seen, as usual, it being a county hospital and all. There's a stack of files on the front desk a mountain high, and everyone in those files seems to be waiting with us. We wait and wait and, after a while, as we move up the hallway, there isn't even a place to sit, and Casey's on crutches. I tell her just to sit in the lounge and I'll come and get her when it's her turn, but she's so frustrated that she says, "Fuck it. Let's get out of here." And she storms out of the building, with every intention of keeping those stitches in her forever.

So I tell one of the doctors Casey befriended after the surgery fiasco, a woman Casey told me she really liked, that Casey is outside smoking a cigarette and she's about to bail because she's too fed up with the bullshit. She tells me to go get Casey and they'll sneak her into one of the examining rooms. I feel a little bad cutting the line, because what about the other people? But if we leave, we're just going to have to wait all over again, and I worry that the stitches may get infected or worse, so I run to get Casey and drag her back.

Casey lies prone on the table as the doc looks and seems to pinch at her leg, which looks like a badly sewn leg of a piece of furniture. At the top and bottom there seems to be a shortage of stuffing, but in the middle, the exposed stitches seem to stretch and bulge, trying to keep the clumped-up insides from spilling out.

Then he moves his eyes off Casey's leg and up to her face, "A little inflamed, but not terrible," he says. Then, as if in great doubt, but trying to be jovial and conceal it, "You've been staying off it plenty, haven't you?"

Casey turns her head towards me and with a critical scowl barks, "I told you we shouldn't have gone skating, ya boob."

I say, "Well, how should I know?"

The doctor practically faints, until we both crack up and he realizes we're just playing with him.

Then they go ahead and examine her stitch by stitch and begin to unthread where they've cut out the cancer. When they're finished, the only thing left to do is talk about the future.

"The surgery went well," the doc says. "But I have to tell you, we had to go very deep. It looks like we got it all, but that doesn't mean we did. If it comes back, there won't be anything left to cut."

"Which means?" I blurt out.

"Which means we strongly recommend chemotherapy."

"No," Casey says.

"Casey," the doc then says, "If you don't get chemo or some kind of radiation, it is our medical feeling and opinion that you probably won't live to see thirty."

I can't quite believe what I'm hearing. I know how Casey feels about chemo and radiation, because her dad has tried them both. And I know she has just had her second operation to remove a huge chunk of cancer.

Now they're saying that isn't enough. It's like being in a dream when you just can't stop the bad guy, and you know they're really going to get you, and you try like hell to scream, but of course, no sound comes out. That moment of irrevocability, when you just can't make it go away, not the bad guy or the bad news. You can't make what the doc said be different than what he said, and death becomes that thing that you turn over and over in your mind trying to picture what it's like. Trying to define what death really is. Puzzling over what it feels like not to be here anymore, ever.

I start shaking a little, trying to fight off the tears that seem to be dripping down my face, but I want to shake the doctor and say, "Okay, doc, where's the joke in that? Cut to the punch line, already."

I hear Case saying, "I really don't believe in that," and I think to myself, what is she saying? Believe in it? Like it's some kind of philosophy?

Then I say, "Isn't there anything else? Like a laser or something?"

His response is, "Fifty doctors and I were trying to figure out that very question just this morning."

So Casey promises she'll think about it, and the doctors say good and that she should let them know and the sooner the better, and we walk to the car, and I try to think of a way to make her really think about it, because I'm pretty sure she has no intention of thinking about it at all.

What really scares me is that I may be the only person besides Casey who will ever hear the lowdown the doctor just revealed. She's trying desperately to keep everything from her mother because of her heart condition, and from her father who has a brain tumor, which is keeping her mother's heart plenty busy. I feel a suspicion gnawing at me that she isn't going to tell Jay, either. I know I can't get out of the car without making mention of what the doctor said, but I know she isn't going to want to talk about it.

So I ask her what she thinks about what the doctor said. She tells me she doesn't like the idea and prefers to consider more holistic options.

By the time we get out of the car, I make my position about her position clear.

"If your life depends on it, you should really think about doing it, and then you should do it."

I know she doesn't like having me tell her that she should do something that is going to make her feel very sick and make her hair fall out and maybe even create sterility in her at the ripe old age of twenty-three, but what kind of friend would I be to ignore the only options the doctor spoke of?

"I have faith in God and I believe in homeopathic living and healing," she says.

"If you want to live, homeopathically or otherwise, you'd better quit smoking," I yell at her, then try to calm down.

"Case, I understand how you feel about holistic medicine. And I know how deeply you believe in God. And I think that both of those beliefs are really important. But don't you think that maybe holistic medicine and God could counteract the negative effects of chemo?"

"I really don't think of it that way. It just seems unnatural to me and I don't want to do it."

"But doesn't the cancer seem just as unnatural to you? If God can't keep you from getting it, how's he gonna help you to get rid of it?"

"I don't know. I just have to take care of myself and have faith."

"But how are you taking care of yourself? By praying?! Fuck, Case, I pray for you too, every day. I pray it'll go away. "

"Just because it's not how you would do it doesn't make it wrong."

"I don't know how I would do it, because I'm not the one who's sick. I really don't. I know it's different, but I also know what I heard them say."

She doesn't say anything for a minute, but I can see her thoughts formulating something, and I can tell she's mad.

"Do I look sick to you?!" she yells.

"No. And I never want you to."

"But you're okay with my hair falling out and my teeth turning green."

Now I'm quiet for a minute. It's gotten dark out and I'm glad, because we can no longer see each other's faces too well. I've begun to cry a little, and I think if I can just keep quiet, she won't hear it in my voice.

"I just don't know what else to do," I finally say.

"Well, the good news is, *you* don't have to do anything. This isn't about you."

She says it with such finality. Like we've had the discussion and it is now over. She's sick of me and my help and I'm helpless.

I think as I drop her off at her place, not knowing what else to say, that people like Casey, who really believe in God, are the ones that always get hit the hardest. Her father has cancer, her mother has a bad heart, and she may not live to see thirty. It's like a bad joke, yet she still believes.

Me, a nonbeliever, I'll probably live to a ripe old age, in excellent health.

CHAPTER 23

I CALL CASEY IN the morning, feeling horrible about what I've said, or at least, how I've pressured her. But she isn't home, and she doesn't call me all day. I go to work and it feels like my own slow death.

Everything actually looks darker than usual, though I don't know how that's possible. Maybe it's the artwork. They're all black-and-white photos, and the main theme stringing them together seems to be people in, and places of, misery. I smoke and I drink tonight, not even trying to hold back.

After a few Scotches, I ask Jonie to tell me about God a little, because she's such a believer.

"When you pray, do you actually hear God's voice speak to you?"

"God speaks to me in different ways. It's not usually through an actual voice. It's more something that happens that guides me in a particular way."

"But do you talk to God when you pray? I mean do you ask him for things or tell him what's going on in words, or do you just think your way to him/her like some kind of meditation?"

"Oh, I talk to him."

"Uh-huh," I say, nodding my head as if I understand, though I don't.

"How's your friend?" she asks.

"Well, it's not 100 percent clear, but it doesn't look so good."

"I'm really sorry," she says. "I'll pray for her."

"Oh, would you?!" I say, sounding like I've won some kind of prize. "Could you send him a message from me, too?"

"Sure, sweetie," she says.

"Could you tell him to guide Casey to do whatever she has to do that will keep her alive on this earth with me?" I say, and start gushing with tears before I even finish my sentence. Jesus, I sound like a three-year old making complex requests of the tooth fairy via messenger. I break a glass trying to clear too many at the same time, and I cut my finger. The blood is bright red and I soak it up with a bar rag, wondering how I will dispose of it.

"Oh, honey, I'm so sorry for what you're going through," Jonie says, grabbing cocktail napkins to help me soak up the mess on my face and now my hand. "You know, you can pray, too. It might help."

"Yeah," I say, smiling. "It might." But it doesn't. I've tried.

Jonie's off to deliver the tear-filled concoctions I've mixed for her, and I top my water off with a little more Scotch. I'm drinking Dewar's, even though it's not my favorite, because its light color may possibly pass for ginger ale.

I like all kinds of Scotch. Glenlivet, Glenfiddich, Glenmorangie, Glenforres, all the Glens. I like Pinch and Chivas, Red and Black (Johnny's) and definitely the Macallan clan. We carry the twelve and the eighteen but we don't carry the twenty-five. People come in asking for it and I always have to tell them we don't have it. They get this scrunched-up look of confusion on their faces as they try to figure out what to order instead, but not before they ask me if I've ever had it. When I tell them I haven't, they let me know how divinely good it is.

I'd never even seen the twenty-five until one time when I went to a bar called The Scotch Bar, devoted strictly to Scotch. Every shelf was sparkling with gorgeous bottles of Scotch. That's where I saw the twenty-five, and I was so tempted to order it, but I didn't, because I figured it cost at least as much as its age, and that just wasn't a part of my budget—not even that night, when I felt like splurging.

All lined up in a row, the twenty-five looked pretty much like the twelve and eighteen, only a little bigger and a little older. The 25 itself stood out and caught my eye.

Someone sitting right next to me at the bar, obviously on a different budget, went for it. He had a deep-brown tan and silvery hair, and he took his snifter with the twenty-five in it up to his nose and practically stuck it in, taking a very deep inhale. Then he swirled its honey-red color around, watching as some of it fell to the bottom of the thin glass and some of it clung to the sides in finely toned legs. Bringing it to his mouth, he wet the inside with it, and set the snifter down onto his bright white cocktail napkin. Then he sank down into his bar stool, resting his arms comfortably on the bar. He turned his head ever so slightly, and from under his silver hair, he looked at me and smiled. It was a smile of complete and utter satisfaction.

I wish I could put a smile like that on every face at this bar. I try to put one on my own by freshening my drink and bumming a smoke from Melissa.

"Oh, now you're smoking?" she says, lighting me up.

"Well, if it isn't the pot calling the kettle black," I say, semi-slurring. When Mel walks away in what looks like disgust, I say, "Isn't that how the saying goes?"

She just smiles and shakes her head at me.

Back to my Scotch, I think how the first sip usually isn't the best. It's a flavor that grows. A rich flavor that just gets richer.

Straight up in a little shot glass or snifter, that gold, reddish-brown color shining through, it's like a tiny bonfire inside you. And when I take a taste the flavor lingers on my tongue like a good hot pancake syrup.

Over ice, it makes the cubes fall all over themselves, melting some while heating the others up. The cool miniature ice blocks mix with that fiery liquid caramel, and it all goes down smooth and slippery.

And once it does, it has a slow mellowing effect. I can still carry on a conversation after a few, though clearly I'm feeling it. It has a virile effect on me. Some of my friends particularly like when I drink it, because there's no telling how bold I'll become. I like to shoot pool and listen to music when I'm under its influence, and flirt with men I don't know. I'm stronger, less shy. I laugh more, but I fight the slur.

I say things more quietly and calmly, my way of asserting that I'm *not* drunk. The words come out of my mouth so precisely, as if this whole communication thing were a science and I a great professor of it. My tongue rounds the vowels, but when it comes to the consonants, I relax my jaw and let them fall out casually. This enunciation combination makes me sound sober, or so I think.

Yet tonight, somehow, its effect is different. I'm not speaking so clearly, though I'm conscious of really trying.

"What would you like?" the slow-motion voice says as if it's trying to disguise itself. It's like the sound of those people on television who are trying to hide their true identity.

"I'll have a . . ."

Yeah, yeah? A what? Come on.

"I'll have a drink . . ."

No shit.

"A margarita."

Brilliant. "Would you lick it with salt—like it with salt, blended, up, rocks. How would you like it?"

"Blended, with salt."

"Great," I say, happy to be moving again. Unhappy to be moving to the blender, but you can't have everything. Although next time somebody asks me for a blender drink, maybe I could tell him or her it's broken.

Lots of ice, lots of tequila, moderate amount of sour shit, nice dose of triple sec, and the machine blocks out all the other noise. Whirring and revving, it sounds like a motorcycle right outside your front door. Mel waves at me trying to get my attention, but I pretend to be deep in concentration on the task at hand, watching the white froth whip around like a tornado. Then I throw a fresh-cut lime on the edge and am careful not to lose a drop of the icy Slurpee-like liquid as it aches to spill over the sides, shaking ever so slightly in my hand as I wobble back over.

"What's your poison?" Steve asks me, bellying up to the bar.

"Ice cold ginger ale," I say, lying through a snake-like smile.

"Yeah. I like a nice cold ginger ale once in a while, too," he smiles back.

"What's the news?" I say.

"No news."

"I got news."

"Well, come on."

"Me and Phil are splitsville."

"You're kidding me."

"Nope. We're done."

"I thought you were working things out. I mean, you went to Florida with him and everything. What happened?"

"Well, we went to Florida, for one thing. And the other thing is, another thing. Anyway, I'm happy to be out of it, let's drink to that."

"Cheers," he says.

"To freedom," I say.

"Freedom," he says, lifting his freshly made Absolut and cranberry.

But then he says, looking really blue, "God, I thought you were so settled down. I'm just kind of shocked."

It's like I've let him down. Like he was counting on me to be stable for him.

"I'm sorry," I say. "But now I can be more like you, you know. Hit on everything that moves." Having said it, I like the idea.

"Yeah, but you're not like that. You're so together," he says, insisting.

"Okay, forget it," I say. But I don't want to forget it. It gives me something to look forward to. It's like a plan.

"Nick, you're a one-man woman. Don't kid yourself."

"I am? How do you know?"

"I just do."

"Whatever," I say, grabbing one of his Marlboro Lights.

Sonny walks by and gives me a funny look, like he's trying to figure me out. I wrinkle my nose and raise my eyebrows right back at him, like I'm trying to figure him out.

"How you doing, Nick?" he says.

"I'm doing great, handsome. How's tricks with you?" I say, with what must be a flirtatious-enough smile to scare him off my track, because he keeps moving, back toward his cell.

There's a funny burnt smell, which I can't figure out.

"Shit!" I shake my hand and throw my cigarette-on-fire-at-the-wrong-end into the sink.

"You all right?" Steve says.

"I'm fine."

"Have you been crying?"

"Hey, could you back off? You're suffocating me."

"Sorry, honey," he laughs, lighting a smoke *for* me.

"Tell me something funny."

"I still don't have a job."

"I said funny."

"I'm still with Janine."

"That's sort of funny, in a sad way."

"I'll work on it."

"Good," I say, off to make my rounds.

"You want some coffee?" Mel says, pouring herself some.

"I can't drink coffee. It makes me nauseous."

"Well, why don't you go to the bathroom and throw some cold water on your face or something?"

"Did anyone ever tell you you're very subtle?"

"No."

I go to the bathroom, far away from everyone. I don't feel as fucked up as I look. It's the smeared make-up, I think. And maybe that I've lost track of how much I've had to drink. But where before I felt drunk, now I feel like I've got it under control. That thing where you get so fucked up you can't feel it anymore, and then you just kind of level off. The cold water does feel good, and I would love to have a toothbrush right now. I love when I'm this way and I can still manage to brush and floss my teeth. It makes everything better again. I find a fresh Band-aid on the shelf and wrap it around my wound.

I give Mel's butt a tiny little pinch to let her know I'm back. She just looks at me and shakes her head. I love her.

"Who's that guy?" I ask her, noticing a sweet-looking guy comfortably settled in her station.

"He's a friend of Alex's. They golf together. You think he's cute?"

"In a quiet kind of way."

"He's not my type."

"Mine either. That's what I like about him."

I'm glad he's popped up. Gives me something to focus on, to distract me. I have an iced tea to counter the alcohol, and it seems to help. Enough to allow me to charm Alex's golfing buddy, Billy, into thinking he likes me.

CHAPTER 24

HIS PLACE HAS clean cream carpeting, a balcony, two bedrooms, and underground parking. It's my day off and the sun is still up, which I love. I love to start a date in the daylight and let it linger on into the dark of night. In the center of the living room sits a big, bald Buddha on a bench with incense surrounding him. Bells and wooden clappers sit neatly beside him. One of the first things Billy told me at the bar the other night was that he was a follower of Buddhism.

This fascinated me almost immediately, because of my own state of being at the time, and because of the serene, soft, quiet glow he seemed to exude. It doesn't surprise me to discover that part of his practice is frequent meditation.

"Is this where it all happens?" I ask, indicating the shrine.

"Usually," he smiles. "In the morning I sit in my bedroom."

"How often do you sit?"

"A few times a day."

"Wow," I say. "It must be hard to find time for other things."

"Actually, it helps me to have more focus and energy for other things. That's what I've been finding lately, anyway."

In the course of this little conversation, I decide that I want him. On top of being into Buddhism, which at this moment I find exotic and peaceful, he's a mechanic. He owns his own garage. A Buddhist mechanic, rugged and sensitive and seeking enlightenment—it's working for me. I mean, there is a fine line, and if he crosses over it, fanatical may be the word I'm left with, but for now I'd like to understand more. So I ask a lot of questions.

"So what is the significance of Buddha? Is he like the God of Buddhism?"

"The definition of Buddha is: an awakened one. But usually it refers to Siddhartha Gautama, the Indian prince, who people know as the historic founder of Buddhism."

"A prince founded Buddhism?"

"He left all his royal treasures and sought and sat for a long time."

"Do you have books on all this?"

"Quite a few."

"Could I maybe borrow one?"

"Sure. I have a really good one that gives an overview and tells of the beginnings and practices."

"I'd be really interested in the story of the prince. How that came about for him. Where he started, how he came to it, where he ended up. I love stories, but something about a prince finding a spiritual path that turns into a religion, that sounds a little like a fairy tale."

"It kind of is."

"So to be an idiot and try to understand this in a Western way, is Buddha like Christ in Catholicism, or God in Judaism?"

"You're not an idiot, and no. In Buddhism, you don't pray to God, you find your way through yourself. It's not about an outside force. It's about an inside force."

"And that's why you meditate so much."

"Yeah."

"That makes sense to me."

It really does. It's seems so much simpler than the other religions. Man against himself. Seeing the way through self. Finding more truth the deeper you go. Right now, I can relate to this existence, search, way of knowledge, more than I can understand the God Casey and Jonie believe in. Casey still hasn't called me back. It's been three days.

We have dinner and drink wine. I feel very comfortable with him just talking and laughing. He has an intense clarity and ease.

After dinner we sit around the living room talking, and we kiss. Before I know it, we're both buck-naked, just lying around his living room like it's the most normal thing. We're touching each other everywhere and it's very hot and I'm very excited and I want to. So I climb on top of him, and next thing I know he's squirming out from beneath me, putting on the brakes.

"Nicky?"

"What? What's the matter?"

"Well, I really like you, but this is happening a little too fast, you know?"

This is happening? Weren't we making this happen?

"Well, do you have protection?" I ask, thinking this is an important issue to slow down for.

"I do, but it's not that, it's just that I'm not looking for anything serious right now, you know?"

It's really weird how nervous he suddenly looks. All color has drained from his face. Minutes ago, we were in on it together, a team, peeling each other like bananas, but now he seems to think I'm the devil attempting to interrupt his personal quest for self-discovery, that path that will allow him to find peace of mind and relief of tension. I feel sure, now, that I am a mere obstacle. A lowly pleasure he can't afford to indulge in.

But more embarrassing than the rejection itself is that he thinks I'm madly in love with him and want to spend the rest of my life with him, simply because I want to have sex with him right here, right now. (I mean it's not like he's T who seems to have fallen off the planet.)

I want to tell him that I'm not interested in getting serious either, I just had a feeling it would be incredibly good to fuck him. It's just that now that seems so wrong.

Instead, I feel I should go with the madly-in-love-with-him idea. Because why else would a beautiful, smart, interested-in-Buddhism woman have gotten naked with and crawled all over a devout Buddhist on the first date, unless she was completely and uncontrollably head over heels for the guy and assuming it might actually be the love that lasts a lifetime?

"Oh, God, yes. You're right. What was I thinking? This is crazy," I say jumping into my clothes as if I can't understand how they and I got separated.

"I mean, I'm really enjoying hanging out with you, but maybe we could just cool down the sex a little for a while, you know?"

"Yeah. Absolutely, sure," I say, feeling like a total idiot, but then remembering how into it he seemed to be before I grew horns on my head and that red suit. "It was just so hot for a minute there, I didn't want it to stop," I say, brushing myself off as if to rub it away, but somehow very sexually, hoping he'll have great pangs of regret.

"But I'm glad you reined me in. That would have been a big mistake. You're right," I say. "I'm glad one of us is thinking clearly," I say, smiling humbly and finishing my last button, proud to have clothed myself so quickly.

He smiles, pleased that I've backed off, but also kind of excited that he had to back me off, I think. We talk for a little while longer so it won't be too awkward, though it certainly is. He loans me that Buddhism book he mentioned earlier, which concerns me, seeing as I can never call him again. Even the slightest effort on my part might make me appear overanxious, and I would be, because let's face it, I'm not having a great week. And if he calls me, and I'm stupid enough to get together with him, it'll be terribly awkward, because he'll be thinking the whole time that I wish we were having sex, and I will be. And if he actually has a change of heart and wants to have sex, he'll have to beg me for it, and that's a long shot. So I really don't know how I'm going to get his book back to him.

"Thanks for the book," I say. "And dinner."

"You're welcome. Nicky, I'm sorry about the sex thing. It's just I really find you attractive, and even the other night, at the bar, after work, it was very hot, and it's just, you overwhelm me a little, and I'm just coming off this long relationship and I don't know, it scares me—"

"Hey, don't worry about it, I understand. If it makes you feel any better, you're not the first person I've ever overwhelmed."

"What do you mean?"

"I just feel like people often feel I'm too much."

"Well, I like that you're too much." He smiles at me warily.

I grab my purse and he says, "I'll walk you to your car."

It's a beautiful night, warm and starry. I toss the Buddhism book and my purse into my car, and just before I hop in, I press my whole body up against Billy's and, just barely touching my tongue to his, kiss him goodnight. It's maybe the sexiest kiss I've ever given anyone. I can't help myself. I'm too much and I've just gotten out of a long relationship, too.

CHAPTER 25

"**H**i. what're you doing?" I say, trying to keep the annoyance out of my voice. It's been a week since I left my apology message on Casey's machine.

"I'm going out to lunch with Gigi. What about you?"

"Nothing. Did you get my message?"

"Yeah. Sorry I didn't call you back, I've been really busy."

I said I was doing nothing. Why doesn't she ask me to go with them?

"So you guys are going to lunch?"

"Yeah, in fact, I better run, she's gonna be here any minute."

"Okay. Well, what're you doing later?"

"I'm having dinner with some neighbors. They invited Jay and me over months ago and we're finally returning the invitation."

"Hey, Case, is everything all right?"

"Oh, yeah, it's good. I'm sorry I'm just in a rush. I'll call you later, okay?"

"Sure. Talk to you later," I say, again trying to sound normal, because I feel like crying.

Lunch with Gigi, dinner with friends I've never heard of. She hates me. Suddenly hungry for lunch, I decide to go shopping and make myself some. I'm not much of a cook, but every now and then I find it comforting.

I pick up a salmon (a poor dead salmon that Beau probably didn't catch) from the fish market and some green beans from the little vegetable store down the street. I'll sauté the salmon with rosemary and steam the beans and whip up a little wild rice.

Aunt Sarah's kitchen is neat and clean and easy to work in. It's fun preparing the food, timing everything just right, watching the colors come together. The only problem is, by the time it's ready I don't feel like eating anymore. I can't let go of the fact that Casey and Gigi are out to lunch without me. I wonder if Casey is telling Gigi how insensitive I was with the chemo situation. But then she'd have to tell Gigi about the chemo in the first place. Maybe she just wanted some time alone with Gigi. That's fine. It's just she wasn't that nice about it. She could've said, Gigi and I never get to spend any time alone, so, you know, nothing personal, in case you were wondering, especially after I haven't called you in days and days. But she didn't. Instead, she was just in this big hurry, like God forbid she should keep Gigi waiting. No problem keeping me waiting after I called her to apologize for trying to be a good friend in the first place.

I wrap the salmon up, thinking maybe I'll bring it to work, leave all the dishes and pots and pans and go rollerblading. Casey and I used to always go blading together. Well, she roller-skated and I bladed. I could never get the hang of those roller skates. Casey would cruise around, backwards, forwards, figure eights. I couldn't move on those things. She laughed her ass off the one time I tried it.

"Yeah, very fucking funny that I can't move," I told her, bent over and stuck in the middle of the bike path, pissed off that she had swept by me.

Then she came back for me and tried to show me how, which only made it funnier when I couldn't grasp it. She was pretty good on blades, though. She rented them after my roller-skating failure, I think to make me feel better. She couldn't go backwards very well on them, but otherwise she did really well. She just preferred her skates. She'd had them forever and liked that—these old brown suede ones, perfect for Casey. Vintage.

But we haven't gone in forever, now. There's no sunscreen strong enough. No sunshield big enough. So I haven't gone for a while, either, and it feels good to be out, gliding up and down the streets, listening to my Walkman, drinking in the sun like it was good for you.

When I get home, I check for messages, but there's only a big zero. It's already time to get ready for work and tonight I don't mind so much, because I want to be around people.

Unfortunately, when I get there, there aren't any. Well, Mel and Jonie, but they don't count. So we just hang around, smoking and hoping our luck will change.

"So did you ever go out with Alex's buddy?" Mel asks.

"Yeah."

"Well, what did you think?"

"He's a very nice guy."

"But you didn't get any?"

"No. And why is that the point?"

"Because you're holding out, and I figure it has something to do with that. What happened?"

"Not too much."

"Yeah, but if he's such a nice guy, why not? You're just not interested?"

"I don't know."

"Are you gonna see him again?"

"I doubt it."

"Why are you acting so weird? What happened? Do you like him or don't you?"

"He thought I was in love with him and got scared."

"Why did he think that?"

"Because I was in love with him."

"Why? You don't even know him."

"Hey, he was very charming. That's all I needed to know."

"Were you really in love with him?"

"No. But I was probably a little intense."

"Oh, here come some live ones. You want to have a drink after work?"

"I want to have a drink right now. Join me?"

"Sure."

We only have one, because the night picks up and we're too busy rockin' and rollin' drinks out to get drunk ourselves. After work is another story.

We all sit around the bar and unwind. Loosen our ties, open up our vests, sit around in our t-shirts. Mel and I finish off a bottle of red wine that Sonny lets us have. We've worked really hard, been stars for a few fleeting hours and made some good cash. One of the cooks from El Salvador lives in Santa Monica and needs a ride home. I offer, if he'll drive. He's still cleaning up and he's not drinking.

He's tall and young—like twenty-five. On the few occasions when I've had to go back to the kitchen to get something, we've caught each other's eye. There's something sexy about catching the eye of someone working in the kitchen. Something about them being so inaccessible back there. You can't get to them and they can't get to you—caged animals, in different cages. That's kind of how it was with Phil and me, at first.

Behind the wheel of my car, Alejandro looks like the star of some foreign film.

"Is this where you live?" I ask, as he pulls up to the curb.

"Yeah. You want to come inside?" he says, with the slightest grin, as if he's been reading my mind.

"No," I say, but he pulls me to him and I inhale his mouth. No wonder I scare them. I overwhelm myself.

"I thought you have a boyfriend," he says after the kiss.

"You want to be my boyfriend?" I say, slurring a bit.

"Sure," he says, and takes me inside. He's not afraid of getting serious.

Early in the morning, I kiss him goodbye, lightly, before he's actually awake. He grabs for me to pull me back into bed, but when I slip through his fingers, he doesn't make too much of a fuss.

At home, I shower and try to get some more sleep, but I can't. Instead, I open up the Buddhism book and find myself comforted by it, and rather absorbed. I read all about the prince, Siddhartha Gautama. Like a fairy tale, his path is not straight and simple. He has to go through many trials before he can find the truth he seeks. Each time he feels that he can't go on, after enduring starvation and pain and fear and suffering, he does go on. And with each obstacle he grows stronger and clearer. When he finally evolves enough to discover true enlightenment, he is free of fear, pain and suffering. But then he must make the choice: to live and enlighten others, or die and be free.

I love the way this story is told. Because you get to see the sacrifices the prince makes, and the meditation he commits to, the main goal of it to explore and understand the most basic parts of life. Parts that I'm embarrassed to bring up and inquire about in the world, most of the time (except to myself, all the time), because I've grown so accustomed to these suffering parts that I believe they're a malignancy inherent in life. They come with the opportunity. We have to endure them; it's just, how do we get through them?

Yet here, the prince examines and finds resolution with these parts of life that we, as ordinary people, suffer and expect to suffer, like death and the fear of death. The prince presents the notion that these feelings of fear and suffering might actually be avoidable. Though I don't delude myself that I, personally, will ever be able to live the Buddhist life, following the steps to enlightenment and thereby ridding myself of these torturous feelings of fear and suffering, I do get to feeling a kind of calm reading it, because I become mesmerized by the whole discussion on death. I'm hypnotized by the idea in this theology, ideology, that not only is death not something to fear, but it is its own opportunity and we should treasure the time when we are allowed to pass. I know I'm leaving out some vital parts of the discussion, but it doesn't matter, because it's the whole being at peace with death idea that makes me happy.

It helps to remind me that we all die. That it is a universal experience, no matter how different our deaths. Something about the fact that everyone does it, sooner or later, eases my anxiety. And when I get to feeling down about how much I'm going to miss Casey if she dies soon, it helps me to consider that maybe missing someone is only one aspect of death. And though it's a painful one, maybe death itself isn't. And when I feel scared for her to die it soothes me to remember that I will die, too. And that maybe death (unless you're murdered) is actually the most natural part of life and completely different from what I've been trained to believe.

I keep trying to get together with Casey, but she'll have no part of me. She cloaks everything in her busyness, but I know it's not that. So I hope for an audition, read, and look for a place to live, because my aunt will be back within the month. In the meantime I work, collecting a fairly decent stash while I'm rent-free.

When I finish the Buddhism book, I drop it off at Billy's front door when I know he'll be at work. Then I go to the library to check out some more.

I read whatever I can, especially when I'm feeling particularly down. Though much of what I read soothes me, my newfound study still doesn't keep me from drinking too much, or working out to excess. I think the extremes make me feel more alive than the living death of the bar.

CHAPTER 26

I TRY TO GET my keys out while I juggle my gym bag and my juice, but it's awkward because on my doorstep is a big bouquet of flowers and with it, a note. I put everything down and grab the envelope. It's from Philip.

Today, like never before, I've felt the coldness of impending closure; the door shutting, and me standing there like an idiot trying to keep it open. I know that with all things that the end is really another name for the beginning—one said in sorrow, the other in joy. And that, although our relationship has ended on one level, there are many more levels yet to explore.

I thought of many things to say and especially of something you alluded to, and that is that I can't call up those "special" things we shared, even in this letter of love: our movie, our song, our special place. How is it that I allowed those to not exist, and is that just more evidence of a relationship that wasn't meant to be? And what's worse, for me, anyway, is the realization that a hundred years from now, you won't be pulling a shoebox out of a closet and opening it, dusty and decaying, and retrieving a bundle of letters tied up in a fading ribbon, and reading with difficulty because of my handwriting, all the expressions of my love for you; showing those letters to your granddaughter when she asks grandma about love.

And now I try to make up for that.

Nicky, you have been more special to me than anything I have ever known. The times we've shared have been the peak moments in my life so far, and your influence on me is like Mother Nature's silent voice telling the caterpillar to awake from its cocoon. You are such a special person, more than you know yourself. There is a fire inside you that rages and I have lavished in its heats; sometimes it mellows to a candle flame and I have relaxed in its soft glow. I only regret that I can't be there when you truly touch it and forge a flame so great as to dim the sun—and you will, for it is inextinguishable. Its fuel is the core of the universe, that which drives the souls of all who search beyond that which is known. Someday, somehow, I'll truly be able to express our relationship and dig deep into that hiding soul of mine and truly know you. That'll be a big day for me. For now, though, one last gasp of affection.

Know that as long as I have shoulders there's a place for your head.

Know that as long as I have hands, there's someone to rub your back.

Know that as long as I have ears, there's someone to share your deepest thoughts, wishes, desires.

Know that as long as I have eyes, there's someone to see your accomplishments.

Know that as long as I have breath, there's someone to ease your pain.

Know that as long as I'm alive, there's someone to share your love.

"Happy Birthday, Nick."

Talk about timing, huh? Call me if you want to share any part of it.

Love,

Phil

So I sit on the doorstep, sweaty from the gym, salty from my tears, and slightly hung over. With all kinds of mixed feelings, I sit and reread. And I wonder, again, how it is possible that we don't have a song, movie, place to call our own. What were we to each other? What thread kept us tied?

I'm struck that someone who has lived inside my heart and alongside me for so long can see me like that, so large. Relieved when I think that no time is wasted time when spent with a person you've loved, no matter how ugly love's end. Sad that those feelings I've just absorbed can't transform our relationship enough to forge us into the future to-gether—into that attic whose wood I can smell, and whose cobwebs I can see, pulling down that shoebox as that thick stack of letters defines for our own grandchildren what love is. Wondering if he thinks he will die first, leaving me to share the shoebox with our grandchildren, or if he thinks that I would just be the natural one to share it while he sits downstairs smoking a pipe and reading the paper. Pleased to have this letter and knowing that now that I have it, I will always have it, evidence of our love, in spite of itself.

But on top of all those feelings, there's a queasy feeling rising up in me. It begins in my stomach, an empty burning that churns through to my chest, then all the way up to my head, making it ache. Out of no-where, there's a smell, a rancid one, and though I don't know if it's real or imagined, I storm into the bathroom. Suddenly possessed, I rip off my sweaty clothes, desperate for a shower that will perhaps allow me to escape my own skin, or at least the parts that he's touched.

I make the water especially hot and I stay under until I'm sure I don't smell anything but the sweetness of my pear antibacterial soap. I cover every inch of myself with it and scrub until I feel certain that I've eliminated every last germ.

When I get out, I don't call Phil to thank him. Instead, I tuck his "love letter" into the safety of my dresser drawer as a kind of reminder, and I go to call Casey.

Unbelievably, there's a message on my machine from her. She's re-corded that song, "You Say It's Your Birthday," and then she sings to me and tells me to call her because she wants to take me out to celebrate.

As I look for the phone, I play air guitar to the song, jumping up and down like a rock star, replacing the words with, *she called, she called, she called.* Before I call her I play the message over a few times, to make myself believe it. She doesn't sound mad anymore. She sounds normal.

I guess that's what she meant by later: when she said she'd call me later, she meant much later, like weeks. I call her all the time anyway, but she's always running somewhere with someone, and she doesn't call me back. I miss her and worry about her, but when I try to ask her what's up she always says, nothing, she's just so busy catching up with her life now that she's out of the hospital. Then I say, "Well, fucking call me, okay?" Then she promises she will, and I believe her because she sounds like the Casey I know, but then she doesn't. Then I don't know what to say or do. But today's my birthday and there's a message from her and she's singing to me!

It was actually on my birthday that we first became friends.

One night when we were working at Halle's she came up to the bar to pick up her drink order and asked me what I was doing on Tuesday night, one of our mutual nights off.

"Tuesday night? Oh, Tuesday night is my birthday!" I found myself saying excitedly as if it was a very cool thing to announce your birthday to someone you didn't know that well.

"It is?!" she echoed enthusiastically as if it *was* actually cool. "Well, you have to come over. I'm having some of the girls over to watch Madonna's Blonde Ambition tour. It'll be a kick. I'll bake you a cake."

"That sounds like fun," I said. "What's your address?"

When I got there we all sat around scrutinizing Madonna's sculpted limbs, horned tits, and indulgent gyrations. We watched as if it were a sporting event, eating popcorn and following song by song with cheers, hisses and boos, as any sports fan might. Afterwards we obsessed, analyzed and dissected our fearless icon over birthday cake.

"Remember when she was fat and didn't shave her underarms?"

"Yeah."

"I really like her hair blonde."

"Me too. I really like her everything. She must work out like five hours a day. She's hot."

Fortunately, conversation distracted focus from any humiliating birthday singing. But Casey had gone to the trouble of getting me a present, which I remember really meant a lot to me, new at Halle's and unsure of who I would end up being friends with.

"I thought of you when I saw these," she said, handing a little wrapped box to me.

I opened it up and found earrings—a pair of big, jingly, jangly, silver, make-noise-when- you-walk, Señoritas dancing.

We go to lunch in Hollywood at a place near the house she and Jay are renting. They've just moved in together. It's incredible how well it's worked out between them. Sometimes I think maybe that's another reason why Casey and I haven't been hanging out as much, but Jay and I love each other, so that doesn't make sense. (But they don't even let me help them move, so who knows.) He knows everything about Casey's cancer situation, except maybe the-live-to-see-thirty-with-chemo-plan. I don't ask him about it, because if he doesn't know that's sure to cause a fight between them, and if he does know and doesn't feel as I do about it, then why am I butting in? In any case, he's a rock for her and they're really in love. They're the goofy, offbeat couple, and for lack of a better word, it's very, I hate to say it, cute.

We eat salads, drink iced teas, color on the tablecloth and talk about a colonic retreat she's going to in two weeks. There she'll drink wheatgrass, rest, flush her system, and, I guess, in our wildest fantasies, make the cancer recede into a faraway land, never to intrude on her young life again.

But death hangs in the air—her death and the death of something between us. Yet it's invisible. I can't touch it and so I can't tell if it's real. Everything she says points to how fine she's going to be. How she's got it under control, how it's going to get better. And when I believe it, I want to take hold of her hands, or maybe her shoulders, touch her and look her in the eye and say, "So that means we're going to be friends again, for real, forever?"

But then I don't believe it. And so I don't say anything like that. I don't believe we're going to be real friends the way we were, or forever. I can tell her what I really think, but it won't change the way things have changed. It won't keep her from dying if she's going to. It *will* make her avoid me more and it *will* make her angry.

"Why do you want to make me out to be sick? I'm taking care of myself. Look how healthy I am," she's probably thinking.

So I don't say anything. Because I want to be whatever kind of friend to her and with her that she'll let me be, for however long her forever is.

We go back to her house after lunch because she wants to show me how they've sponge-painted the walls and rearranged the furniture. We stop at a bakery on the way, getting sugar-free desserts in honor of my birthday.

"So, thirty, huh?" she says to me, commiserating. "You look a little older, too, you know?" she says, squinting at me funny and then laughing when I push her.

I am in a bit of a panic over it, but it feels excessive to complain when we don't know if she'll be making it to thirty.

"How do you feel about the whole Phil fiasco?" she asks.

"Mostly relieved that the end is finally here," I say. "Free."

"Did you work last night?" she asks.

"Yeah. And I tied one on after."

"At the bar?"

"Yeah, with Mel. Then I went home with Alejandro and jumped his bones."

"You did not."

"Yes. I did."

"Because of Phil?"

"Just because."

"Well, do you feel better, now?

"Yes and no."

Just sitting there talking to her makes me feel like crying. I feel like I shouldn't have said anything about the chemo in the first place. I mean, what do I know about it? Or maybe I should've worked my way up to it more, giving her a chance to let the doctor's words settle in, because I don't want her to die. But if she has to, I want her to go out in a way that she feels right about.

But, even now, as I sit here trying to hold back, I have to fight such pushy impulses. How can she know a way to die that she feels right about? Is there such a thing? I want to ask if she's planning anything beyond the retreat. I want to know if she's got a plan. But I don't ask, and she doesn't tell.

So instead, we sit around looking at magazines and just hanging out, which is what we do best together anyway.

"I can't believe you really quit smoking. That's so cool," I say. "Now who am I going to bum from?"

"Yeah, I know," she says. "And it's not as bad as I thought."

She does look really well. The swelling in her leg has diminished a lot and her skin is probably as close to Snow White's as a real person can get, especially one who lives in Southern California. She has a peacefulness about her, as though just being out of the hospital is enough to make a person feel fulfilled. We take bites from each other's desserts. Hers is a rich chocolatey something and mine is a banana crunch cake with a gooey cranberry filling.

"If it's sugar-free, what do you think they make the chocolate with?"

"It's probably unsweetened cocoa combined with that fructose stuff."

"But it really tastes chocolatey, you know?"

"Yeah, it does. Did you ever get the chocolate-covered donuts?"

"Those are so good."

"Sooo good."

I wish I could freeze-frame this moment.

CHAPTER 27

OR DINNER, BEFORE work, I cook again. It's so unlike me. I cook all these delicious things that I never knew I could, but I don't really know if they're delicious because I don't eat them. Instead, I bag them and bring them with me to work for the homeless people who hang around the bar and the parking lot. It's becoming an odd habit. I mean, I eat, I just don't eat what I've cooked, yet somehow I find the cooking itself both fulfilling and compelling.

So today I turn thirty. Three weeks ago I had four auditions and three callbacks for producers. But, today, on my thirtieth birthday, I'm back home behind the bar like I never stepped out from behind it.

Nobody cares, now, where I got my interesting raspy voice, or how I stay in good shape, or if I'm funny because I studied comedy, or if I was classically trained in New York—it really doesn't matter. All that remains is that I'm still here.

The job seems to become me. My customers are my fans, and the good ones adore me. They call me beautiful and we laugh together.

I feel that I've become it. The color of the walls and my skin seem to grow closer in hue, something in the yellow family. I'm not sure whether the smoke seeps into my pores or out of them. The specks of sun-induced brown spots on my hands remind me of the nicks in the wood I lean on to pick up ashtrays and light cigarettes.

And yet, it's like a good dress. It fits me. It hugs my curves and reveals just enough of me to be sexy. I can let my hair down without taking off my clothes. I can hide here in the dark, the dark smoky room where I'll never be discovered.

But tonight there isn't even enough business for me to stay on—too slow a night for us all to stay till closing. So I jump out from behind the bar and sit at it.

I feel like there's a hose pumping bourbon through my body. No matter how cold, it still feels hot to me. Burning in my chest, my eyes, my thoughts. I taste the heat as it trickles into my throat, my belly, my lap. Like a fireplace, the bottles warm me. They soothe my skin.

What I really want, though, is a hot bath. I always want one when I'm here. The later it gets, the more I want one and the more I know I'll be too tired to go to the trouble.

My days are controlled by these nights in front of the bar or behind it. I can't wake up until late afternoon or early evening. Getting out of bed is a complete struggle. I just want to close my eyes. I don't want my feet to have to touch the floor. I don't want to go anywhere or do anything but stay in bed and sleep.

Once out of bed, the bath is like a magnet. I'm so drawn to it I have to plan each of my actions very carefully to avoid the strength of its pull. But sometimes I allow myself to be tricked into it.

I eat breakfast, and then I convince myself that a bath would do my aching limbs good. Once I get into the bathtub I'm doomed. The water is as hot as I can take it, and it lulls me into a false sense of security. I run my fingers through the water and I swish my body around in it, sinking to the bottom to get my head under. I convince myself that going under a few times will wake me up, but it just makes me more tired. Soon I'm telling myself, just a small nap will do me good. I climb out of the bathtub, moving my books aside, the ones I was going to read in the bathtub but was too tired to pick up, and I dry myself quickly.

Having made my decision that falling into bed for a short nap will do me good I'm in a hurry to get there. I strip the towels from around my body and my head and I pull the flannel covers back, slipping under them. I'll only sleep for an hour, I say to myself, feeling shame and guilt that it will be longer. And when I awaken, whether it's been two or three or only the one I've given myself permission for, I feel terrible when I open my eyes. Ashamed of all the time I've wasted sleeping. Guilty, when I think of all the people working hard that really could've used my nap. And I wonder, why am I so tired lately?

I feel this way right before work sometimes, when six o'clock or seven rolls round and I'm finally waking up. Finally ready to face the day, and wishing I could be going someplace other than the bar now that I'm ready. Awake at last and sorry that I couldn't be this awake earlier, when I had all the time in the world to get stuff done, important stuff, stuff that mattered to me.

Somehow, now, even though it's late, I find myself at Phil's front door. I knock. Sweaty and rough, I think, like I need to get it out of my system. Kind of like fucking the life out of it. It reminds me of one time when I was in college and my boyfriend Derrick (the same one who said I was so demanding) and I did crystal meth and then fucked the whole night long. We were insatiable, and yet it felt so good until the sun came up. Then I remember saying, "Get away from me. You're actually making me sick."

Maybe it's the bourbon, maybe it's my birthday, but I'm here to fuck the life out of it. I'm here to kill it off till it's truly dead, as though coming back must make it right to have stayed so long in the first place—whatever. I just want to let it be whatever, because last times are like that. I wish I could go to Casey's, but I feel ridiculous talking about any stupid thing I'm going through when I think she might not live to see her thirtieth birthday, when I'm frantic about losing her and she doesn't seem to be afraid. It seems like there's not one thing in life that doesn't seem trivial when you compare it to death.

But I must not crave death enough, because I don't climb into bed with Phil.

"I think we haven't seen the worst of it with Casey," gurgles from the bottom of my throat.

"They don't think they got it, you mean?"

"They don't know, but they highly recommended chemo and she's not going for it."

"Why?"

"She doesn't want to."

"What do you think?"

"I told her I thought she should, but she didn't want to hear it and I don't know if I'm right and she feels fine, anyway."

"Well, maybe she will be."

"Yeah, that's the thing, nobody really knows. They don't see any cancer now, so she could be. Or not. But she can't live normally like she used to, you know? It's like she has to be careful just going outside. She really shouldn't work too much either. Too stressful."

"I'm sorry. It sucks that this is happening to her. How's she holding up?"

"She's strong. She just takes it one step at a time and keeps going. She's either in denial or she has complete faith in God taking care of her. I think it's both."

"I didn't know she was so into God."

"Oh, she believes it's all under his control, part of his plan. I'm starting to believe it a little, too. Only she thinks he's going to save her ass, and I'm thinking he's going to take it away to his side where he could probably use someone like her."

"I'm so sorry, Nick. I wish I could say it's all going to turn out fine."

"I know."

He hugs me into his chest and I let myself fall apart. Crying out loud, in short breaths and long guttural ones, just letting it rip like a baby. He rubs my back and holds me, then wipes my black mascara off my face with a tissue.

"You know, it just makes me look at life differently. It makes me think about how every minute really counts and that sounds so cliché, but why would you want to waste a minute complaining, punishing yourself, or just standing still, when in the next minute you could die or lose your best fucking friend."

"Yeah," he says stroking me like I'm a cat.

I fall back onto his chest, just resting for a little bit.

"You don't have to go, you know. You can sleep here."

"Thanks. But I can't," I say, making no move to go.

"You know, we haven't talked for like a month, and now you're here. Why don't you just slow down for a minute? Try to relax. Stay."

I hear his words as I drift off into sleep for a bit, and each word compels me to do exactly the opposite of what he's saying.

Wake up and fight, focus, get out, go.

I hug him and thank him and leave.

"Thanks for the flowers and for being my friend," I say, finally feeling some real closure, then I collapse back into tears as I hurry down his steps.

As I trudge up the stairs to my new home, I know I will not sleep, which turns out fine because, like me, my new home is a mess.

A film of grime seems to coat the walls and counter and floor, slick and sticky. The silverware is caked with food, and even the clean glasses in the dish rack are cloudy with spots, the once-neat kitchen now a trashed victim of the cooking frenzy. Everything from tiny pieces of dried-out fish to crusted charcoal grills and thickly oiled frying pans congealed in grease, everything lying about the kitchen in rotting piles.

The hardest part is starting. Facing it. It makes me queasy just to look at it all, and I can hardly proceed. But I do, because I know when I start to pour the hot soapy water over the filthy particles, the scent of the lemony soap will start to replace the garbage stink wafting through the house, and I'll be able to breathe again without gagging.

Scrubbing, soaping, spraying, wiping, I can't seem to get anything clean enough. The grease clings to the walls in big long streaks. But there's something so reassuring about scraping it all shiny clean, wiping it all away. Getting into the cracks and under the refrigerator. Catching the crumbs before they slide in between the stove and the counter top, never to be seen again. Scouring and polishing, disinfecting, shining, turning chaos and disarray into order as the rhythm lulls me into a feeling of calm. What was dirty slowly but surely becomes clean, tidy, manageable, and then somehow everything seems easier.

CHAPTER 28

"**N**ICK? IS THAT you?" says a familiar but unrecognizable male voice as I fumble with the phone.

"Yeah," I clear my throat, trying to make it sound like I haven't been sleeping.

"You asleep?" he says.

"No."

"Well, wake up. You awake?"

"Yeah."

"You got the prison thing."

"The prison one?"

"Yep."

"I did?"

"Yeah, congrats, honey. It's probably only a day's work, but still, I'm proud of you."

"Are you sure I got it?" I say.

"You shoot it next Wednesday. Why don't you drop by some time today and pick up the script, so I can give you a big smooch and all the details."

I can't believe it. It's just how I pray and hope it will be every time I pick up the phone. I always picture myself saying, "I did?" Like it's just going to happen to be my agent telling me I got a part. I always picture it—the phone ringing and a bit of news so fantastic it changes everything. But then this morning I'm out cold, sleeping in the middle of the day, and there it is. And yet it isn't exactly the call I've been waiting for, because it wouldn't be very sane to quit my day job for one day's work. But, as my agent said, it's something to feel proud of.

I could tell they liked me at the audition. In fact, I really thought I had it, because they were cracking up at my delivery, two women, one the producer, one the director/producer. But then, so many times I've thought I had it and never heard about it again.

They said, "You're funny."

Then they laughed with each other and asked me to do it again.

So I did.

They laughed again.

Then they said, "Thanks, Nicky, we'll be talking to you," which usually means not in this life. Except I guess sometimes it does.

What's strange to me is that it's such a small part, and yet the process is just as big a deal. Which is kind of great because I've been waiting for a big deal for so long.

So you audition, they pick you, they call your agent, he calls you. Then you get out there and say two lines, which in this case happen to be the same one repeated twice.

But when I get to the set I wonder if I've missed something, because I discover that I've been assigned my own private trailer. It has my character's name on it, which is Freckleface (though no one seems to address her or speak of her by this name), and it's mine for the day. I cautiously await the moment when I'll be yanked from the trailer that surely was meant for someone else with a bigger part, while at the same time hoping that I've been missing some pages from my script and I actually have a bigger part. Neither of these things happens, so I go inside, letting the door shut behind me as though I'll be needing to get right to work.

I'm a prison chick. I'm supposed to be slightly insane, and obsessed with paranoia that people are staring at my tits. Or at least that's what I've come up with, since my two lines are: "Quit staring at my tits."

I guess they were laughing at the audition because when I said, "Quit staring at my tits" for the second time, I cocked my head to the side, sort of turning it upside down to meet the focus of the male prison guard's eyes, which I'd imagined glued directly to my huge hooters. I personalized the situation, which wasn't too tough with tits like mine.

Now, inside my very own trailer, it's clean and private and I don't have a lot to do. I fantasize about becoming a star. Because this could, of course, lead to something bigger, and that's what I have to hope for when I start to feel badly about the fact that I don't have much to do.

I sit around pretending to be a star. Pretending I have a script in front of me and it needs real focus and attention for me to get into character—that I have been given this very private space and time to work on creating a very real person, in a poignant but rough-edged story that will climax with my character making some kind of miraculous transformation that will somehow save lives.

When the knock on the door wakes me from my dream, and I'm told "Five minutes to make-up" (which is a lot better than, "This trailer isn't for you after all, didn't you realize you only have a tiny part?"), I snap out of it and try to focus on my two separate cues that lead to my two identical lines, because nobody actually talks to me, and it's not obvious from the text when I would say "Quit staring at my tits."

It's a little part, but I love it. In my mind, I'm a prisoner, and I've got enough to deal with—I don't need any horny guard staring at my tits. I've decided that I'm in for armed robbery, and even though I haven't shot anyone, one of the guys in my gang did, so we're in a heap of trouble and I'm never getting out. Five minutes is enough time for me to get into character, and I'm off to make-up.

Unfortunately, make-up makes me look uglier than I ever dreamed possible.

I mean, whatever works for the character, but I would've thought the grotesque size of her breasts and the focus on that would have been ugly enough. I would have been wrong.

I wear a pale green tank top, with my breasts smooshed together and protruding through the material as much as possible. I guess this might look sexy on someone else, but with my small stature, cornrowed hair and dark-blue eye shadow, it looks whatever the opposite of sexy is.

I have to admit I'm disappointed. I looked as good as I could for the audition, and this is what they had in mind for me? Why does she have to be ugly? Is there any rule that says all prisoners are ugly? Wouldn't it be more real if I was a regular person with tremendous breasts, guilty of a crime and with some obvious problems, without making me into some kind of big-titted freak?

I think back to when I starred in a show Off-Broadway about a young woman, a priest, and her Italian family. The show spanned three time periods, in one of which somebody else played my younger self. But because of the time frame, I had to wear all kinds of period clothes, like Capri pants, saddle shoes, bobby socks. It was fun. The clothes were cute. I remember shopping for them with the costume designer in the Village. I even had to have my hair specially cut for it. My bangs were cut so short they fell somewhere smack in the middle of my forehead. And that wasn't something you could change between shows. It must have looked funny when I wasn't working, but I was so proud of what I was doing I didn't care. I was working Off-Broadway in a great ensemble cast of actors who had done everything from voice-overs to Broadway to big movies.

We got reviewed in the *New York Times* and it was a damn good review. The day it came out, a friend of mine from college picked it up early in the morning and read it to me over the phone. We were cracking up because we couldn't believe how good the review was.

I didn't care what I looked like because it made sense to me. It had a context. There was a point to it. But this prison garb, this is ridiculous.

Ready to go, in my green chino prison pants, it's time to meet the stars of the movie for a read-through. They are prisoners, too. They look great.

As sorry as I feel to be all dolled up and looking like a monster, I'm still so happy to be here, to hear the words, to see the exchanges, to be involved with the work. I love just to sit and listen and watch. It's like any rehearsal, everyone reading their part, focused on what they're here for. I only have to keep reminding myself that after my lines, I'm gone. I don't get to come back and sit around the cell with them, or show up later for work duty, or sit out on the yard for outdoor time. I have to savor what little time I have here.

After the read, we go back to our trailers and wait to be picked up and taken to the set. There are five of us that travel to and from the set together: the stars, Annabella Sciorra and Rae Dawn Chong; two other actors with parts like mine, maybe bigger (couldn't be smaller); and me. To my dismay, we're all considered principals.

When we get to the set, the PA has to go up inside the back of my bra to mike me because there's a lot of surround noise. But because of my tiny tank get-up, I can never show my back to the camera or my mike will be clearly seen.

We go ahead and do a couple of takes, just like in rehearsal, but for some reason it's not working out. The crew tells me it's a technical problem and not to worry as they adjust my mike, apologizing as they inadvertently graze my breast.

When we go to take again, the director tells me to stick out of the line-up. I think I do, but she says it a couple of times and then seems annoyed. There's lots of stuff going on around us, and she's talking to someone else while we wait to do the next take. Annabella touches my hand and says, "Just take your time. Don't rush. It's your time."

"Okay," I say. "Thanks."

"You're doing fine," she says.

This time the director says, "Nicky, step out of the line."

"Okay," I say, not at all sure what is going wrong, but knowing something is. But before she said stick out and now she's saying step out, so I do.

I step out of the line, and she says to make sure I'm on an angle because otherwise my mike sticks out. So I do my best. She says we're going to roll for tape.

Just before we do, Rae says, "Just go crazy, you know. That's what I'm going to do. Go really crazy," she says again, this time kicking something.

"Yeah, okay," I smile.

Annabella smiles at me and says, "You're doing great."

And then within seconds, we're rolling. Having been cheered on by the toughest prisoners on the cellblock, I feel confident. I step out of the line, cock my cornrowed head and deliver my lines, precisely and deliberately enough to scare anybody who would even think of fucking with me.

"Cut—that's it. We got it," the director says.

Moments later, I'm being disconnected from my mike and sent on my way home. I see Rae on my way down the hall.

"See you later," she says.

"Bye," I say, wishing I would be seeing her later.

I go up to Annabella and say good-bye to her.

"Are you done already?" she asks. And yes, it's sad but true.

"Yeah. That's it for me. Thanks so much for helping me out."

"Sure. You did a really good job, you know."

"Thanks. See you and good luck with it."

"Thanks a lot. See you."

And that's it for me, for now, anyway—short and kind of sweet. But finally, when people ask me if I have any tape, that much-asked question in Hollywood, I can say yes.

CHAPTER 29

T HE REAL REASON I don't tell anybody I graduated Magna Cum Laude (or even that I graduated at all) is because, under the circumstances, it's embarrassing. Announcing that you're good at something because you don't have any other way of proving it.

"Oh, you were an A student in college so you could serve me drinks in a smoky bar? How enterprising of you."

If they believe me they feel sorry for me, and if they don't, they also feel sorry for me. It's like telling people that I'm a really gifted actress. It's just not the right environment. It doesn't work to confess "truths" about yourself in this setting. It doesn't ring true. It doesn't fit the role. And that's the real truth.

Because that's what it is—a role. And I've been working so hard at playing it well. I laugh, I smoke, I drink, I take care of everybody, but I don't reveal myself. It would be like breaking the fourth wall. Like throwing an aside to the audience: "I'm not really a bartender. I just look, smell, and act like one."

But play a role well enough, long enough, and isn't what they see what you get? I put on my uniform, I climb back here, I "talk the talk," "walk the walk," and suddenly I'm it. And it's easier to be it than to explain who I really think I am and why. I would rather be one of them: a person who likes what they do, or at least is happy enough pretending to.

So sometimes I imagine that this is what I've always wanted: to be this, just this and nothing else. To make money and laugh with strangers at night so I can have my days free just to kick around. When I play this game with myself, and I do it a lot, a big sense of relief washes over me. It calms me. And that's when I really get into it. I get good at it— because if this was what I really wanted, I could be tops, the best. And when I'm able to convince myself that the fast action, the lively pace, the people dancing and talking and flirting and fucking, is exactly what I want, I feel good about being here.

But I have to become a part of it or there's no way I can be convinced. And that's why I have to dive into my role so fully. I take it on with gusto, and I climb into the character's skin in such a way that I can survive anything. Because this is a role about survival, and the quickest way to lose in a role like this is to show your bare ass to a bunch of drunks. The problem is, along the way I get lost in their stories and my heart breaks a little for them, and I realize I don't have to pretend to be one of them, because I already am. The other problem is, I forget what I'm struggling so hard to survive for.

I'm only able to reflect on this role as bartender because for two minutes I got to play another one. Got to be somebody else. It pulled me out of my comfortable, uncomfortable little hideaway behind the bar long enough to remember myself—the self that was just pretending to be a bartender so that I could do what I loved and wanted more than anything else.

Now, back in the pit, I can't stop obsessing about those times when I came so close to really getting something. I can't let go of it. Like that time two years before I left New York when I had three callbacks for the movie "Last Exit to Brooklyn," for the lead. We thought I was so close that my Mom and Dad took different stances on whether I should take it or not if they offered it to me.

She thought I should. "It's a great part. That's what acting is. Everyone will know you're acting and that's not you, as long as you do it brilliantly."

But my Dad thought the better I did it, the more it would typecast me as a big-titted, ruthless gangbang victim.

I wasn't sure what I thought, but I figured I'd worry about that later.

On my third callback I met Uli Edel, the director, and the casting directors taped the audition. We were all asked to do a monologue for the tape because the script wasn't finished yet. So I worked hard on a monologue of this real tough-girl type. One of the hardest parts was finding the appropriate piece, because there aren't that many great women's monologues that haven't been done to death, and this one needed to be specific. So I put it together from a novel. Then, of course, making an out-of-context monologue work on videotape would be its own challenge.

But by the time I had finished preparing, I felt ready. And after I auditioned I actually was afraid I might get it, because there were some brutally graphic scenes in Hubert Selby Jr.'s book (which I had read cover to cover), and the film was supposed to be based on it. In addition, the casting directors had asked "right up front" if I had a problem with full frontal nudity. I had responded that I did have a bit of a problem with it, but if they were asking me if I'd do it, the answer was probably yes.

Uli was a very nice man, soft-spoken, German, and I felt he was genuinely impressed with my work. I'm pretty sure I would not have turned down that role, even knowing, now, that the film wasn't a big hit. But what I would've done mattered very little, because a few weeks later they gave it to Jennifer Jason Leigh. I wondered why they had bothered with me when they probably wanted a star in the first place. But then, maybe not every star would want to play that role, and Jennifer might have needed time to figure out if she did.

What I really wondered, then and now, and couldn't and can't let go of, is why, after three callbacks and meeting the director, nobody so much as offers me some little whore, prostitute, drug-addict part, of which there always is one. Was it that my agent didn't say, "Maybe

Nicky'd be right for something else"? Couldn't any of the casting people see it? So okay, you're up for some mammoth part that you don't really expect to get, maybe you're never even as close as you think. They give that part to a star or the daughter of a star, but why can't you be the girlfriend, the sister, the cocktail waitress, the cop?

What irks me more is that people always say, "But they'll remember you for the next thing." How can they remember me for the next thing when before they've even finished casting this one, they've forgotten me?

CHAPTER 30

S PEAKING OF FORGETTING about me—T comes in and tells me he got a new job and it's in Seattle. (So not another planet, but Seattle.) He's with Paul, and Paul asks me how my vacation was. I haven't seen him since I got back from Florida with Philip, even though that was months ago.

"It wasn't so great," I say, still trying to digest the fact that T's moving to Seattle. The thing I most know about Seattle is the postmark of the Seattle Repertory Company, as I've sent them a letter a year for about the last five, requesting an audition. All requests denied.

"Bad weather?" Paul asks.

"No, the weather was beautiful. It just wasn't that much fun," I mumble, and walk away. I close out a check and make a couple of margaritas for a guy and a girl clearly on their first date.

Soon I'm back, getting Paul a beer. He drinks Red Tail Ale just like T, only not as many. He's fit and lean, where T's big in a muscular sort of way. I imagine Paul, being a neurologist and all, prefers smoke to drink, anyway. So, I bring him a beer and ask if I should get T one, because he's not there at the moment.

When I put two cold ones down, he says, "So what could make a trip to Florida not fun?"

"I didn't get along with his family," I say, referring to Phil's family.

"Really?" he says.

"I had a big fight with his dad, and I didn't get along too well with him, either."

"No kidding," he says, like he's sorry, but also like this bit of news has excited him.

"Yeah, the fight with his dad was so bad I wasn't allowed into his dad's house afterwards."

"And what about you two?" he asks, eagerly, I think.

"I moved into my aunt's place until I can find a place of my own," I tell him.

We both just look at each other as T returns to his stool and says, "Oh, thanks," taking a long swig of his beer.

"You're welcome," I say, as I move along to get somebody else's order.

I watch them out of the corner of my eye. I see Paul talking and T listening. By the look on T's face, I guess this new information about me and my now ex-boyfriend is registering, and I can't help but watch for his reaction. He catches me, and I feel something funny in my stomach. I look away, and I don't dare go over until they're ready for their check.

When I give them their change and receipt, T says, "Nick, Paul tells me you moved. Do you have a phone number I could call you at? I'd like to give you my new address."

"Sure," I say, scribbling my aunt's phone number on a piece of their receipt. "When do you leave?"

"A couple of days," he says.

"Wow, that's so fast. I'll really miss you."

"I'll miss you, too," he says.

Paul leans over to me and says, "More than you know," I guess implying something about the way T will miss me. Then he gives T a little pat on the back and smiles.

"I'll be by to keep you company, Nicky," he adds, as they head for the door.

As they exit through the glass doors, I see T giving Paul a playful little jab in the ribs as they break into a boyish horse fight.

The next morning the phone rings. It's Casey.

"I don't want to alarm you," she says, "but I had a seizure."

"A seizure? Fucking great," I say.

"Yeah, I know," she says. "It happened when I was driving, and I had a little accident with the Mustang."

"Oh, shit, are you all right?" I say.

"Yeah, but the Green Hornet doesn't look so good."

"Is it totaled?"

"Yeah, kind of," she says. And she's laughing, because she knows how fucked up it all is, and how much worse it's maybe going to get, and I think because she wants me to react calmly, like she just told me she overslept for work or something.

"Also, the doctor says it metastasized to my lungs, and the next place for it to go is my brain."

"Your brain?" I say.

"If it goes there I might not be able to recognize things so well, and maybe people, too."

"Your brain? How does it get to your brain?" I ask, as if she would know. I had asked Paul, because he was a neurologist, how the cancer might lead to death, if in fact it did. I had asked what form of illness it would manifest itself as; because it's always something specific that kills you. It's not like you get cancer and then boom you die of it. It's what the cancer does to you. We had talked about the possibility of pneumonia. But the idea of it traveling to her brain had never occurred to me.

"So it could affect your motor skills?" I ask, stalling.

"Yeah. That's what he said."

Then there's a long period of silence between us. I don't know what she's thinking, but I'm thinking about how strange human existence is. One minute you're walking around, trying on new clothes, and the next minute you're spasming. Your body is jerking this way and that, and even if you're conscious enough to see what's happening, you can't make your brain tell your hand to stay steady on the wheel. You can't tell your brain to do anything. It's your brain that tells you. And you are really nothing without your brain.

I hear myself saying, "Are you surprised?"

She says, as if she's been thinking about it all right along with me, "Yeah. The doctor said it's really uncommon, too. Usually melanoma is too fast traveling and it never reaches the brain. I really wanted you to know, just in fucking case, you know?"

"Yeah," I say.

In case she can't recognize me, in case we can never have another conversation like this, in case next time she can't call me.

"And they're sending someone over from hospice in the morning. Jay doesn't think it's a good idea for me to be alone, so Gig is coming over tomorrow afternoon for a little while . . ."

"I'll come by after I teach my class," I finish her sentence.

"Thanks," she says. "Was it really cool meeting them?" She means Anabella and Rae.

"Yeah, they were really nice."

"And you had your own fucking trailer?"

"Yeah, but I sure wish you were doing my hair and make-up."

"They made you look gnarly, huh? Still that's so cool somebody finally cut you a break. I know you're gonna be awesome. I can't wait to see it."

CHAPTER 31

I GO TO CASEY'S every day after the seizure. And so I watch as her demise begins. Little by little, like an elderly person, she's losing her functioning capabilities. First she can't drive. Then she can't walk. And before you know it she can't move. That first day after the seizure, the vomiting starts, and Gigi and I realize that it's begun. This is what it's like. The lack of control, fine one minute, not able to hold anything down the next, including the seizure medication or the pain medication. And that's how it's going to be. Only worse.

At first we just sit around, waiting for her to call out to us what she needs: a bowl for vomit, a pill for pain, a walk to the bathroom. We sit around just marveling that this is what the end is really like: the helplessness of it, our helplessness in it.

But in what feels like such a short time, she stops calling out. She vomits and shakes with seizures and we have to keep up with the remedies. We look to the pharmacy of pills the doctors have left us with, because that's all they've left us with. They've abandoned anything more than keeping her comfortable, believing she's a goner. But how to keep her comfortable is confusing, because the medicine that keeps her from convulsing causes her to vomit, and the only way she can get the pain medicine is if we give her a suppository, and she doesn't want us to because it makes her disappear. Even the simplest thing, like a shower, is difficult, because her motor skills have begun to fail her. In the shower Jay will tell her to hold on, and she'll yell back at him, "I am holding on!" her body collapsed and sinking toward the hard porcelain.

After that first couple of days, everyone who loves her comes to her bedside, changing bedpans, feeding her chocolate Ensure, frozen, because that's the way she likes it best; dabbing that little pink spongy thing in her mouth to moisten it, dehydrated because she can't keep anything down.

It's happened so fast our heads are spinning, but that's how they say it goes when you're so young. Every day something we take for granted slips from her, and then the morphine takes over. In her moments of clarity she always asks how you are, wanting to be there for you, only occasionally cursing the loss of an old skill and the diaper that it necessitates, incredulous at what is happening to her.

She tells her friends back home in Philly that she'll be coming home for a visit, and some believe her, because she can pull it off over the phone. When the phone rings and I answer it, I have to tell them I don't think so, even though Casey's telling us the same thing.

"She'll be coming home, but not the way you're thinking. If you want to see her, you're going to have to come here."

I can tell everybody that except for her parents. I can't tell her mom and dad that because her dad, ironically and unbelievably, has his own brain tumor eating away at his last weeks or days of life, and so he probably wouldn't understand anyway, and her mom is so busy caring for her dad and his brain tumor that flying out to California to see her twenty-four-year-old daughter who claims she'll be home for Easter just doesn't make sense.

The Green Hornet sits in the driveway all smashed up, like an omen. Each day as I travel from home and work to her house and back, spending every free minute I can with her, I think that the chemo wouldn't have helped, because it was already too late. It had her. That shouldn't matter now, but somehow that doesn't keep me from obsessing about it over and over.

"That's *so you*, tortured," her voice echoes through my thoughts.

As we sit huddled around her, willing her to live, we worry that she might—go on living like this, with all the life inside her draining away as her brain decomposes and her dark-brown eyes stare out at you trying to speak, but unable to form the words. Death is not like those other things in life that get better with time. With time, the dying embody death more and more, until you almost long for their last breath.

CHAPTER 32

WHEN THE PRISON movie finally comes out, everyone gathers around Casey's home hospital bed to check me out. Casey always wanted to see me in something, but now, given her condition, her excitement doesn't look like much. Her eyes are like glass. Her face blank, sometimes it seems like she is almost smiling but mostly I think it's my imagination. The movie feels so tangible compared with the vagueness of dying. Something you see and hear in black and white, with a dramatic arc, instead of "Maybe she'll feel better tomorrow, maybe she'll feel worse. Maybe she'll die soon, maybe she won't."

I have to work. I absolutely can't get out of it, so Jay promises to tape the film for me.

As I cruise up and down the bar, I feel a mixture of excitement and fear, layered on top of the regular Casey's-dying depression. I've forewarned everyone that it's a small part, that if you aren't concentrating, you might miss me. But still, it's on HBO and I'm in it. I've been waiting for this moment for so long, when I would finally be on film, and people I know and people I don't would watch me doing the thing I most wanted to do in the world, which I was meant to do, after all. It's supposed to feel good, but with Casey dying, I feel ashamed when I let it.

At least now there's something to look forward to. It's almost like tomorrow will be different. Like people will start seeing me in little parts all the time, and new customers in the bar will wonder out loud why I look familiar.

It won't feel so bad to pour drinks if I can feel that hope. The hope that this really is a stepping stone, not a gravestone. Everything is different when you don't feel it owns you.

But around eleven o'clock I get a call from Jay. They've just come to the part I'm supposed to be in, but all they can see or hear that resembles what I've told them is someone who looks vaguely like me on the screen for about thirty seconds, yelling at a guard in a Hispanic accent to "Shut up!"

"What?" I say, struggling to hear above the bar noise.

"It didn't sound like you, and there was nothing about tits."

He's speaking in the past tense. That great moment that I so longed for has come and gone, only it sounds like it hasn't come at all.

"Was I in it, though? Maybe it hasn't come on yet."

"We couldn't really tell, it was so fast, Nick. But it definitely wasn't your voice."

"They dubbed over my stuff?"

"Maybe. I don't know. You couldn't see who was talking, you know? I'm really sorry, Nick."

"That's okay."

No, it sucks. God, that sucks so badly. It's, it's, I don't know, so cruel.

"Were you able to tape it?"

"Yeah."

"Okay. Good," I say, as if it matters. Good, they've taped a stupid prison movie that I'm not in.

"Thanks. Fuck. Is Case still up? Did she see?"

"She kept her eyes peeled open for as long as she could, but she's sleeping now, so I'm not sure. Are you coming by tomorrow?"

"Yeah. I'll be by. I guess I really fucking sucked for them to cut me up and dub over me, huh?"

"What? No. Don't say that. It might not have had anything to do with you, you know that."

"Yeah, yeah. I know. Thanks for calling, Jay. I'll see you tomorrow. Oh, and Jay?"

"Yeah."

"Don't tell Case what happened if she didn't see, okay?" I say, feeling nauseous.

"Sure, Nick, don't worry about that," he says.

"I can't wait to see it," she said when I first told her. Now she never would.

But the next day, when I go over, I tell her I was great. She's so out of it, and I know she doesn't have long. She can barely talk. Once in a while she'll say a word, but mostly she's got this blank stare on her face, and we wonder if she can hear or understand us at all. A few days, I figure, maybe even less, and I can't see the point in telling her the truth. So I tell her I was really great and I'm so sorry she missed it, but not to worry because Jay taped it. I act really happy about the whole thing because I feel like, as much as she can understand, she needs to know that I'm going to be okay. She really seems to need that.

When I think back to that torturous stretch of time when she stopped calling me and started hanging out with everybody but me, I understand it better now. I think she was trying to protect me, to let me down easy. Trying to get me to move on, so my heart wouldn't break into a million pieces, so I wouldn't glue myself to her bed, so I wouldn't fall apart so completely that even alive I would be more dead than she would be when she died. I think she was trying to say, "If I die you won't have a best friend. You'd better do something about that," and I want her to think I have. I want her to believe I'm going to go on living and that I have that thing I've always dreamed of to hang on for.

It doesn't matter that there's no sign of me on that tape, or for that matter, that Jay never actually taped it. He meant to, but for some reason it didn't work (which often seems to be the case). But it doesn't matter, because the life is drifting out of Casey's body. She's very still and she's got these puffy purplish bumps on her feet, which are actually tumors, and her mouth is always so dry because she can't eat or drink anymore, and we feel like she can't hear us, even if she can.

So there's no need to show her my big debut, anyway. No need to prove anything. Yet, as out of it as she is, she knows I'm lying about being great, because she knows me.

I know this because the next night, when nobody's around, I come back to be with her. I basically want to be with her for every last minute she has. Nothing else really matters. So I'm sitting by her side, thinking how surreal it all is. How beautiful she looks. How young. How sick. And I'm praying she'll talk to me, praying—as religious as I'll ever be—that she'll look over at me and come out of that faraway place that the cancer and the morphine have banished her to and say, "I love you and I'm going to miss you, my friend."

It's then, that night, for the briefest moment that she does come back. I had seen her do it one other time, when Jay shaved off his beard. She had come from that faraway place, where she lived most of the time the last two or three weeks of her life, and was instantly in the present with us. She had reached up and touched Jay's face. "I like you without the beard. You're so smooth and soft," she said, rubbing her chin against his and smiling the sweetest smile, and then—right back to that place.

And though I'm hoping for some communication and trying to figure out what meaningful thing I can say to her that'll allow her to go peacefully, and allow me to feel some peace with her going, I'm shocked when she actually speaks.

She says, as if we've been talking all along, "That part doesn't matter. It wouldn't have mattered if they didn't cut you. It wouldn't have made you happy, or me either. You're gonna do other things, though. Those things will be for real. Those things will matter. But you know what, lover? You better get your ass out of Dodge first."

And then, like in a movie, her face turns back to stone.

"Case? Casey?" I yell into her blank face, begging her to come back again. But she doesn't.

I wouldn't have believed it if someone had told me that could happen, a day before she died, but it did. She was so present when she said it, like she'd never been sick for one minute of her whole life.

CHAPTER 33

THAT NIGHT BEFORE she dies, I finally get up the courage to whisper into her ear, "I love you, but don't hold on for me or anyone else. You've been so strong, let yourself rest."

And when she lets go, that next morning, I feel a bittersweet mixture of pain and relief.

It's a sun-drenched day and we all gather at the house, after the men take her little body away—those of us who have been here for these last days and weeks and those who haven't.

Those who haven't seen her sick must think the rest of us odd, because we walk around with a kind of lightness, an energy in our feet, a laughter that peaks and then relaxes into calm, a peacefulness that suffuses us all, releasing us from the suffering and endless loss that overwhelmed the house when Casey was dying in it. It's as though she's been locked up in a dark, cramped dungeon for too long, and now we all feel better knowing she's set free.

The Mustang no longer sits smashed up in the driveway. Jay had it taken away a week before the men came to take her. We had joined hands around her bed that same day, as a priest we had invited over read her the last rites. I went back and forth between irrepressible tears and a panic that she would wake up from her deep, drug-induced sleep and bark, "What the hell do you guys think you're doing?"

Last night, before she died, when Casey spoke to me so clearly from her deathbed, it coursed through my brain that maybe all the failures and disappointments I'd been experiencing were just checkpoints on the road to something else. It coursed through my brain like I imagine heroin might course through my veins—in that you will at a certain point do anything to make the pain go away. There was no way I could find anything positive in Casey's illness, but maybe if I looked at my own life from a slightly different angle, (a little heroin-coated maybe?) I could, at least, get out of Dodge. I wondered if Casey, teetering on the brink of death, was having a vision for me, if she could actually see me doing great things, or if she was just hoping and trying to give me hope. I'd like to think that when somebody's in that place, they're able to see farther, clearer, more. But, vision or hope, if I can find even a tiny part of myself that believes in it as much as she believed in me, no matter how many other parts of my life are screaming **LOSER,** I can go on trying to do what makes me happy to be alive.

And I thought that if I could believe in her vision for me, I could come up with one that I believed in for her, too.

So I've come up with one very much like the near-death stories I've read about, where the people almost die but don't, so they can tell you exactly where they were headed, because they saw what was coming.

There's a long tunnel, where she gets to say goodbye to everybody she ever loved, because on the way to death she's no longer sick and there's lots of time and she's all clean in a cream-colored something, just floating along. And then, as she gets to the end, there's this brilliant light, warm and golden, and it just hugs her, warming her up, and then kisses her, too, all over her face. The whole time God is right there with her, by her side, closer to her than she ever dreamed possible, guiding her, and everything is white and clean, so clean.

But best of all, when they've passed through to the other side, God asks Casey to design her own wings and some of the other angels', and she's allowed, in fact encouraged, to devote herself to it, making them exquisite and detailed, out of the richest fabrics of her own choosing. And there are all kinds of antique chairs there, thousands of them, of all different centuries and sizes. And while she's busily working her magic on those wings and other important heavenly attire, God is filling her in on why he's brought her here and why she was down on earth with us, before. And why her strength, her courage, her love, her sense of humor, her savvy, and of course her wonderful sense of style, are all so needed, here, now.

I find comfort in the fact that her vision and mine are both a little over the top.

So with each day that goes by I revise both hers and mine, and it gives me something to strive for. Because if I can make her last words more real, maybe my blissful vision for her will also become real. If I can keep her vision for me alive, working hard to find ways to fulfill it, maybe she can stay alive inside me.

I love wearing her clothes. Of course she had great taste, the kind you can't help but notice on the street—a great hat or jacket or just the right color shoes. But mostly, I like wearing her clothes because they were hers. It makes me feel closer to her, and I want that. Sometimes when I put on something of hers and I'm buttoning it, the buttons will pop open, and it makes me feel like she's goofing around with me, trying to send a sign. Other times I wish she would send some kind of sign, because I can't find her, and I feel as if her clothes are the only things that keep her from fading away entirely. Other times, I actually think I see her: rounding a corner, buying shoes, driving. When I catch myself and realize it's not her, I sometimes think, well, when's she going to get better? When's she coming back?

Much as I love wearing her clothes, I don't have very many of them.

I went back there on a rainy day. The house still smelled of her—that good smell of her—a combination of earth and some of the scents from the perfumes she collected, and everything remained but the portable bed from the hospice. She'd needed it towards the end because it was impossible for her to get down the three steps to their bedroom and onto the futon that lay on the floor.

When the cot first came it looked so strange sitting there in the middle of their living room, a metal-framed bed lifting and lowering, smack in the middle of Jay and Casey's sponged walls and distressed furniture. Soon after that first day, though, when Casey couldn't hold anything down, the whole house started to look like a hospital, and that cot began to blend in with the dozens of pill bottles and diapers and cans of fake food and the general medicinal aura that surrounds death. Now that the cot was gone, with nothing new in its place, the room felt very empty.

Aside from the brown pinstriped vest, I took a tan jacket with big brown buttons and a little belt in back, and a black-and-white dress that she used to wear with maroon lipstick, and a pair of grayish-blue trousers and a black lacy shirt.

I always get compliments on the jacket and the trousers. They're both big and funky and masculine in a feminine sort of way, yet very classic. The dress isn't really a dress at all. It's sleeveless and chiffony, but actually more of a shirt, because the little white buttons only go down to your bellybutton, so you have to wear something underneath. Casey used to wear it over leggings and black high-top Converse sneakers.

Jay said, "You take this. It'll look good on you," and he tossed the black lacy thing at me.

I didn't know if it would even fit me, but it was getting late and we'd been at it for hours, and I could feel that he was beginning to drown in her clothes and her smell and her stuff and her death, and I didn't want him to feel like he was sinking into quicksand any more than I already did. So I took that black lacy thing, too.

"Thanks," I said, stuffing it into my bag.

I was glad when he offered it, because I hadn't always liked it or wanted it, and I felt better about taking a thing that I hadn't always wanted when she was alive. That's why I guess I felt so funny about taking any of her hats—because I loved them and I always had.

They hung in three horizontal rows against the long closet wall. A cream velvet one with rings that went all the way around was almost like a beret; only it had a longer front and back and sat higher on her head. A gold one, almost a little pillbox, she used to wear sometimes with big, chunky white shoes. There were black hats and brown hats and blue hats, and one of my favorites, a plum one with a simple round rim. I used to borrow that one all the time. The two of us bopped around town in funny hats and combat boots. She had hammered a bunch of nails into the wall and thrown the hats on those, and it looked like a cross between a shop in the East Village and a museum exhibit.

She bought a lot of them on Haight Street in San Francisco—right after we left the hospital, after those specialists picked and probed at her like some kind of science project. Right after that, we went on that little shopping spree on Haight Street, popping into stores, trying on hat after hat and laughing at the seriousness of cancer.

We passed a couple of cops walking their beat, and they casually said, "Hey, how's it going?"

We smiled and responded with the automatic "Fine, good."

A millisecond later Casey looked at me with a mock-crying face and said "Well, actually, I've got cancer," and somehow that cracked us both up.

The only hat I asked for was the one she put a deposit on the day I drove her home after her second operation. The doctor had told her to take it easy and stay off her leg, but she insisted I take her shopping. Didn't she deserve to be out in the world a little after being cooped up in the hospital for all that time? She was trying on dresses even though she was on crutches, and her leg was looking like my grandmother's did sometimes, all swollen, when she came across this hat and fell in love.

It was a woven material with rusty-peach and white flowers on it and a forest-green stem. The leaves of the stem looked real, and there was bone-colored lace that attached the leaves and flowers and a finely gold-embroidered ribbon. You could wear it a lot of different ways, but she wore it pulled way down, so the brim was pressed flat against her forehead like a flapper's, which not many people could get away with.

It was a great hat, but it would never have looked like that on me. She talked the salesperson into putting it on layaway for her, even though they didn't ordinarily do that, because together we only had fifty bucks on us, and it was more and she really wanted it.

After she died, I told Lee, one of her best friends from her hometown, Philly, that I wanted it. Lee and I had grown close in those last weeks of waiting for our friend to leave us, and he must've told Casey's mother, because when Jay and I got to Philly the night before the funeral, she said, "I have something for you, Nicky," then ran off upstairs. When she came back down, she had that hat in her hands.

It made me feel special. And I really did want that hat—to look at in a specially appointed place in my room. To keep a piece of her with me forever, but never to infringe on its sacredness by putting it on my head and going out in it. And I guess that's why I had found the courage to ask for it.

Flying home from Philly with that hat on my lap I thought of all those other hats that hung on her wall like a part of her character and wondered what would happen to them. I felt so stupid for having worried about taking them. I wish I had. I'd throw some nails in the wall and make an art display of them.

In fact, I feel like it would be a good thing to go out and find some special hats of my own.

CHAPTER 34

LAINEY IS IN tonight, T's sister. We teach at the same gym. We're friendly, and sometimes I cover her class for her if she needs a sub. She's the queen of the aerobics world; I'm just a visitor.

She's having a drink and then dinner in the restaurant. She looks a lot like T. Beautiful black hair down her back, smooth, hairless Asian skin, lean muscles perfectly sculpted; beautiful like him. Having a drink right in front of me, like he used to. We chit-chat about the gym for a while: complain about the stereo breaking down, gossip about some of our mutual students. Is anyone making any good new music?

Then I ask about him.

"How's he doing? Does he like it up there?"

She mentions, very casually, that he's going to be in town. "Hey, we're going to have dinner together Tuesday night. You want to come?"

She says it as though the idea has just occurred to her, but I'm wondering if T could possibly be behind this invitation, or if he doesn't know about it but wouldn't mind, or knows but didn't suggest it himself, or is completely oblivious to any of it. I hear myself saying, "Sure, I'd love to."

The host comes by to tell me Lainey's table is ready. I tell him her check is cleared, and he comes over to escort her.

"Oh, what do I owe you, Nick?" she asks.

"You're all set," I say.

"Hey, thanks," she says sweetly and then, "I'll call you about Tuesday."

"Great," I say. "Have a nice dinner."

It's so busy I can't tell who she's having dinner with, but I got her two drinks, so I know she's not alone.

Tonight feels easy. They're in, they're out. The music is fun and the people seem happy. It gets a little hectic when Melissa has to go to the bathroom and people need their checks closed out before they sit down. I track their checks and sometimes I have to track the people down, too, but they're pretty quick with the money tonight, so it doesn't get too stressful.

Lainey passes by on her way out and tells me that dinner was really good. Then her friend joins her and says, "Yeah, the macaroni and cheese here is delicious."

I know her friend. She works out at the gym too. She's really pretty, with blonde hair and blue eyes, and though she's a little on the big side it doesn't detract from her very good looks.

They say 'bye and Lainey says, "I'll see you Tuesday."

And then her friend says, "Yeah, see you Tuesday."

I know the friend's name. Lisa. I know she hangs out with Lainey some and takes Lainey's class. I also know she's dated T a few times. What I don't know is if they still see each other, if he's in love with her, why she has to come.

Now I really don't want to go, but it would be so awkward to back out.

"Yeah," I say, "see you Tuesday."

On Tuesday night, the phone rings just as I'm trying to figure out what to wear. Over a year of knowing a person and he's only seen me out of uniform once.

"Hi, it's Lainey," the voice says. "T is stuck at his shoot 'cause they're running late. Are you starving?"

Starving? I forgot all about the food.

"No, I'm fine," I say.

"I'm so sorry," she says, "He called to apologize and said he should be out of there soon. Do you want to just come over here whenever you're ready?"

"Sure," I say, glad that I don't have to rush my clothing selection.

"Okay, see you in a bit," she says. "Oh, by the way, Lisa's sick, so it's just the three of us."

"Oh, okay," I say, thinking maybe I should say I'm sorry Lisa's sick, but I don't. "See you soon," I say, and we hang up.

When I knock, I hear the two of them laughing together about a bicycle he's helping her fix. She gives me a hug and he says, "Hi, it's great to see you," and I think he's noticing what I look like in real clothes. I'm definitely noticing what he looks like in clothes, and while I'm at it, wondering what he would look like without any.

We go to a favorite Japanese place that a friend of theirs owns. I love sushi, but I'm not too well versed in the names and neither is Lainey, so we make a couple of suggestions and T orders the rest. Then she orders sake, and I don't much like sake, so T asks if I want to get one of those huge beers, and we can share it.

When everything comes he serves it to us, always making sure to refill my beer and my sparkling water when they get a little low. I'm shy, but not uncomfortable. I like them both and I get this strange feeling like we've done this before, or we always do this, like we're family.

The owner, their friend Mike, joins us and we all have a drink together. After dinner, we go next door to Mike's brother's place for coffee.

It's pretty late by now and there are only a few straggling customers besides us. Mike asks us if we mind if he smokes, and breaks out some cigars. T's eyes light up. Lainey and I sip cappuccinos as the boys tug on cigars. I know Lainey smokes cigars now and then, too, but not tonight.

I expect the conversation to change, for Mike, his brother Jim, a friend of Jim's and T to focus on sports or business talk. Instead, they puff on cigars and talk about books they love.

They discuss one book in particular that they all have read. I can't follow the details because I haven't read it. I've only just gotten into reading books again. For a long time I haven't been able to focus my thoughts long enough to comprehend and sustain interest from one chapter to the next, having read only plays and scripts. It's only now that I'm rediscovering reading and loving it, like a good first kiss. And I love to listen to these guys talking about books while smoking cigars.

T takes a nice draw and says, "This cigar is really a treat."

Mike says, "You're a treat, man," pulling his arm around T and smiling.

Then T worries that he's keeping me out too late. I do have a class to teach very early in the morning, which I dread, so I say it's not a problem, but I really should get going.

On the way to my car, which is parked near Lainey's, T teases me.

"Well, it's really nice to see you outside of the bar now that I live in Seattle, Nicky."

"I know, it's a real shame," I say.

I want him to drive Lainey to her front door and then drive me to my car, so I can have a minute alone with him (speaking of first kisses).

But he doesn't. Instead, I hug them both goodbye, and on my way home I have to keep reminding myself that he lives in Seattle now.

I awaken to his voice calling me from the airport.

"I just wanted to tell you I really enjoyed spending time with you last night."

"Oh, thanks," I say. "It was really nice."

Then he says, "I know you're enjoying your newfound freedom," (I'd told him how happy I was to be free of Philip and free in general), "but I was just wondering if I could reserve some time with you next week?"

I blurt out, "Why?" because I'm a little scared. Scared because I've known him for a while, loved him from a distance, and always had an excuse not to get to know him at all. Talked myself out of liking him, and wondered if I was lying to myself.

He says, laughing, "Because I really enjoy your company. I have to come down anyway, to meet my family for a trip we take every year at Christmas."

So we decide to get together, but in the daytime. I tell him I'm working almost every night that week, which is a lie.

He picks me up at my aunt's and we take a walk along the beach. We hold hands, walking along, and he tells me about a book he's read that he thinks I would like.

"It's about these two sisters. They're really close, but they're so different. One lives in Nicaragua, caring for the poor and war-stricken, and the other in the hometown where they grew up."

"It does sound like something I'd like. My sister and I are really close, but very different."

"Yeah," he says, like he knows this.

How does he know? Have I told him before, at the bar?

"Is she still working with computers?"

"Yup, she is," I say, awed by how carefully he's been listening to me. What else does he know about me that I've forgotten I revealed?

"I'd like to read it."

"You can have my copy," he says, giving my hand a little squeeze.

I like his hands. I did right away. They're strong and big, with big knuckles. But when he uses them, say to twirl a glass or sign a voucher, they look quick and agile, like fine tools. I like to watch them. I like the way mine feels linked with his.

Stopping in for a drink at a restaurant on the beach, I wish I could call in sick, because tonight I really am working, and now I wish I wasn't.

"How about an early dinner before you abandon me for work?" he asks.

A delicious bottle of deep purple Cabernet finds its way to our table, and I have some, despite the fact that I'm on my way to work. Sitting by the window we can see the cold on people's faces. Inside, next to him, I don't feel the cold or the time. I just listen to his gentle voice.

"I'm so glad we could get together," he says. "You know, Nicky, I've always wanted to have some time alone with you."

"No, I didn't know," I say. Or did I? I don't know. I don't know if I want to know now. But I hear myself say, "Or maybe I did. I'm happy to know it now, anyway."

He looks at me and smiles. "You know, the first night I saw you, I was with a bunch of people from work, a bunch of women, actually. We were sitting at a table in the dining room, and I couldn't take my eyes off you."

"I definitely didn't know that," I say, laughing.

"They were egging me on to go to the bar and talk to you, but I liked just sitting there watching you fly around and laugh with people and work every inch of the bar."

His dark-brown eyes look right into mine as he talks to me, almost like he's looking through me. I have trouble putting into words what it is about him that makes me feel so good (besides the obvious flattery), but I think it has to do with a gentleness about him. That calm delivery of his words calms me, and his carefulness in choosing them lets me see his thoughts at work. Even when he's being at his most direct and it scares me a little, I want to know more.

"So then what happened?" I ask him, as if he's telling me a story I know nothing about.

"I came back the next night and sat at the bar."

"That must be the first time I saw you. I noticed you and everyone else got kind of blurry. I tried not to let on that I was checking you out, though, because of the Phil situation."

"Nicky, I was married once," he says.

"You were?" I say.

Married? To a woman? I don't know why I should be shocked. Then I realize it's not shock, it's that I don't want to believe it. I want to believe I'm the only woman he's ever looked at this way. But then a compulsion comes over me to find out every last detail. How long did it last? What went wrong? Was she beautiful and smart? Was he crazy about her? Is he still?

But I have trouble asking the questions, because I'm hit with an immediate and overwhelming desire to possess him. The knowledge that someone has had a claim on him before, a married claim, makes me intensely aware of my own wish to claim him.

But I remain calm and just say, "When?"

"A few years back," he says, like he would answer anything I asked. I don't think he's still in love with her.

"Were you in love with her?"

"I cared for her, but we were more like friends. Unfortunately, we were very mismatched. But it's helped me to feel so much clearer about what I want in a relationship," he says, looking straight at me, as though I'm *it*.

But now, instead of jumping for joy that it *might* be me, I feel scared again, because I really like him and I can feel myself *wanting* it to be me. I can see myself, down the road, desperate for it to be me. I'm ashamed to be thinking this way, and it also scares me, because I know it can't be me: the bartender with the foul mouth and the crumbling acting career. The one who's lost her best friend, the one who's not clear about anything right now.

Yet, because I *am* me, I have to probe further anyway.

"Like what?" I ask.

He takes a sip of his wine and then swirls it around in the glass.

"Like somebody who takes big hungry bites out of life even when they sometimes might not taste so sweet."

I want to take a big bite out of his butt right now. Instead, I pull his very prominent cheekbone to my mouth and kiss it.

"Mmm, sweet," I say.

After dinner, when he drops me off, he asks if he can stop by to see me later. I don't answer right away, and he senses some awkwardness and quickly says, "I won't stay long. I just want to give you something."

There's something about a guy that I like coming to the bar specifically to see me that makes me a little uncomfortable. I guess it's that everybody's watching me, and there are always a fair number of male customers around, and I have to give the appearance that everyone receives the same attention—unless, of course, I've declared someone mine, in which case I can subtly let it be known. But if I haven't come around to that declaration with myself, if I'm not sure enough to reveal that change in my status, then it conflicts me, the pressure burning down on my neck to decide one way or the other.

"Okay," I say. It's two days before Christmas.

When he comes in I feel incredibly shy because I've just been telling Mel about him and I've got a little buzz on from dinner, or at least I think that's why. He gives me earrings with a rabbit and compass on them. The rabbit because in Chinese astrology I'm born in the year of the rabbit, and the compass, well, I think of it as a guide.

I see him again before he leaves on his trip, and I give him a Christmas present, too: a box of stationery—perhaps not as subtle.

CHAPTER 35

RUMORS BUZZ OF the bar closing. Being bought, being sold, being shut out by the place across the way. Those same rumors go around wherever you work. It's more everyone's wish than it is based in any kind of reality.

It's so you can think more comfortably about where you would go, what you would do, if you had to.

Still, wherever I work, whenever the rumor surfaces, it excites me. You come to work one night and the doors are shut. The music is off, the lights are out, the people are gone, and in a way, you're free. The choice is taken from you. You can legally go on unemployment and really think about your next move. Maybe you find a way not to go back. Maybe something turns up.

It's like a sign. A sign that if this one died, they'll all be dropping like flies soon. And so you can't go back, because there's nowhere to go back to. It's over and you can start fresh.

"You think it's true?" Jonie asks me as she picks up a few stray drinks.

"It's never true, but I don't know. You never know," I say.

Ludwig shuffles by. On his way he lays a cigar on the lip of the bar, then another.

"You give you boyfriend," he says.

"Thanks," I say, not having the heart to tell him I don't have a boy-friend anymore.

"You okay?" he says, looking me over.

"Sure," I say.

"Nicky, you a pretty girl, but don't forget, not just pretty, you smart."

Now, as I watch them file in from the place across the way, I feel anything but. They've already spent their money over there and now they just want to linger until the last call is yelled out, permitting them or forcing them to go home, if they have one.

Steve keeps me company, but he's on the wagon, more from short-age of funds than true commitment, but it's more of a challenge now to keep him happy. This night is the opposite of those nights when Marvin Gaye's singing gets everybody movin' and groovin', and yet they hang around, hoping.

Hopefully I'll get to go home a little early. It's so slow they're sure to try and get rid of one of us so they don't have to dish out any more of that minimum wage than necessary. I need money, but not so badly that I'd willingly stay these last few hours that last for days.

"Hey, Nick, do you think I'm boring?" Steve asks.

"No more so than when you were a drunk," I say.

"Thanks," he says, sincerely.

I see him struggling with it. Comparing everything to when he was drinking. Was I bigger, better, stronger, funnier, happier? I imagine how hard it is to be in the same exact place, surrounded by the same people, smells, things, with just that one element, the one that you lived for, gone. No wonder you don't see that many reformed guys hanging out in bars.

"It's just a phase," I say. "You're a little down. You'll snap out of it. You'll see. You'll be your same gallivanting, obnoxious self in no time."

"Thanks," he says again, and I hope I'm right. I also hope that he's gotten rid of Janine for good this time. On again, off again, on again, off again, talk about torture.

At the back bar, I fiddle around with the cigars that Ludwig left. Surveying the room for available men, I feel pretty sure there aren't any that I will go off smoking into the sunset with, so I stash the cigars in my backpack. Then I start to arrange the credit cards with their appropriate tabs, making sure I don't give John's to Bill or Bill's to John, because that can be a major problem. Out of the corner of my eye I see Shell, my white/Hispanic storyteller. I haven't seen him in a long time.

"Hi, Nicky," he says nervously. He looks kind of green.

"Hey, how've you been?" I ask, a little afraid to serve him.

"Good, good. Can I have three Rolling Rocks?" he says, between grinding teeth.

"Three? Isn't that a lot of beer for you to be drinking by yourself?" I ask, trying to check out his intoxication level, see if he's okay, aside from the obvious coke problem.

"Two of 'em are for my friends," he says, gesturing towards two fidgeting, scrawny-looking guys in leather jackets, guys I've never seen and would wager that he hasn't either before tonight.

"Oh, sure," I say, making my way over to the cooler. When I come back to deliver, there's a twenty on the bar and Shell's on his way to the men's room. I ring him up, drop his change and try to find something else to do. But I notice he's gone for a while, and one by one, each of the scrawny guys disappears, too.

Ricky and I shoot the breeze for a while.

"Shell looks like shit, man," Ricky says.

"Yeah, he doesn't look too good."

"Too much drugs," Ricky says, shaking his head.

"Yep, I think so."

Nobody's asked me to go home yet, so I take the initiative.

"Hey, Sonny, you want me to go home?" I call out to him, as if I've come up with a novel idea to save them money.

"No, no, it's too soon to tell," he says, and then, "Have you seen Shell?"

Ricky and I exchange a look, and with shrugged shoulders I say, "Bathroom?"

As Sonny heads towards the men's room in hunting mode, Ricky says, "Uh oh, honey, I think trouble."

A few minutes later, Sonny is escorting Shell out of the bar. He drags him out, reminding me of a cat with the scruff of one of her little ones between her teeth.

"He puked on the floor in there, and his two greaser friends were snorting off the counter," Sonny says.

"I only served them one drink, and they never touched it," I say, trying to keep my hands clean.

"Shell's 86'd," he says.

"Okay, boss, you got it," I say.

"You have credit cards for everybody?" he says, throwing his weight around, trying to remind me that he's important.

"You bet," I say.

I wonder if Sonny confiscated the scrawny guys' stash as I pocket the change from Shell's twenty.

At this one place I worked in New York, people would pass coke off to me as a tip. They'd slide it into my hand like they sometimes did with money, only in this case, whether I wanted it or not, I was stuck with it. I couldn't politely refuse and try to pass it back because if anyone caught the exchange it would look like I was dealing over the bar. Throwing it away in front of the customer was all wrong, and putting it in our community tip jar wouldn't do either. At that bar, my coworkers were a couple of old guys who supported their families with the job, bald guys who had been there for fifty years—no joke. If they did coke I certainly didn't know about it, and if I did it I certainly didn't want them to know about it. So I usually slipped it up my sleeve and discreetly into my bra when I was fairly sure no one was looking. Sometimes I did it, sometimes I was afraid to, 'cause who the hell knows what these guys were giving me.

"I told you so," Ricky says, shaking his head and grabbing a roll to munch on.

"You sure can call 'em, Ricky, man," I say, pulling his cheek off his face with a pinch.

Finally Sonny asks me if I want to go home.

"That's putting it mildly," I say.

"Another half hour," he says.

"What are you, trying to torture me?" I ask.

"Me and the wife might move out to Colorado," he says, as if he's answering me.

"What're you talking about? You live here. This place is your life," I blurt out, shocked and beginning to wonder if the rumors might not be rumors at all.

"I know," he says. "But you know, there's some opportunities over there and we're looking into 'em."

"Who would hire you, you bum? Is Trevor closing?" I ask.

"It's not that. Annie's pregnant," he says.

"Wow. That's great," I say. But just the thought of it is so hard to believe. The idea that Sonny, who loves his very important managerial station in life, would ever leave this place never occurred to me. The idea that he would leave before me is mind-boggling. Then again, maybe he was just talking. He likes to talk, but you never know.

"Hey, wait a minute," I say, grabbing my backpack. "Here. Have a cigar."

"Thanks," he says with what looks like a paternal grin. "Start closing your bank, and I'll meet ya in the office in five."

Sonny out of here—he's the carpenter, the bouncer, the plumber, and the manager. Without him they might as well be going out of business.

CHAPTER 36

I 'VE ONLY BEEN to Philly once before, for the funeral. But it's
Casey's birthday, and they're having a special on American Airlines,
and I want to bring her some flowers. I probably wouldn't have felt
the need to bring them to Philly and the cemetery, because I'm not
that literal and I don't really understand the whole grave thing. When
I feel her presence it's more around me than in a particular place. But
she had been specific with regard to only one thing, and that was where
she wanted to be buried, so I feel that's where she might've liked all, or
most, correspondence directed to.

She didn't like to talk about stuff like that, but I remember the one
conversation we had about it. I had come over to her place in the morning, the day after the hospice people had been over.

"How was it?" I asked.

"Kind of depressing," she said.

"What do you mean?" I said.

"Well, she kept asking me if I had made arrangements."

"Like final arrangements?"

"Yeah."

I remember thinking about what she'd said for what felt like a long time before I spoke. She was right. That would be a depressing visit, but then again, no more depressing than the facts themselves.

"Well, you know what, Case, I know that's not a lot of fun," I had said. "But if you think about it, we're all gonna die. So we should all probably make arrangements. But with three or four doctors telling you you're gonna die sooner than some of the rest of us, maybe it's not such a bad idea that you start making some arrangements now."

"Well, I know I want to be buried in Philly," she said.

"Okay," I said.

Lee is picking me up from the airport, and I'm very grateful for that. His sister, Dana, was Casey's best friend from childhood on, and Lee was one of her closest friends, too. Their relationships were, of course, different because Lee's a guy, but needless to say, their whole family got hit hard when Casey died.

We give each other a big hug when I get off the plane and then Lee asks if I'd like to go to the cemetery first or to see everybody. I tell him the cemetery, feeling I want to see Casey first, becoming acutely aware, in that moment, of how very much I would like to see Casey.

We pick up flowers at a little flower shop in town Lee knows, and I get flooded sporadically with a feeling of foolishness as I search for the perfect ones. I buy some orchids, knowing that they die more quickly than some of the others, but, loving their beautiful rich color and maybe even their impracticality, I don't allow that to spoil my choice.

Once at the cemetery, I'm surprised at how much I like being there. Buying the flowers, getting in the car, going there, it's like a real outing, and as we make our way to her gravestone, I feel excited that I may actually be with her soon. It feels a little like a visit to my grandma's used to. The preparation and the excitement as I anticipated spending the night with her—lamb chops or spaghetti for dinner? Pajamas and a movie together in her old and special living room, just the two of us, so quiet in the late night.

As we get out of the car, I hear Lee say, "It's over here. I don't know if you remember."

"Thanks," I say, following him.

"Take your time," he says. "I'll be right over there," moving off to the side so I can be alone with her—alone with her grave.

I talk to her in my mind, but not aloud. At first I talk in sentences, trying to actually talk to her, but I keep feeling like she's looking down at me from somewhere, shaking her head and making a funny face, saying, "You are such an ass."

I felt kind of like that at the funeral, too. And I know Jay did, too. Maybe because we're Jews and it was so surreal, with Jesus Christ hanging off the cross, and Casey in an outfit that she had always looked good in, just lying there in the coffin below him looking great, her hair and make-up done beautifully by Dana and her other close friend, Lisa, who used to be morticians, and all those candles and flowers. Every time I started to get the slightest bit weepy, I kept feeling like Casey was going to leap up out of that coffin and look at me funny and say, "Cut it out. I'm not really dead. Sometimes you're so ridiculous."

So now I just stand here thinking about her. Not talking to her, because that does seem ridiculous, but just kind of communing through those thoughts that aren't really articulated in your mind, yet are there. Like about the two white stone columns she had in her one-room apartment, before she moved in with Jay. Or the way we used to go skating together, her dancing around backwards on her weathered brown roller skates, me on my blades. Or talking to her while I sat on a closed toilet seat staring at her collection of little glass perfume bottles on the vanity shelf, waiting for her to finish applying that final touch of dark-brown lipstick.

Thinking here like that, without any real point to make, makes me feel closer to her—and I don't feel her laughing at me now. Instead, I feel like she understands me. Understands that I love her, understands that it hurts, understands what I'm doing here.

I lay my flowers down next to the other pretty flowers. There are lots today. Lee lays his flowers down, whispering something tenderly as he does, and then we go back to the car.

"Kind of weird, huh?" he says to me.

"Yeah. Weird, and also very not weird. I'm glad to be here."

"Yeah. I'm glad you're here, too," he says. Then he tells me this fluky story about how a crow landed on her grave the other day, and it was so strange, like Casey was talking to him.

Back at Casey's mom's house, there's a gathering celebrating the fact that Casey was ever born at all. Dana's here with a new baby, her second, and I can't help remembering all the stories Case used to tell me about her best and crazy friend, Dana, and the wild times they used to have. Lisa (her friend the former mortician) is here, expecting, and one of her friends, Allison, who came out for a few weeks towards the end and took care of her night and day until she died.

The same people are here that had invited me to join them in giving the eulogy at the funeral. We had all stood up and stepped forward on that church stage, and then each of us had said something about the way we loved her and the way she loved us, and I didn't cry because, again, she wouldn't let me. It was as if she was standing behind me the whole time, coaching me: "That's right, say it, say it, good—uh oh, no crying please, cut the melodrama, good, go on, tell them how great I was . . ."

There are lots of people here: her sisters and their children, her nieces and nephews, her mom; everybody handling things in their own way.

Her mom seems well, but she's very angry at God, which is making this difficult time even more difficult. She tells me this, struggling with the fact that she can't let the anger go, no matter how hard she tries, because she can't accept a God who has let her daughter die before her. And I don't blame her, not at all. But I hope desperately that, like a miracle, God somehow finds a way to make his presence known, and gives her something she can understand and hold onto, because, just like Casey, she has always been a believer. The thought of losing your daughter and your belief in God all in the same time frame is just too painful for me. Especially because I have just begun to believe there really may be a God, one that has some kind of bigger plan and knows what he's doing, the only explanation that makes a kind of magical excuse for her being gone.

We hang around for quite a while, laughing and crying as we reminisce. Then Lee and I go back to his place and have a couple of glasses of wine before we head out to all of Casey's favorite clubs, where we sing and dance till the last call kicks us out.

CHAPTER 37

I'M BACK AND Brendan's here. He's the to-go delivery guy. He's a high school student trying to make a few extra dollars, and that's probably all he's making, because we don't have very much of a to-go business. We used to kill time together when I worked the day shift, but I don't know what he's doing here now.

"Hey, what are you doing here?" I say.

"Oh, just came in to pick up my check," he says.

"Yeah. How are you doing? How's school going?"

"Pretty good," he says. "How about you?"

"Still here, but I'm pretty good," I say.

I really do feel good. After visiting Casey's home and seeing her family and friends, my feet are light on the mats and the smoke doesn't penetrate. I feel refreshed and hopeful.

"Too bad about Ludwig, huh?" Brendan asks.

"What about him?" I say. I haven't seen him since I've been back, but I just got here.

"You didn't hear? He's out of here."

"What do you mean?"

"Holly hadn't seen him for a few days, so she called his hotel to see if he was okay, and the front desk said he was no longer staying there."

"I didn't know he lived in a hotel."

"Me neither," he says.

"Did they give her a forwarding address?"

"They didn't have one."

"That's funny."

"It's strange to think of him never hanging around here anymore, isn't it?" he says.

"Yeah," I say, but notice I've got the slightest grin creeping onto my face. I'm not sure why.

Then we don't say anything. We just stand around quietly, like we used to sometimes when Ludwig was here, almost like we're waiting for him to come waddling through the door, yelling.

"Where do you think he went?" I ask.

"I don't know," he says.

"But you think he's really not coming back?"

"You know, the guy came in here every day. If he didn't come in for one or two days, I might wonder, but going on a week, it feels permanent."

Brendan always used to be here when Ludwig made his grand entrance. Lots of people thought of Ludwig as an eccentric character, but Brendan really liked him. They'd talk for quite a while, I don't know what about. Ludwig was like a father figure to Brendan. His own father was kind of mod: had a young girlfriend, smoked pot, and drove a Porsche. Ludwig represented an old-fashioned goodness.

I wonder if he went back to Germany with the son he was always bragging about. I imagine him taking a cruise ship back to Europe. Smoking a cigar on deck and finishing off a nice cold Beck's as the moon shines down on him and he looks out on the glistening whitecaps of water that extend on into forever.

Of course, I can only imagine, because nobody really knows. That's the thing. Working in a bar, you might see a person every day for years and years, but then one day they just stop coming in, and you never know what happened to them.

I think of Ludwig's sun-spotted little head and smoke-wrinkled fingers. I think about the way he talked so loud all the time, maybe because he was hard of hearing. Maybe because he just liked to get under people's skin, or maybe it was his way of broadcasting to the world that he had made it and was proud to be a survivor.

The early evening music is classical. It dances into my head on little figurines like the ones you find in music boxes. Like the boxes I imagine Ludwig used to make. I love music boxes. I always have. I love the way they look and feel, and that they're a secret until you open them up and then there's a whole world alive inside them.

A couple of customers come in. It's Tom with a couple of friends. Tom's a regular. He sometimes has lunch at the bar, but today it would have to be dinner. He knows Ludwig.

I throw a few cocktail napkins down with a cheerful, "Hey guys, how you doing?"

Tom says, "Pretty good, Nick," but he's looking around like something's missing. Then he says, "You haven't seen ol' Ludwig, have you?"

"No. Word has it he's moved on."

"Isn't that funny? You get to feeling some people are fixtures in a place, and then they just up and go."

"Guess he had us fooled," I say, and again I'm surprised by the strange tickle I feel inside.

I grab a few menus, and when I make my way back over, Sonny has joined Tom and his friends. I hear them reminiscing about Ludwig, talking about things he used to do and say, behavior uniquely his.

I make their drinks, eavesdropping on their impressions of this man I hardly know but somehow feel bonded to. Then Sonny becomes brusque and businesslike, cutting short what I think of as a pretty intimate conversation.

As he heads back to his cave of an office I ask, "Hey, Sonny, where do you think he went?"

"I don't know, but Ludwig was a pretty sick man, you know. I wouldn't be surprised if this move was health-related," he says, picking something up off the bar and quickening his pace as though he's got something very important to do, or just is very important.

The way he says it makes me think it's such bullshit. "Oh, he was a very sick man." Like now that Ludwig's gone, it would be the logical conclusion that he must've been sick, and he'll probably be dying soon, too. As if death was his only ticket out.

He didn't seem sick to me. Oh, he coughed a really phlegmy cough, but I figure anyone who smokes cigars all the time might do that.

Brendan grabs my shoulder on his way out. "Take it easy," he says.

"Yeah," I say. "Thanks for the update."

I'm glad somebody who actually likes Ludwig was the one to fill me in. And I'm glad the news wasn't anything as tragic as Sonny would like us to believe. Because it's hard enough to believe somebody's dead when you've seen their light go out and their body go into the ground. But when nobody knows what happened to a person, where they went, what condition they were in when they went there, there's nothing tangible to hold onto—nothing real to convince yourself of.

Sonny passes through again and I ask him, "What about his business?"

"What business?" he says, as if he never knew he had one.

"Hey, Sonny," I say, trying to slow his pace, "how did Ludwig get out of Auschwitz alive?"

This is something I've always wondered about and think will be fascinating enough material for Sonny to expound on. I figure he may've been blunt enough to come right out and ask Ludwig what they did to him in the prison camps and then elicit the sadistic details. But his answer is simple.

"The war ended," he says.

That's Sonny, I guess. One of the waitresses has told me that he's having a vulnerable day. He will be moving on after all, and he's expressed a sadness to her about leaving his family—by which he means us, the staff. He has told this same waitress for the last five years that he doesn't care if everyone hates him because he's the manager and he doesn't want to be friends with anyone, but that's Sonny, too.

I touch the wooden surface before me. I like the way it feels under my fingertips. Smooth in some places, a speckled roughness in others where it's worn from years of people leaning on it and reaching across it. People made up mostly of shoulders and heads, the bar obscuring from my sight everything from their hearts down to their toes.

I pour some oil on a dry cloth and rub it into the wood, making it shine, noticing that it's not just a piece of wood, but a place; a place where people like Ludwig and me might meet.

Then the initial thrill I felt tickle through me upon learning of Ludwig's journey to a new destiny dies out. I picture one of the candles' flames being extinguished: it's that fast that my excitement turns to sadness and leaves me with a little patch of emptiness.

I'm uncomfortable with this feeling, but it begins to make sense to me when I think about everyone having a story and his or her story being a part of my story. If they disappear before I've had a chance to get more than a glimpse of the intricate details of their story, it's probably normal to feel a little robbed.

It's like having a puzzle, and as you're putting it together you discover you don't have all the pieces. You're missing some of the important ones that would make the picture whole.

Or like when you're an actor and you have to create a bio for the character you're playing. You only have the text, you make up all the rest. You make up all this great stuff about where your character's been and what's happened to them in the past. And it's great stuff not because it's necessarily so brilliant, but because of how richly it contributes to who that character is in the present, as the past always does.

But if that present is taken away because a person disappears, then you can make up as much shit as you want to about the person, but the only thing you'll remember is what you know. I didn't even know he lived in a hotel.

I probably should've asked him more questions, but Ludwig wasn't the kind of person who talked a lot or told you much when he did. His was more the kind of story that reveals itself over time, and it never occurred to me that I'd run out of time. I miss knowing that he'll walk in that door, that he'll shuffle back and forth, smoking and drinking, hanging around, surviving, here with me.

A guy comes in and asks for a Beck's. I put it up on a fresh white cocktail napkin and I say, "Beck's. It's the best, you know? The best beer."

The guy just smiles, taking a swig. I'm smiling, too, liking the sound of the words coming out of my mouth, while at the same time feeling the wetness of a tear rolling down my cheek. Tom catches it, too.

"Hey, Nicky," he says, "I think that's nice that you feel that way. What if I never came back one day?"

CHAPTER 38

I 'M WORKING TONIGHT, New Year's Eve, mostly because I've got nothing else I really want to do. I don't want to be with anyone just to be with *someone,* and I don't want to be alone because I can't stop dwelling on the fact that Casey should be here, that one year ago tonight, she was here.

Last New Year's, one of my customers hired us a limo for the night. His name was Red, or at least that's what everyone called him. He'd been a customer of mine at Halle's, and when I left, he followed me to Fioreca's. He was a great customer. I never kissed his ass even after I found out what a great tipper he was, and he loved that. I loved that I could be my New York–style cut-to-the-chase self, and he never got offended. I haven't seen him for a while now, though.

But last New Year's he wanted to do something special for Casey and me—he knew about the cancer and all—and he hired us the limo. We cruised by Halle's, had a few. Came by here, had a few more. Then we went dancing across the street at Green Trees.

Casey looked her usual awesome. Black pants with a red, long-sleeved, off-the-shoulder halter-style back, big old black boots with a chunky heel that she could really dance in, and a black man's-style hat. I felt great that night, too. I wore these silk navy pants that kind of ballooned at the knee, and I had a sleeveless, skin-tight white turtleneck on. Jay had to work for a little while, but then we had the limo go back and get him, too. Even Jay got dressed up in his very Jay way—he wore a Hawaiian shirt with his black work pants, and snakeskin cowboy boots. Then we just cut up all night, laughing and dancing.

I thought about calling Jay tonight, but then I didn't think it was such a good idea, because if he wasn't depressed, I would depress him, and if he was depressed, I would only depress him more.

I thought of T and wished he wasn't away on that annual Christmas trip with his family. I felt like we could've gone somewhere, anywhere, and talked and drunk wine and been happy. I felt like he would've been okay if, in a tipsy haze, I got a little hysterical about Casey. I told him about her the last time we went out, and he listened and held my hand.

But instead, here I am, prepping for the big bash. We've got buckets of Champagne chilling in every station and rows of flutes tucked into corners. Coolers stocked to their fullest capacity, and Sonny dressed up and scurrying around, making sure everything is just so, checking the taps, the ashtrays, the candles, the flowers.

It's Mel, Alex and me.

"Do you think it's gonna rock?" I ask Mel as she glides her red lipstick on.

"It could. There're a lot of reservations," she says.

"Yeah, but are they diners or are they drinkers?"

"That's the question," she agrees.

The last time I worked on New Year's I was in New York. It was typical of how most New Year's turn out—tons of anticipation and preparation, very little reward and a big hangover the next day. But who knows?

"Alex, did you work last year?" I ask.

"Yeah. It was mediocre. But tonight there're a lot of reservations, so it could be all right. Probably won't get going till later, though."

"Yeah," I say painting my own lips and noticing as I scoop my hair back that my eyes have lost their red, crusty swelling. Instead, they look soft and velvety.

Sonny's still hurrying about, chasing his own tail, checking on cherries and oranges and lime wedges.

"You got enough Champagne?" he asks.

"Shitload," I say.

"Okay. Don't forget. The music's got to come off at five to, and the volume on the TV comes up."

"Okay. You think it's gonna be busy?"

"Are you kidding?" he says, as if I'm ridiculous.

Mel just smirks.

The place looks great, anyway. The lights are down low, and the white tablecloths covering the bar reflect the flames of the candles, making our faces glow a little. We've got big golden streamers and black-and-gold party hats, not the conehead dunce cap kind, but the cool kind, like an actual hat, stacked up along the bar. There are roses everywhere and even the artwork seems illuminated. They're all still lifes this month. Big wooden bowls hold luscious clusters of grapes on wooden tables and benches, which sit on top of creaky old plank floors, making me feel the warmth of a country home.

Or is it that I'm feeling a warmth of my own? A little fire blazing inside me, both comforting me and burning a hole in me as it spreads, as I stand here imagining what it would be like to stay here forever, admitting to myself that I've been here almost that long.

"Two Champagnes, please," a guy orders for himself and his lady friend when the doors open.

That seems to get the ball rolling. Little by little they start rocking up to the bar, into the restaurant, laughing and smiling and getting excited about the New Year.

And though it starts as a trickle, it steadily grows, and soon I can hear the cha-ching, cha-ching, of the register as if it's a part of the instrumentals flowing through the speakers.

Martinis are poured from icy premiums stored in the cooler, margaritas are premade in pitchers, shots of Patron Tequila, specially discounted for tonight, stand lined up in rows, temptingly.

"Hey Nicky, you and Mel, drinks on me, let's go, you choose," one of our Friday night regulars calls out.

Mel and I look at each other, then pull the Patrons out of their neat little rows, bringing one over to our regular and downing the others with a big crash of glass and a loud "Cheers."

Then back to business, because that trickle is now a steady rush of rapids, but they're people acting like we're giving it away, and Jonie has got tickets flying all over.

"Drinks! Orrder!" she yells, clearly not thrilled that I've chosen this moment to enjoy a libation.

"Ricky, beer," I yell hoping he'll have time to grab a case or two.

"Whut you need, honey?" he says, seeming to recognize that sweetness *and* speed count tonight.

"Corona and Rolling Rock," I say, helping Jonie load her tray with Sea Breezes and G/T's, Bloodys and, of all things, coffee drinks.

"You got it, baby," Ricky says, burning some calories down to the basement.

Boom, boom, boom. "Who needs what?" I yell to the crowd, with lots of new faces mixed in amongst the old.

And then I hear a Southern twang that I could never mistake.

"Well, Ah don't lahk to be kept waitin'," it drawls.

"Talk about waiting. Where the hell have you been?" I say, reaching over and giving Red a big hug.

"I had some surgery," he whispers. "But I'm okay now."

"Are you sure? You look a little skinny or something."

"Special diet. But I'm off it for tonight, girl. How bout a CC and ginger?"

"Sure," I say, going to get it.

When I come back with it, he's got a whole bunch of his regular buddies with him, and he detains me, asking them, one by one, what they want and then telling me.

"Hey, did that surgery do something to your head?" I say. "I don't have all day to be taking your order. Get it together, mister."

He smiles, confers with them, and then shoots out, "Okay. Jack and Coke, Stoli and OJ, Wild Turkey rocks."

"Better," I say. I'm starting to get a rhythm now, so I make his round, run his credit card, and then I'm off.

"Keep it open," he shouts.

"Of course," I shout back.

Ice, glass, liquid, sometimes it's so pretty. We're bopping along, mixing, spinning, laughing, lighting, cruising. I do kind of feel like a machine, but it's a well-oiled machine that knows perfectly what to do when. Then, out of nowhere, some guy offers me fifty bucks for my shirt. It's very strange, but I guess when you're in a bar, anything's possible. Before I can respond, Red flags me down in a big hurry.

He pulls me over and says, "Tell him I'll give you sixty."

I feel a little ridiculous, because why would anyone want my shirt, especially since I have no intention of stripping it off right here in front of him? But I just work here and the customer is always right, so I tell the guy, "The gentleman down there says he'll give me sixty for it."

He looks down the bar, checking out Red, who gives him a big smile and a little wave of his hand.

"Tell him seventy," he says.

So I go back over to Red and tell him seventy and he says eighty. Some of the other customers are starting to check out the action now. Steve passes through the back layer of people and smoke with a couple of girls draped over each arm.

"Hey there, gorgeous," he calls out to me, blowing a kiss. But this is a rare appearance now that he's not drinking, and he just passes right through.

The crowd is made up of a lot of men tonight, I guess those who couldn't find dates or didn't want them to begin with.

As the bidding continues, Jay comes in.

"I knew I'd find you here," he says.

"I'm glad you did," I say, climbing on top of the bar and throwing my arms around him. The truth is I'm more than glad.

"What am I getting you?"

"How about a Stoli Cosmo?" he says.

"How about it indeed. You see Red's here?"

"No shit," he says, making his way over to him and patting him on the back.

"We're up to a hundred," I tell Red when I deliver Jay's drink.

Ricky scoots in front of me and, big eyes popping out of his head, says, "Omigod, honey. Que pasa?"

"Well, let's cut to the chase and tell him I'll make it two hundred and fifty," Red says.

"C'mon, Red, this is getting silly."

"What's going on?" Jay asks.

"There's a bidding war for my smelly shirt," I tell him.

"Well, that's a sin," he says, Casey style.

"It really is," I agree.

"Go on and tell him," Red insists.

"All right, but you're nuts," I say.

So I do and the guy, naturally, folds. I come back and ask Red if he wants the shirt now or what. I've already let him know in no uncertain terms that I'm not going to take it off in front of anybody. I told the other guy the same thing, but for some reason it didn't stop the bidding.

"Sure. Now's good," he says.

"Okay. I gotta talk to Sonny," I tell him. I have Mel watch my back while I try to explain the situation to Sonny and get permission to get out of uniform.

"So they both wanted your shirt?" he asks.

"Yeah. I don't know what's gotten into everybody tonight, but you know, it was kind of a show."

"How much did you get for it?" he says with a dirty little grin on his face.

"Two fifty."

"No shit? Okay," he says. "There're some Fioreca's T-shirts in the office. You can grab one of those for ten bucks."

He *could* just give it to me, but Sonny's gotta feel like he, synonymous with the house, is getting something out of it.

"Thanks," I say making my way to the office.

When I bring my shirt back—a Fioreca's shirt, too, only it's a man-tailored one with a special iron-on patch for the New Year—I give it to Red.

"Thanks," he says. "Now, let me close out my check, and why don't you bring your shirt over there to my bidding friend?"

"Really?" I ask.

"Yep. Go ahead."

So I close out his check with the two hundred and fifty dollar tip attached to it, and I show it off to Mel and Alex, who've gotta love me now, and I give the weird guy who wants my shirt my shirt. He, of course, goes over to Red and says he can't take it, and I wash my hands of the whole situation, having done my part.

Jay grabs a stool at the bar and slips out his hand for a low five.

"Smooth," he says.

I low five him, then I high five him.

"Hey. Where's the old guy?" Jay says, looking around.

"He's gone," I say.

"What do you mean?" he asks.

"We hadn't seen him for a week and Holly found out he checked out of the hotel where he lived, and that's all we knew. Then, just yesterday, we got a letter from his son saying due to circumstances beyond his control he had to put him in a home. But he wanted to thank all of us at Fioreca's for looking after him all these years."

"What kind of circumstances?"

"I wish I knew. And where's the home and what's it like and can I visit?" I wish I knew all of that.

I refill Jay's drink and put it in front of him.

"Cheers," I say.

"Cheers," he says back. Then he takes a sip and says "Smooth" again.

"It's one of those funny nights, you know?" I say, looking at my watch. And when I do, what's smoother still is that it's five minutes to twelve.

"Cut the tunes and crank the tube," I yell. And when I do, a hush comes over the bar, conversations trail off, and everybody's eyes shift over to the screen for that moment when everyone's clock is exactly the same and the old year ends and a new one begins.

Then everyone kisses and hugs, and Jay grabs me in a headlock and makes kissy noises all over the top of my head. Then he says he's going back to Halle's and invites me to come by later if I feel like it.

"Later?" I say.

"After hours," he says.

"Like they're going to let me in after hours."

"I'll let you in."

"Maybe," I say.

"Yes," he says nodding his head up and down, overruling my "maybe" as he slips off his stool and disappears into the smoky crowd.

As soon as the kissing and the cheering simmer down, the TV is turned back to mute and Marvin Gaye's voice is quickly piped into the room, causing limbs to move as pelvises gyrate in spite of themselves.

Mel, Alex, and I meet in the middle for a toast.

"1, 2, 3, Drink!" we shout in unison, over the chorus of the crowd.

Then we all pause to soak up the glory of the moment, looking out at them, while they twist and turn and dance and laugh and grind together, as if at a rock concert. The bar stands solidly before us, protecting and elevating us like a stage.

As I go to the cooler to grab the millionth bottle of cold white wine for the billionth glass, I am sidetracked to the cabinet next to it, the one with our personal belongings in it. The pull is strong, like a magnet to metal, and I close my eyes briefly, allowing this force of gravity to suck me in and have its way with me. Then my hand grabs the cabinet door handle, at first for what feels like balance, but then I'm opening it. Inside, my backpack sits on top of my leather jacket. As if for a moment all the activity freezes to a surreal halt, I, in what feels like slow motion, pull off my apron and slip my bar towel off my shoulder. I hang them over the dimly lit sconce, just above my register. Then I slip my arms through the straps of my backpack, grab my bucket of tips, and dump it into Mel's, giving her a kiss along the way.

"What are you doing? Where are you going?" she asks.

"I'm going out there," I say gesturing with my chin.

"You coming back?" she asks.

"I don't think so. Can you handle this crowd?"

"Yeah. Sure," she says smiling, slipping some money into my front shirt pocket. The last I see of her, she's lighting a cigarette and shaking her head.

I crawl out from under the bar, and pull Jonie's apron string undone on my way up.

"Hey! What're you doing?" she yells. As she grabs for her apron, I mess with her hair and give her a playful one-armed hug around her neck.

"Oh, come on. Cut it out," she laughs, swatting me away. "Go on," she says. "Get outta here."

"Yeah, thanks," I say, swinging my leather jacket over my shoulder and slowly, casually, gliding through the smoke and the people and out the front door.

There are a million stars in the sky, and even though the moon is not full, it lights up the night so it almost looks like day. And if ever a day felt like it, this one feels like that amazing last day of school. You feel that overwhelming sense of freedom, and you're not worried about what you're going to do next, because you believe you can do anything.

ABOUT THE AUTHOR

Credit/Sean Lim

JULIE PEPPER LIVES in Northern California with her two children. She is a recent Master of Arts graduate of San Francisco State University in Communication Studies and works for *Tikkun* magazine seeking to heal and transform the world through love, kindness and generosity of spirit. Julie is a playwright and has been writing plays for the last ten years. This is Julie's first novel. She is currently writing her second book which takes place fifteen years later entitled *Stirred Up but not Shaken.* ■

Made in the USA
San Bernardino, CA
16 July 2013